Raves for Stephen Blackmoore's Eric Carter novels

"For a book all about dead things, this novel is alive with great characters and a twisty, scary-funny story that teaches you not to tango with too much necromancy. My favorite book this year, bar none." —Chuck Wendig, author of the Miriam Black series

"Breathtaking . . . Carter's wry voice is amusing as ever, but the grief he carries is palpable, adding depth and a sense of desperation to this action-packed adventure. Readers will be eager for more after this thrilling, emotionally fraught installment."
—*Publishers Weekly* (starred)

"Not only met, but exceeded, my expectations. . . . Plenty of action and magic-slinging rounds out this excellent second novel from one of my favorite authors." —My Bookish Ways

"In *Dead Things*, Stephen Blackmoore expands upon the Los Angeles supernatural world he first conjured in *City of the Lost*. Blackmoore is going places in urban fantasy, and readers fond of dark tales should keep their eyes on him. Highly recommended."
—SFRevu

"Blackmoore can't write these books fast enough to suit me. *Broken Souls* is hyper-caffeinated, turbo-bloody, face-stomping fun. This is the L.A.-noir urban fantasy you've been looking for."
—Kevin Hearne, author of The Iron Druid Chronicles

"Eric Carter's adventures are bleak, witty, and as twisty as a fire-blasted madrone, told in prose as sharp as a razor. Blackmoore is the rising star of pitch-black paranormal noir. A must-read series."
—Kat Richardson, author of the Greywalker series

"Fans will find plenty to enjoy in the long-awaited third outing of necromancer Eric Carter. Blackmoore infuses his increasingly detailed and dangerous urban fantasy landscape with grim yet fascinating characters, and ensures that every step of Carter's epic journey is a perilously fascinating one." —*RT Reviews*

*Novels by Stephen Blackmoore
available from DAW Books:*

CITY OF THE LOST
DEAD THINGS
BROKEN SOULS
HUNGRY GHOSTS
FIRE SEASON
GHOST MONEY
BOTTLE DEMON
SUICIDE KINGS
HATE MACHINE
CULT CLASSIC

CULT CLASSIC

STEPHEN BLACKMOORE

DAW BOOKS
New York

Copyright © 2023 by Stephen Blackmoore

All rights reserved. Copying or digitizing this book for storage, display, or distribution in any other medium is strictly prohibited. For information about permission to reproduce selections from this book, please contact permissions@astrapublishinghouse.com.

This is a work of fiction. Names, characters, places, and incidents are products of the author's imagination or are used fictitiously. Any resemblance to actual events, locales, or persons, living or dead, is entirely coincidental.

Cover illustration by Chris McGrath

Cover design by Adam Auerbach

Edited by Betsy Wollheim

DAW Book Collectors No. 1942

DAW Books
An imprint of Astra Publishing House
dawbooks.com
DAW Books and its logo are registered trademarks of Astra Publishing House

Printed in Canada

Library of Congress Cataloging-in-Publication Data

Names: Blackmoore, Stephen, author.
Title: Cult classic / Stephen Blackmoore.
Description: First edition. | New York : DAW Books, 2023. |
Series: Eric Carter ; 9
Identifiers: LCCN 2023013174 (print) | LCCN 2023013175 (ebook) |
ISBN 9780756417673 (trade paperback) | ISBN 9780756417680 (ebook)
Subjects: LCSH: Carter, Eric (Fictitious character)--Fiction. |
Demonology--Fiction. | LCGFT: Fantasy fiction. |
Paranormal fiction. | Novels.
Classification: LCC PS3602.L32544 C85 2023 (print) |
LCC PS3602.L32544 (ebook) | DDC 813/.6--dc23eng/20230407
LC record available at https://lccn.loc.gov/2023013174
LC ebook record available at https://lccn.loc.gov/2023013175

First edition: July 2023
10 9 8 7 6 5 4 3 2 1

ACKNOWLEDGMENTS

The first Eric Carter book, DEAD THINGS, came out February 5th, 2013. As I write this it's just a touch over ten years old.

Ten years writing about this guy who I like to think is really trying to not fuck up and, sadly, failing spectacularly. When I came up with the idea he looked like Guy Pearce's character Leon from MEMENTO. He was a broken drifter with a screwed-up past confronting dangers nobody else could see.

Ten years. It's been a wild ride and I couldn't have done it without a long list of people helping make it happen. There's my editor Betsy Wollheim and the amazing people at DAW, my agent Lisa Rodgers, my wife, Kari and most importantly, all of you who took a chance on an author writing about ghosts, zombies and really poor life choices.

Thank you.

Chapter 1

The air is filled with the screaming buzz of high-powered engines as F-1 racecars zip by below. Long Beach Grand Prix. Every year they shut down some streets near the marina and turn Shoreline Drive into a racetrack. Stands are filled with fans under a blazing sun. Some places in April are still under snow, but out here in Southern California we barely know what rain looks like.

I've never really gotten the appeal of car racing. It's like baseball. When it comes down to it, it's all just a bunch of guys running around in a circle. Although racing at least has the added benefit of one of them occasionally flipping over and exploding. If that happened in baseball, I would watch the shit out of that.

"Which room?" I say. Danny hands me his binoculars. We're standing on the roof of the Long Beach Performing Arts Center facing the Hyatt Regency hotel.

"Twelve up, eight in from the left," he says. It takes me a second to find it and focus in.

"Yeah, that's her," I say. Nicole Hawthorne. A trim black woman who used to do the whole sex-kitten routine to get what she wanted. It's been almost thirty years since we met and she could still pull it off.

She's also one of the more dangerous mages I've met. Not for her specific magic, though believe me she's no slouch, but because of her patron, a talking head named Jimmy Freeburg.

And when I say talking head, I don't mean some guy behind a desk on cable news. I mean a literal talking head. Jimmy's an Oracle, a terrifyingly powerful artifact with the ability to tell the future by dint of being able to manipulate the future.

Jimmy sees patterns, consequences. It then finds the one or two events that would make things work out differently and changes them. They're not usually big changes. They don't have to be. They're a zig instead of a zag, a single domino tipping the wrong direction.

"Actually, it isn't her," Danny says.

Danny's second generation Korean American. Short, maybe five-two. Built like a fireplug, arms like fucking tree trunks. He hands me a different set of binoculars. They're dark blue with a crystal embedded into a socket on the top. I look through the new binoculars at the window and instead of Nicole I see silhouettes of five figures. Three are definitely men, not sure about the other two. They're all slightly different colors.

"These aren't thermal," I say.

"Auras," he says. "Handy for punching through illusions."

I pick the regular binoculars back up and look again. "It's a damn good illusion."

"Oh yeah. Unless you're watching for a long time. All she's done for the last two hours is pace in front of that window."

"I assume that's bait," I say. Of course it's bait. And of course, it's a trap.

"You would assume correctly. Your fans are getting cleverer. Bounty's up to a couple million bucks."

"Seriously? I'm barely worth a buck fifty. This mean you're upping your rates?"

"Excuse me," he says. "I'm a professional. I won't sell you out for anything less than six."

"Always nice to know what a man's price is."

I've been looking for Nicole for the last three months. She's also been looking for me. Only where I've just got me and some occasional help from Danny here, she's been hiring teams of mercenaries. This is the sixth time we've done this particular dance.

From what I can tell, she doesn't want to kill me, just capture me. Only problem is that she's been sending normals, people with no magic, to take me on. They don't usually last very long.

"This changes things," I say.

"Damn right it does," Danny says. "That is one fucking good illusion."

"At least one of them's a mage," I say. "Where did you hear about this?"

"You're gonna laugh," he says. "Leather Charlie."

"Charlie's still alive?"

"Yeah. Fuck knows how. He was dropping your lady friend's name like it was hot coals."

Danny and I go back to before I was run out of L.A. We weren't terribly close, but we ran in similar circles. Both of us fought at a place called Quick-Change Alice's Bar and Brawl, an underground mage fighting ring. Think MMA with fireballs.

We shared another thing in common at the time: we both did a lot of cocaine. Charlie was our dealer.

Danny and I ran into each again years later in Miami. He was doing security. He needed someone who could deal with some local ghosts. We worked a couple of jobs together over the years.

"She's not at this one either," I say. Nicole wasn't at any of the previous attempts to take me on. Why would she need to be? All she has to do is throw money around and let her mercs do the rest.

"I'm thinking their plan is that they figure I'll see this, come to the room expecting to find Nicole alone, and instead find myself face to face with five assassins."

Another reason I think she isn't here is Jimmy. Since Jimmy can see potential futures, it's real hard to sneak up on the damn thing. If I find Nicole, then chances are it wants me to find her. That's the trap I'm really worried about.

There are only two people Jimmy can't "see," the people who created it. It doesn't perceive things the way it did when it was human. Instead of sight, it perceives chances and possibilities.

One of those people is Nicole. It can see her to an extent. She's hazy, like static. That's because she's been its keeper for the last going on thirty years. Proximity has made her easier to see. She's as much a victim of the situation as anyone its influence affects.

As to the other person who made it? That would be me.

"What it looks like," Danny says. "It's a stupid plan, mage or no. You'd be walking into a kill box or going through the window and they'd be waiting for you."

"Nicole's the bait," I say. "They're the trap."

"You'd be stupid to go in."

"Yep," I say.

"You're going in anyway."

"Yep. Can you hit them from here?"

"I would be vaguely insulted, if I didn't want to show you my new toys," he says. "I've got the same aura rig on my AR-15. Got it chambered for .338. I can take them down before they know what hit 'em."

"Okay. I'm gonna head over there. I'll let you know when I'm at the door. Leave one of them alive and try not to pop too many heads. Might need to talk to a dead one."

"I ever tell ya you necromancers are fucking creepy?"

"Few thousand times. You good?"

"Yeah. I'll be set up by the time you get over there."

The hotel's soundproofing is impressive; I can barely hear the cars outside. The room's easy enough to find. Twelfth floor, eight in from the left. The hallway's empty. From what Danny could see the rooms to either side are empty and the rest have two or three people in each doing pretty much nothing. If we do this right, there shouldn't be much noise to get their attention.

I saw Nicole and Jimmy last in Las Vegas. Jimmy had manipulated me into a position where if I wanted to save the soul of another mage, one who I care very much about—Gabriela Cortez—I needed to break it out of a Las Vegas casino vault.

That thing about me being one of the people Jimmy can't see? Turns out that since it can't see me, it couldn't tell the guy who had it that I was coming. I was camouflage. At least that's all I thought I was.

The question was, how was it captured in the first place? Easy: it wanted to be. There was this rock, an opal. One of a set, most of which are at the bottom of the ocean, last I'd heard.

Stupidly powerful artifacts, though nobody seems to really know what they do. Powerful enough that Jimmy can't see them either. Seems they're naturally resistant to its powers.

I do know what one of them does. It can sort of raise the dead, though fucked if I know how. There's a guy, Zombie Joe. Hates it when I call him that. Gabriela has him working for her. He was murdered and brought back using one of them. Now he's got it sitting in his chest so he doesn't go all George Romero and start eating people. I hear it's pretty messy.

So Jimmy couldn't see the Vegas opal, but it knew who had it. Magic? No, just shipping records and a minion who could sort through them.

We break Jimmy out, everything's great, I get what I need. Jimmy gets out with the opal. Happily ever after for everybody. And only three casinos burned down.

And then I find out that Nicole went around later to all the people who had helped us get Jimmy out and murdered them. And not just them, everybody around them. It was brutal and cruel and I don't know why she did it.

Some of them were her friends. At least they thought they were her friends. I guess I'm lucky that way. Nicole and I were never friends.

It'll make killing her a lot easier on the conscience.

"How many is this now?" Danny says. I've got an earpiece hooked to a two-way radio in my pocket.

"Five?" I say. "No. Six? I've lost count." The first two traps were obvious. A couple of normals, people without magic, lying in wait for me, once near my place in Venice Beach and once in Downtown L.A. They weren't very smart. Now they're very dead. After that they got smarter.

This is the first time they've used something as sophisticated as an illusion, though.

"Two of you must be tight for her to go to all this trouble."

"Oh, yeah. Thick as thieves." I just wish I knew *why* she was going to all this trouble.

The thing that worries me is that this is a setup for a setup. That's the thing with Jimmy. It manipulates things in small enough ways that you might not know it's happened until it's too late.

Once I took care of business in Vegas I was too eager to leave. It was when I was too far outside the city to do anything about it that Nicole went on her murder spree. I won't make that same mistake.

This trap might just be maneuvering pieces before the real one gets sprung. I can only think that this is because of that opal.

Because I kinda stole it.

Unlike the opal in Zombie Joe, the Vegas opal seems to be more of a battery. At least that's what Jimmy's using it for. Jimmy had a device built that allows it to project its powers a couple of weeks into the past. Normally, if it wants a thing to happen today, it would have to have set it in motion yesterday or earlier.

The device lets it do exactly that. It's made Jimmy a lot more powerful and a lot more frightening.

I palmed the opal out of it. The device is useless without it. I've seen the kind of effect it can have. Fuck if I was gonna let Jimmy have it.

I press myself against the wall next to the hotel room door. I can't feel any spells being cast. An illusion like the one at the window isn't going to be coming from someone casting it. They'd have to be concentrating to keep it up. Four hours plus is a bit much even for a good mage. Probably a projection artifact. You can buy them pretty cheap if you have the right connections, but this looks like more of a specialty item, meaning these guys are well-funded.

Mages can sense other mages when we cast spells or draw power from the local well of magic that surrounds everything. Artifacts are a different matter. Sometimes we can feel them when they do their thing, but more often than not their magic doesn't register. I've got a straight razor that can cut through bone like it's Jell-O, for example, and it doesn't feel like anything other than a straight razor, even when I make it appear in my hand out of thin air. Or it makes itself appear. It has something of a mind of its own and appears sometimes before I realize I need it.

"Nobody's casting," I say. That's actually a little troubling. No reason I should expect anyone to have a spell running, but I'd at least expect to feel somebody tapping the local well of power, if only a little bit at a time. Do it a little bit at a time in can be hard to notice. But if you know what you're looking for it's easy to spot. I've done it myself plenty of times. But there's nothing.

"I got a shot," Danny says. Fuck. Is this another trick? Some other bullshit to get me to lower my guard? Yeah, we're not playing that game.

"Take it," I say.

"Showtime."

I hear the window shatter as four bullets punch through and find their marks. Hysterical screaming from the lone survivor, who yanks the door open and runs out into the hallway. He barely clears the threshold before I'm on him, arm against his throat, shoving him back inside the room. I kick the door closed with my foot. He trips, falls, and I drop onto him, knees in his guts and a gun in his face.

"Hi," I say. "I understand you're trying to kill me."

I knocked the wind out of him, so he's not saying anything for a minute, but if this is a hardened killer I'm Santa Claus.

He's a stereotypical Huntington Beach surfer dude. White guy, perfectly tanned skin, blond hair with frosted tips, board shorts he's currently pissing in.

I look around the suite. The other four are pretty much the same. Two women, two men. They all look like extras from Point Break. A table in the middle of the room holds a mini keg and a stack of red Solo cups. I'm beginning to get a very bad feeling about this.

"Please don't kill me. Please don't kill me." His voice is barely a wheeze.

"What are you doing here?"

"We got the room comped. There was some lady checking out early so we got an upgrade. And we got a keg and Luke was gonna ask Melody to marry him this weekend and oh my god you killed them you killed them both what the hell."

I dig the gun into his forehead. "Shut it. Who's the woman who checked out?"

"I don't know. Some lady."

Fuck. Fuck fuck fuck. This wasn't the ambush. It was the bait.

"We've been played," I say into the radio. "These are a bunch of surfer kids. You seeing any movement?"

"No, I—Wait. Yeah. Three rooms away on either side just headed out the door. I'd say ten total. I can't get a shot yet."

Dammit. We should have just walked away from this one. The people we saw in other rooms scattered around the floor were the ones waiting for me. They weren't moving around like mercs waiting for their target, so of course it didn't occur to either of us that that was exactly what they were.

"I'm thinking you're about to have some visitors of your own," I say. "Cover your ass. I got this."

"Good point," he says. "If I can, I'll give you some support. In the meantime, don't get killed. You owe me money."

I get up from the floor and pull Surferboy up with me. "You and your friends were set up. It's about to get very loud in here. Go into the bathroom, close the door, get in the tub.

Do not come out until you hear nothing for at least ten minutes."

He's in shock but he's not stupid. He bolts for the bathroom. Better to have him out of the way. Because he's really not going to be okay with this next bit.

I throw out a spell that's got enough juice behind it that if there are any mages in this building who didn't know I was here, they sure as hell do now.

"All right," I say. "Up and at 'em." The four corpses stand up. Danny did a good job. Clean kills right through the heart. They were dead before they hit the floor.

"You two stand over by the door, stay out of sight. Grab the fourth and fifth people who come through after they've passed you. You two get on either side of the entryway. You go after anybody who makes it past you." They hurry to their respective spots and wait.

"What the fuck did you just do?" Danny says. "That was a shit-ton of power and four people just appeared in the room. They have really fucked up auras."

"You really want to know?"

"This is necromancer shit, isn't it?"

"It is. So, if you'll excuse me."

I used to only be able to animate a person like a puppet. But over the last few years I've picked up a thing or two. You'd think the fact that I was dead at the time might have gotten in the way of my learning anything, but it was kind of a job requirement.

This time is easier than the last time and, provided I survive this, I suspect the next time will be even easier. Now I can raise a handful of corpses, give them vague orders, and they'll handle themselves. Not well, but they'll do it. I'm honestly not sure if that's good or bad.

I can hear running footsteps in the hall. If these guys are professionals, and I don't see any reason they wouldn't be, they're going to throw a flash-bang in first to disorient me and, yeah, that's so not happening. I cast a spell that creates a bubble of silence in front of the door, extending into the rest of the room. It doesn't have to last long. I pull a couch away from under the window and get behind it. I'm still not sensing any spells.

The door explodes silently in as they hit it with a battering ram. In comes the flash-bang. I turn my head away and duck, covering and closing my eyes. Even still, I can make out the intense burst of light through my eyelids. As soon as it goes dark I'm up, and I pop a couple rounds into the first guy through the door.

Problem is he's carrying a ballistic shield. Tall shield to cover the entire body with only a slit in the front to look through.

The first shot misses completely, the next two ricochet off the shield, but the fourth one goes through the slit and into his faceplate. I feel him die as he goes down. One of the more annoying aspects of being a necromancer.

The guy behind almost trips over him. Within that bubble of silence, he didn't hear my gunshots. He and the one after him stumble into the room and get a very rude surprise as two undead surfer boys descend on them.

Over by the door the next two are coming in only to get grabbed and yanked off their feet by my other corpses. It's a surreal scene. Like watching a silent 1920s zombie film. I almost expect a placard to appear that says, "RAAARRGHGH!" in flowing script.

Five down, five to go. Or not. I put down one as they come in and the next two's heads explode when Danny hits them through the window. I will my mini zombie horde out the door to get the last two in the hall.

My silence spell doesn't extend to the hallway, so I can only imagine the kind of racket they're making. I feel the final two die under the teeth and hands of the recently dead. When I step out into the hall the sound comes back and I can hear wet, tearing noises as the zombies rip into the corpses.

I don't know why they do that. It's not like they need to eat. Is it me? Do I have decades of zombie movies subconsciously shaping the spell? I'll have to look into that. I kill the spell and all four zombies drop to the floor.

I bend down to one of the more intact mercenary corpses, pull his gun and check the magazine. Rubber bullets. He's got a taser on his belt and a bunch of nylon zip-tie restraints. I roll him over and my hand brushes against them, and I can feel the magic coming off them.

Motherfucker. These are mage shackles.

You can't just slap handcuffs on a mage. They'll turn them to smoke, dissolve them, shatter them, whatever. So, some asshole during the Inquisition came up with these fun little toys. They suppress a mage's ability to cast.

I've seen them done as handcuffs, bracelets, collars, a remarkable amount of bondage gear, on and on. Never seen them as zip-ties before. Makes sense. Go after a mage, you want to be prepared. But why do they have so many?

Could be useful. I reach to pull them off his belt and get a better idea.

I pull two HI, MY NAME IS stickers from a spool in my messenger bag, write YOU CAN'T SEE ME on them, slap one onto the front of my jacket, the other onto the corpse, and shove a burst of magic into them. This whole place is going to get really crowded really fast and I don't want anyone to get in my way.

"All right," I say, "let's go." The corpse pulls itself to its feet, staggers a bit, and then steadies itself.

"Follow my lead, don't touch anybody, and try not to leak too much if you can. You and me, we're gonna go take a drive and have a chat."

"Hey." Danny's voice but tinny and distant. The earpiece has fallen out and its hanging by its spiral cord. I get it reseated.

"Yeah," I say.

"Why weren't you answering?"

"Silence spell. You all right?"

"Yeah," Danny says. "They sent a couple up here all right. Makes sense. This is the only spot to get a clear enough view of the room. But we can compare notes later. Long Beach PD just rolled up with a dozen squad cars and a SWAT van."

"Good to know," I say. "On my way out."

"Hey, uh—Did I just murder four kids?"

"No," I say. "Nicole did."

Chapter 2

I met Nicole right before I left Vegas almost thirty years ago. I went out there when I had to leave L.A. to keep a crime boss from murdering what was left of my family and friends.

Not long after arriving I hooked up with a bunch of other mages robbing private vaults, museums, the occasional bank.

We were children. A bunch of amoral reprobates and psychopaths. I left when the psychopath bit became a little too apparent in a couple of them.

I'm not entirely sure why I did. I think I still had something akin to ethics at the time. But some crack in me was letting all that leak out and I felt like I was losing myself. So I left.

Shouldn't have bothered. Lost myself anyway.

That's when I connected with Jimmy. Decent guy. Not too bright. Did a lot of meth. But he needed a roommate and left me alone. Except for all the times I bailed him out of jail.

I wonder sometimes why I did. I told myself it was because he was useful to me, so I couldn't have him locked up someplace. But that was bullshit.

The thing about Jimmy is that he was a mage who didn't know he was a mage. Didn't even know magic existed. He had one trick and he didn't even know he was doing it.

Every mage has a knack, that one type of magic they're stupidly good at. Some never figure out what theirs is, but most of us still have one. Some people get healing, divination, flight, whatever. Me, I got necromancy. Jimmy got a weird and largely useless form of invisibility. Useless for him, anyway.

He was this sort of black hole to scrying. Magical senses just slid right off him. He didn't ping anyone's magical radar unless they were looking the right way.

And the effect extended to the places he spent a lot of time at; his apartment, a couple strip clubs, the North Las Vegas jail. Which meant it was great for hiding me.

It's funny how much time and effort we spend on justifying all our choices to ourselves. "Because I wanna" never seems to be good enough.

Truth is I felt sorry for the guy. Not exactly a part of who I thought I was. So I lied and pretended that I didn't care and went and bailed him out anyway.

And then he got caught cheating at a casino. Like I said, he wasn't very smart. One, don't cheat at a casino, they'll catch you. Two, don't cheat at a casino run by a mage, they'll make your life miserable.

The mage running the place, one Sebastian McCord, noticed the Jimmy-shaped hole in his awareness of his casino floor and went to investigate.

He found out Jimmy knew me and that's when the fun really started.

"Why is there a dead SWAT officer in my morgue?" Kyle says. Kyle is a medical examiner for the County of Los Angeles. He also moonlights as a doctor and coroner for some of L.A.'s supernaturals here, here being a homeless shelter in Downtown L.A. that caters to humans and supernaturals both. Although the two types of clientele are kept very, very separate.

"One, it's not your morgue, it's Gabriela's. Two, despite the all black BDUs and tactical gear, he's not a SWAT officer. And three, where the hell else would I take him? He's dead."

"I recall you just leaving bodies by the side of the road," he says.

"Give a hoot. Don't pollute."

"Uh huh. How'd he die?"

"Bullet through the heart." Amazingly the bullet didn't hit anything else. But that's magic for ya. Danny's one of the better combat mages out there.

Kyle is a fairly unassuming guy. Bald with little wisps of white hair around the edges of his scalp. Has a weird gait. Arms are just a touch too long. Otherwise he looks completely normal. Unless he's eating.

Kyle's a ghoul. Ghouls eat carrion, preferably human. For the most part they pass as human just fine, more or less. Until they eat, at which point their jaws unhinge, their throats puff out, and you get a good look at the rows of sharp teeth going all the way down their throat like a snapping turtle's. Sometimes they eat things a little more lively than carrion.

"Really, why's he here?" Kyle says.

"I was hoping I could put him on ice for a bit in case I need to ask him more questions."

"Ask him more—"

"Can I use a drawer? He was sitting in the car with me up from Long Beach for two and a half hours with the AC blasting. I've slowed the degeneration down but he's starting to get ripe."

"Fine. Drawer twelve."

"Awesome. You heard the man. Drawer twelve."

The body levers up from the waist and slides off the autopsy table. He walks past Kyle, opens the drawer, and clambers inside, pulling the drawer closed behind him. To his credit, Kyle doesn't even flinch.

"What the actual fuck was that?" Kyle says.

"Figured neither one of us needed a strained back hauling him into the drawer," I say. "He's got legs, he can do it himself."

"I liked you better when you were dead," he says. "You know, I had you opened up on a table down in Mission." I'd heard my body had been cremated with no fanfare so I'm a little surprised it went down to the morgue on Mission Road.

"You take any choice bits home to eat?" I say.

"Oh hell yeah," Kyle says. "Your kidneys were great."

"Glad I was good for something."

Kyle's got a sweet gig at the coroner's office. He has access to some choice cuts of fresh meat. All the guts and the brain from a body get tossed into a viscera bag during the autopsy and are supposed to be cremated. Instead, a lot of it goes into Kyle's freezer.

It's a position some ghouls would kill for and from what I understand have. Things have calmed down but apparently there were some really messy fights among the ghoul population in the sixties, each trying to knock out the competition.

But then the eighties happened, the murder rate skyrocketed, and there was plenty of fresh meat to go around.

"You need me to do anything to your corpse?"

"You already did."

"I mean the one in drawer twelve."

"Right. No, I think he's good." We were stuck on the 405 with nothing else to do so I made the best of the time and had a chat. I had to use a little magic to slow down his body from doing what bodies do. Trust me, you don't want that kind of mess when you're crawling past LAX.

His name is—was—Philip. A Marine, he made it to E-7, gunnery sergeant, before cashing out and going the military contractor route. Did some official stuff in Iraq, some off the books jobs in Libya, Sudan, Somalia, then about a year ago hooked up with a group who only did stateside jobs.

That's where he ran into mages for the first time. He adjusted pretty quickly. Did a few jobs with magical backup. Strangely, the one in Long Beach didn't have anything with magic beyond the illusion of Nicole and equipping the team with mage restraints.

Philip didn't know why. Didn't know a lot of stuff. No idea who hired them, why, what was supposed to happen once they got me into a van. Wish I'd known which one of them was the driver.

But he did know who his boss was.

"Some guy named Miles Kendrick," I say. I've called Danny as I leave the morgue. "Know him?"

"Ugh. Yeah. Kind of a prick. I can get hold of him. Getting any client info out of him is gonna be tough. Or expensive."

"Tell him if he doesn't give his client up I'll fill his house with undead cockroaches."

"You do know that going straight to intimidation is not the best opening move for this sort of thing, right?"

"It's always worked for me," I say.

"Of course it has. All right. I'll give you a call when I know more. Don't get tased and tossed in a van. I'd hate to have to come rescue you."

"You're adorable," I say and hang up.

A few minutes later my phone rings and I think Danny can't have come up with anything that quickly. But it's Gabriela and my day suddenly feels better.

Things have changed between us lately, though I'm honestly not sure how much. We're dating? I guess? She's also dating another mage, Amanda Werther. It does feel a little weird sometimes, but good weird. Usually, I date somebody, they eventually try to kill me. We got that out of the way when we first met.

"Hey," Gabriela says. It's good to hear her voice. Funny. I'm still not sure how I feel about us, but I guess that's a positive sign?

"Hey," I say back.

"You don't sound good. What happened?"

"You got all that from one word?"

"I know you better than you think I do," she says. "What happened?"

"Stepped into another one of Nicole's little funhouse traps. Accidentally murdered four kids. They were bait."

There's a long pause as she processes that. "Is this Long Beach?" she says.

"Already made the news, huh?"

"Fourteen dead, suspect in custody," she says. Christ. Like the kid's got enough on his plate, now some asshole detective's gonna try to pin this on him.

"That won't stick," I say. "They'll figure out all the shots came from a sniper rifle or a .40 and they won't find either one there. Then they'll have to explain how four dead teenagers ate a bunch of armored mercenaries." I give her the highlights.

"Are you okay?"

"No," I say. "Danny's probably worse, though. He's the one who took the shots. I stink of gunpowder, but a change of clothes and a shower and I should be fine. I dropped off my new mercenary friend in the shelter morgue with Kyle. I forgot a bag here with some clothes so I figured I'd stop in instead of driving all the way back down to Venice."

Gabriela is not the typical mage for L.A., or anywhere for that matter. She owns and operates this Skid Row homeless shelter. She has to do a lot of business with the city, goes to council meetings, actively runs protests in support of the homeless, stuff like that.

She's got a recognizable face to some of the normals so she tries to keep a lid on the magic in the area lest someone start putting pieces together.

She used to own an old SRO, Single Room Occupancy, hotel in Downtown Los Angeles that she used for the same thing. Pretty typical for an SRO; old, run-down, barely holding together. Except most of the residents weren't human.

Vampires, aswang, ghouls, she let all sorts in. No judgment. Just don't kill anybody that leads the cops to her door.

It worked out pretty well for her, except that to fund all that she made herself a nice little criminal empire in Downtown Los Angeles. Knock-off Chanel handbags and fake Rolexes down in Santee Alley, mostly. Also robbing the occasional dealer and pimp who strayed a little too close to her territory.

She made sure everybody who needed them had clean needles, a place to get a shower, food to eat. Basically, taking care of her little corner of the neighborhood.

It didn't last.

"Forgot?" she says. I can hear her smiling which you'd think isn't a thing, but, well I can.

"Okay, kind of forgot."

"And wasn't home on the way?"

"Yes, you caught me. I have an ulterior motive of wanting to see you. And dropping a corpse off in your morgue because he was starting to smell up around Torrance, but mostly just to see you."

"A nefarious plot? Whatever shall I do?"

"I can think of a few things."

"Do you want to leave a toothbrush?" she says. "I hear that's the next step in a relationship."

"You want to leave one at my place?"

"I, uh, kinda already did," she says.

"Tells you how observant I am."

"Sadly, I'm not going to be back for a while, I think," she says. "You have anything else going on today besides almost getting tased by mercenaries?"

"Thought I'd live dangerously and go hit Oki Dog."

"I can't believe you actually eat that stuff."

"Come on, a chili, hot dog, pastrami burrito? That's like the turducken of shitty L.A. fast food."

"I admire that you're so committed to gastric distress that you'll cross La Brea for it," she says. "But if you're gonna drive all that way I have a better idea. Got a mystery needs solving. Wanna come play Scooby Doo?"

"Is this a sex thing?" I say. "Because if it's a sex thing I am totally on board."

"Maybe after," she says. "I can dress up as Velma and you can look for clues."

"Tease. Where do I meet you?"

"Simi Valley."

"You're fucking kidding me." Simi Valley is just outside L.A. County at the base of the Simi Hills. Not much around it but scrub brush, so it burns on the regular. In terms of miles it's not that far. In terms of time, it might as well be the fucking moon.

"Yeah, I know," she says. "Take the 118, get off at Erringer and take a left. There's a Motel 6. I'll meet you in the parking lot."

"Gonna be a bit. I need to get cleaned up. Unless you want me to show up smelling like a crime scene."

"Now who's the tease?"

"You want to walk me through this?" I say. "You had a guy up here to check this place and he never came back out?"

We're standing in front of a house nestled off to the side of a fire road in the Simi Hills. We had to walk through a barely visible path through the scrub to get to it. There isn't so much as a driveway.

It's a sprawling Mission Revival property, a complex of terra-cotta roofed buildings surrounded by a wall that encloses an open courtyard in the center. Oil lanterns made of rough glass and wrought iron are spaced along the porch. The owner's commitment to authenticity is impressive.

"I don't know that he necessarily went in," she says. "And he wasn't supposed to. I'm more concerned that he never called in and he's not the sort to do that. And his truck is still here."

"And that was when?"

"Couple days ago," she says.

I met Gabriela at the motel and followed her up to this middle-of-nowhere property. We've parked our cars well away from the house, neither of us trusting whatever the hell this is.

I don't care about my car, I stole it a couple hours ago, but Gabriela owns a dark purple Charger that she'd rather not have damaged or destroyed should whatever-this-is turn out to be dangerous. Having had a sweet Cadillac El Dorado blown up into scrap metal under me, I can understand.

Of course, if it's dangerous to the cars, then it's dangerous to us. Neither one of us really worry about that sort of thing, though.

I go up and touch the wall, check the rough-hewn double door and its hammered-iron handle. There's no lock. Everything looks new, or new-ish at least, but the design is old Rancho California. I work my finger into a crack on a wall and pull out a chunk of mud plaster, showing dried mud and straw underneath.

"This is real adobe," I say. "Who the hell builds with adobe anymore?" There are no power lines I can see, windows are shuttered. At one end of the courtyard there's what looks to be a chapel, the cross on the roof cracked and weather-beaten. "How'd you hear about this thing?"

"The Internet," she says. "If you can filter through all the NIMBY whining it's amazing what you can find out on Nextdoor. Couple people ran across it about three months ago on a hike. Next weekend it was gone."

"And now it's back." I have no idea what Nextdoor is, but knowing people and the Internet, I can guess.

"And now it's back," she says. "Seems to come and go. I had him set up a few trail cams nearby. Streams video. One second it's there, the next it's not. Few hours later, it's back."

"Pattern?" I say. If it's coming and going at regular intervals then . . . it still doesn't tell me what the fuck it is.

"Not that I've noticed," she says. "And we've got good coverage. He was Army Special Forces. Used to do shit like this all the time."

"Special Forces? I didn't know you had somebody like that on the payroll."

"You've been busy." "Busy" in this case being a euphemism for "Dead."

"You catch him on video?"

"Yeah. He walked into frame when the house appeared and then walked out. Doesn't look like he went inside. At least not through the front door."

"You trust him?"

"More or less," she says. "I know he's not going to try something like simply skipping town. And if he'd stolen something from me, I'd have known. He came here and something happened. But I have no idea what."

"I'd write this whole thing off as a loss," I say. "Seal this place up with wards so nobody can go inside. But you won't do that, will you?"

"You wouldn't either," she says. "Much as you'd like to pretend you would. I don't throw my people under the bus. Also, this house shouldn't even be here."

"How so?"

"It's not on any modern planning maps, never been zoned. This should all be scrub brush and coyotes."

"You said modern planning maps? You found something. How far back did you have to go?"

"Old Rancho days. Place was owned by one Jose Miguel Garcia who was granted the title in 1786. It was ceded in the 1850s to the territorial governor when the U.S. took California. At that point nobody owned it and as far as I can tell the whole place was gone by then."

"No heirs?" Usually there's at least one person in Southern California who can say "My great-great-so-and-so used to own that" for just about every piece of dirt.

"There's a story in that," she says. "His son, Don Miguel, married Juanita Hernandez in 1814. Had three boys. Found death records for all four of them. Juanita drowned her kids in a pool in the courtyard. Miguel came home to find her crying over the drowned kids. They say she drowned herself and he shot himself in grief."

Something sounds familiar. And then I have it. "Wait. This isn't—It can't be. That story doesn't even come from here."

"Besides the husband shooting himself sounds a little like it, doesn't it?"

There's an old story, La Llorona, the Weeping Woman. Shifts around depending on where you hear it, but the basics are this: A woman marries some rich asshole, bears him two sons, and then gets thrown over for a younger, prettier version. So, while her husband's off banging his new sweetheart, she snaps and drowns her boys in a river. Too late, she realizes what she's done, and tries to save them, but they're lost to the current. She searches and searches the banks, crying the whole time for her lost boys, until she herself keels over from, fuck, I dunno, exposure?

Anyway, the rest of the story is that she haunts the place

where her children died looking for them, constantly wailing. If you hear her, bad things will supposedly happen to you. Like you'd guess, it's used by mothers to get their children to go to bed, telling them that La Llorona will get them if they don't chill the fuck out.

"I think I met her," I say. A memory from my time as Mictlantecuhtli bubbles to the surface.

"Excuse me?"

"Mictlan. The original story's Aztec. The Hungry Woman. The Starving Mother. Something like that. It's more complicated. Some of the dead gods were involved. Cihuacoatl. Coatlicue. But the woman herself was just as human as everybody else in Mictlan." There's a long pause, something I've gotten used to when I blurt out shit like that.

"How much are you remembering, lately?" Gabriela says. "About being Mictlantecuhtli?"

"The stuff that I was directly involved with, pretty much all of it," I say. "Everything else is sketchy unless something triggers it. I can pull some stuff if I really concentrate. Most times it's like that word that's always on the tip of your tongue. Kind of maddening, actually."

When something does trigger them, memories come flooding in. Sometimes a little, sometimes a lot. Like now. Thinking about Cihuacoatl and Coatlicue. Two goddesses I—sorry, Mictlantecuhtli—couldn't save five hundred years ago when the Spanish took out most of the gods as they were subjugating the people.

I shake off the memory. The sense of failure. The anger. The despair. Those aren't mine, no matter how much they feel like they are. And thinking about those memories won't lead to anything good.

"Anyway," I say, "Seems a bit of a stretch. Doesn't mean it's not related, but it's almost cliche."

"It gets better," she says. "One story is that Juanita tried to raise them from the dead and she drowned herself when it failed."

"That's . . . unusual."

"I think so, too, but I figured before I do anything else, I should call the expert in dead things to take a look and tell me what he sees."

"Fuck all," I say. "There are no ghosts in, around, or within a mile of this place."

"Is that normal?"

"Not even close. This is a literal dead zone. There is nothing here. At the very least I'd expect a couple of Wanderers, maybe a Haunt or some Echoes from a car crash nearby, but this is just a big ball of nothing."

One of the perks, if you want to call it that, to being a necromancer, is the ability to see ghosts, those cast-off shells that are left behind from traumatic deaths. There's a barrier between the living and the dead, which is a good thing, because the dead eat life, they're always hungry, and if they ever cross that barrier a lot of people end up with their souls devoured.

But there's more to it than that. The other side is like a funhouse mirror of the living side. If something's been in a place long enough, it leaves a doppelganger over there. Best example I know is the Ambassador Hotel down on Wilshire where Bobby Kennedy was assassinated in the sixties. It closed down a long time back and was demolished years later only to have a school built on the old grounds.

But on the other side the Ambassador is still there. In fact, it's more than just a hotel. It's been so filled with events and life and mystique during its existence that it didn't just become part of the psychic landscape, it gained a sentience of its own, and now it's a ghost itself. Nice place, good conversationalist, mass murderer. I used to have a room there until I collapsed it on an eight-thousand-year-old djinn.

If this house has been around for very long, I'd expect to see a dim outline of it through the veil, but I don't see anyth—

"Wait," I say. I crouch down and squint. There is something on the other side. "I'll be right back."

I slide over from the living side to the dead to get a closer look. A burst of jet engine noise, the world going from vibrant color to washed out grays and blues. Like I thought, the house doesn't exist on this side. But I do see something.

"It's not here," Gabriela says, sliding over next to me. She's already sweating from the effort.

"I don't know why you do that," I say. Most mages can learn just about any spell. Though Gabriela's not a necromancer, she picked up this trick before I ever met her. But like with most people, the dead side is not kind to her.

"Subverting expectations," she says. "People underestimate me."

"You are good at it." I say. "You see that?"

"Barely," she says, blinking. Most people, mages included, can only stand to be over here for a little while before the environment leeches the life out of them.

I walk over to a series of boulders that probably haven't moved in a few hundred years so they exist on both sides, taking care to not step into the perimeter of the house itself. A black military boot sticks out from behind the rock.

"Found him," I say.

Gabriela walks over. "Fuck. That's Earl." She bends down to take a closer look at the body. She starts to tilt.

I grab her before she can keel over. "Can you get out on your own?" I say.

She nods. "I think so."

"Then go," I say. "I'll bring him out. You don't want to pass out here. Trust me." She nods, wipes sweat from her brow, and disappears.

Aside from having decades of prior experience, I got a crash course in death god studies over the last few years. Before I died and went to Mictlan, I'd be feeling entropy sucking at my soul out here. Now I don't feel a thing. Like I could be here for hours. I guess death has its pluses.

I look over Earl's body and have more questions than answers. If a living person comes over here and dies, it's usually because ghosts ate their soul. They leave distinct marks on a body, deep, cold gouges that look like freezer-burned chicken.

But he doesn't look like he's been attacked by any ghosts. That's not as weird considering there are no ghosts here. Spend too much time over here and the environment itself will leech you dry, but it doesn't look like this.

What he does look is about a hundred years too old. Maybe this is what he looked like before, but I kinda doubt it.

Not going to get many answers over here. I bend down to pick up Earl's body. He weighs next to nothing. I shift his weight and I hear something crackle. Flakes of skin drift to the ground. As they reach the ground I see it.

I set him down and slide over to the living side to look at the spot where his body lies on the dead side. It's just outside a side door of the house. I slide back.

"What is it?" Gabriela says. She's a little ways away, leaning against another boulder. She looks a little green.

"He was inside the house," I say. "Then something happened, he came out here and he died. Or he died and was pushed."

I point out the depressions and prints in the dirt. There are boot prints from him, but they only get a step and stop. But a second set of prints, plain soles, small. A woman's or a child's feet. They stop next to Earl's prints.

"He was killed on the dead side and then pushed over to the living."

"I don't see any blood," she says.

"It was only a quick look, but I didn't see any wounds on him. How old is he?"

"Mid-forties?" she says. "Why?"

I slide over, grab his body, and slide back. "See for yourself."

"What the fuck happened to him?"

"Old age?"

"The hell does something like this?"

I can think of a few things. I have a pocket watch that if you spin the crown, point it at something, and push the button, makes things age scarily fast. But it's about as precise as a hand grenade.

"You think Kyle will be upset if I use his morgue a second time?"

"It's not his morgue," she says. "It's mine."

"You should tell him that."

"Oh, I think I can let the necromancer take all the blame for telling off the volunteer pathologist."

"Ouch," I say. "You wound me."

"That's why you love me," she says. There's a pause, neither one of us knowing what to say to that. We've had a strange relationship. And over the last few months it's gotten stranger.

"Anyway, uh, yeah," she says. "I've got a morgue back at the shelter. State of the art and everything. Cost a fortune."

"I am clearly in the wrong line of work," I say.

"That's okay," she says. "When we go out on dates I'll pay. I'll be your sugar mama. But I expect you to put out."

"Yes, ma'am."

There's a pause. "I do not like where this is going," Gabriela says.

"What, you don't like the idea of me putting out? I am offended. Or is it that whoever did this is a necromancer powerful enough to go over to the other side and take someone with them, while driving all the ghosts out of the area?" I have to take a breath after that one.

"Something like that, yeah," she says. "Would they be as powerful as you?"

"Not sure. But honestly, I doubt it."

"That's something, at least. I guess," she says.

"Yeah. It's something, all right," I say. "But we have a bigger problem."

"Bigger than another necromancer?"

"Yeah. Because only one of them's a necromancer," I say.

"Shit," she says when she gets it.

"If the person who moved Earl over is a necromancer, then somebody else moved a house two hundred years into the middle of nowhere and aged a man to the point that he looks like a mummy." She lets that soak in for a second.

"Don't say it," she says. "Do not want."

"Me either," I say. "But you know that's what it is."

A flare of magic grabs our attention, followed by a scream somewhere between anger and anguish.

I draw my gun, Gabriela manifests a glowing machete in her hand. I reach for the door. Before I touch it there's a sound like thunder and a blast of air that throws us to the ground, knocking the wind out of me.

The house is gone.

"You all right?" I say. I stand and help her up.

"Yeah, I'm good. I fucking hate time magic."

I look down at the body of Earl. The blast of air scattered desiccated bits of him and his gear around.

"I don't think he liked it much either."

Chapter 3

After the L.A. Firestorm, if you read the Times, Firepocalypse, if you read the LA Weekly, or That Fucking Necromancer's Fault, if you talk to most mages, Gabriela bought what was left of the surrounding properties and along with the land she owned under her hotel transformed it into a modern, multi-building shelter that covers an entire block. The money for it all is managed through a complicated series of shell companies to make it look like she has anonymous donors rather than criminal enterprises.

About two thirds is for the human homeless. The non-humans have their own section. She has it hidden from the normals with wards, don't-look-at-me spells, and creative architecture. It doesn't look like there's a secret section in the complex. The extra space allowed her to put in some amenities she didn't have before: a supernatural-focused clinic, job training, space for AA and group therapy meetings. And, of course, her own morgue.

The whole area is set as far from any of the living spaces as possible. You think a rotting human corpse smells bad, you should catch a whiff of a chupacabra.

"What exactly prompted you to put this in?" I say, realizing I just assumed she had a reason and that was good enough for me. Most times it is.

"The residents," she says, pushing open the sterile white double doors at the end of the hall. "They've had to hide their dead for a hundred years to keep humans from finding them. Now they've got somewhere to bring them. We have a contract with a mortuary in the Valley run by a ghoul for cremation. Plus a lot of them want to know how their friends died.

Speaking of friends, you here to take your corpsesicle off my hands?"

"Not quite yet," I say.

We've given Kyle a few hours to poke around while we did, uh, other things. Earl's body is laid out on the autopsy table. He's mostly bald with a few thin wisps of hair across a scalp stretched taut over the skull. He's covered in liver spots, muscle wasted away to nothing, his bones pressing against the skin in deep relief. When I picked him up to put him in the car his clothes were so loose they almost fell off his frame.

Kyle's already got him opened up, viscera bagged. Everything looks sort of gray, like uncooked steak left too long in the fridge.

"Any ideas what killed him?" Gabriela says.

"Old age," he says. He picks up the viscera bag, lays it on top of Earl's open chest cavity so we can see better. "There's the obvious external signs, but in case there was any doubt, we have this.

"You see how everything's sort of a dark brown color? That's lipofuscin. Accumulates in the tissues as you get older. This yellow gunk all over the liver are fatty deposits that you get with aging.

"I'll run a tox screen, too. Results can take a few weeks, but I seriously doubt he was poisoned. There's nothing, nothing natural at least, that can do something like this. Also, it gets better."

"I am so going to hate this, aren't I?" Gabriela says.

"Yeah," Kyle says. "And then some." He picks up the sternum that he's cut through to get into the chest. Some of the attached ribs are cracked and brittle at the ends where the saw went through, but others show clean, straight cuts.

"These broken ribs are what I'd expect cutting through someone with advanced osteoporosis, which he very clearly has. But these straight cuts are what you'd get from somebody no older than forty, tops. No sign of disease. The difference is even more pronounced with the long bones where it alternates along the length. Different parts of his body got old at different rates."

"What do you think?" Gabriela says. "Like your pocket watch?"

"Kind of," I say, "though to be honest I've never dissected somebody I used it on afterward. And this just affected him—how about his gear?"

When the adobe house disappeared there was a small shock wave. Only enough to knock us over. But I noticed flakes of some of Earl's clothes were blown off the corpse.

"About that," Kyle says. "Most of it's fine. And then there's this." He grabs a plastic baggie from the instrument tray. It's full of brownish-gray dust, a brass fixture, and a short chain.

"The fuck is that?" Gabriela says.

"Rabbit's foot. It was still intact when I found it in his bag and the second I tried to move it, damn thing exploded."

"Let me guess," I say. "Old age?"

Kyle shrugs. "Honestly, I couldn't tell you, but given everything else it wouldn't surprise me. And it's not just this." He points to a table where he's laid out clothing. There's a belt in pieces, a boot cracked down the middle. "Leather, cotton, anything natural as far as I can tell."

"How old would you say he is?" I say.

"How old were you expecting him to be?"

"Forty-ish," Gabriela says.

"Yeah, he's quite a bit north of that. Depends on which parts of him you're talking about, though. Oldest bits maybe a hundred, hundred and ten. Youngest, yeah, I'd say forties."

"Any ideas?" Gabriela says.

"None you're going to like," I say.

"If this is magic shit," Kyle says, "you take it outside. That's just gonna make me nervous and I'm nervous enough dealing with this fucker."

"I don't think whatever it is is catching."

"Yeah, well, I don't know. Which is why I'm wearing a smock and a face shield."

"Do ghouls even get sick?"

"Mostly just indigestion," he says. "Now get out. I got work to do."

We get about halfway down the hall before Gabriela says, "Don't say it."

"Figured I didn't need to," I say.

"I fucking hate time magic."

"Good to know. I'll make sure I don't get you any for your birthday."

Time magic, chronomancy, is rare. More rare than necromancy, and my kind are what you'd call thin on the ground. I've met very few other necromancers and no chronomancers. As far as I know. It's not like we walk around with signs on our foreheads, after all.

I know ridiculously little about chronomancy beyond what my pocket watch can do. I suspect it can do a hell of a lot more, though if it can, I honestly don't want to know about it.

Near as I can tell, chronomancy mostly deals with bending time, making it go faster or slower or stop altogether.

Amanda Werther, Gabriela's girlfriend, has her family estate inside a pocket universe with rooms where she can do exactly that. She has the body of her murdered father frozen in one, the uncle who murdered him frozen in another, and her backstabbing aunt frozen in a third just because she pissed her off.

They're not a very tight-knit family.

"I don't even know where to start with this," Gabriela says. "And I don't even know who to ask."

"There's gotta be somebody," I say. "Beyond whoever it is that did this."

"None that want to talk to me," she says. "Maybe. I'll have to check on that. How about you and this other necromancer?"

"Only one I'm on speaking terms with is dead and sitting in a Las Vegas jail cell. But whoever they are shouldn't be that tough to track down. We're not really big on subtlety."

In fact, if there's another necromancer that powerful in

town, I should have found out about it by now. Everything about this feels wrong.

"I should—" she starts. "No. There's nothing I can do about this right now. It's weird and fucked up but I promised myself I'd actually have a life." She pokes me in the chest. "And you're part of that."

I honestly don't know what to say to that. Gabriela and I are—I don't know what the fuck we are. Fortunately, she doesn't give me a chance to make this awkward.

"What are you doing later?"

"Not getting ganked by mercenaries?" I say.

"Amanda and I are going to a club in Hollywood," she says. "You should come with."

Okay, not *too* awkward.

When Amanda Werther inherited her father's estate, money, resources, and power, things changed for her. She went from being the daughter of the most powerful, well-connected mage in L.A. to being the head of her family and inheritor of everything her father had, not all of it good. There are agreements, obligations, debts.

Politics.

Everybody's been expecting her to start acting like her dad and they don't know what to do with the fact that she isn't. Case in point, clubbing.

Clubbing is to Amanda what golf is to old white men. Before, she was a princess. Now she's the queen. The clubs Downtown and along Sunset Boulevard are her court.

All of her connections have been fostered over the years in clubs and on dance floors. She's brokered deals and negotiated complicated truces between mages with nothing but her brains and her father's reputation to back her up. To say she's part of a new generation is an understatement. Her father was a couple hundred years old when he died.

And now that she's in charge everybody's coming out of the woodwork looking for an audience. And to see if she can swim now that she's been thrown into the deep end. If not, they want to be there to hold her down so she drowns faster.

Most mage families are like old money. They're controlled by stodgy old farts who last poked their heads out into the world sometime around the Nixon administration. They won't set foot inside these places, which is part of the point. If they want to deal with her, they'll do it on her terms and on her turf.

This has been changing the power dynamic in the city. Now the younger generation are gaining influence since, well, they're the only ones who'll go into the clubs. Dealing with a younger, potentially more progressive crowd has made some things easier for her.

But we're still talking mages here. No matter how progressive any of us might say we are, we're still a bunch of power-hungry narcissists who think we're better than everybody else. The truth, of course, is that we just have more ways to justify our complete lack of morals. Mages are assholes no matter how old we are. Even when we try really hard not to be.

An important fact that people don't seem to be paying attention to is that her family's been trying to kill Amanda since she was born. She was the heir presumptive, and a lot of people want to wear the crown.

So unlike a lot of the mages she's dealing with, she's been playing high-stakes politics her entire life. When your family's repeatedly trying to murder you, either you get really good at playing the game or you only live long enough to be an object lesson.

"You do remember who you're talking to, right?" I say.

"Yeah, I just thought you'd—"

"I can think of about half a dozen reasons that would be a bad idea, not least of which you seeing me do the white man's overbite."

"Really? That bad?"

"Trust me. I'm not a dancer. Even worse than I am at politics. And you know the sort of crap that'll start."

She pinches the bridge of her nose. "I am so fucking tired of the politics. Sometimes I just want to say fuck everybody and burn this whole town down."

"Not as cathartic as you'd think," I say. "What's going on? This isn't like you."

There's a long, worrying pause, and then: "Everybody knows you and I are—whatever we are," she says. "And that Amanda and I are a couple. People see the Werther Queen and La Bruja together and they lose their shit. They see you and I together and they lose their shit."

Amanda pointed out to me once that power in mage politics is concentrated in five main players. Three of them are families with lots of power, resources, and pawns to move around the chess board.

Gabriela is talked about the same way. She's on an equal footing with the rest of them. She's built up a following over the years. If she wanted to put together an army, there'd be no shortage of volunteers.

But the one that did surprise me, is me. Apparently, I'm the scariest motherfucker in town. Hell, in two towns. I went to a club in Vegas and when I told the bouncer the owners were expecting me and who I was, he almost pissed himself right there.

Mostly because I was in a wizard cage match a few days before, witnessed by thousands of mages, and ended it by parading my opponent's severed head around the ring, covered in both our blood. But still.

Gabriela and Amanda worry people. Gabriela and I scare people. Gabriela, Amanda, and I fucking terrify them.

"You know what'll happen if the three of us are seen together," I say. "And I don't mean 'Oh, what will the vicar think?'"

"I know," she says. Frustration is creeping into her voice. "I'm tired of hiding. I hid who I was at college. I hid behind La Bruja. And now I'm just hiding. Does that make sense?"

"Yeah," I say. "You want to be who you are. I want you to be who you are. So does Amanda. If you really want to do this, then let's talk to her and arrange it. Springing it on her when I just show up out of the blue is probably not the best way to go about it."

"Yeah," she says. "That would be fucked up, wouldn't it? I won't do that to her." She laughs. It's a bitter sound. "We'll have a coming out party." I step in close and hug her. She presses herself into me.

"You realize that any party we have is likely to end in gunfire," I say.

"And machetes."

"Blood, definitely."

"Ghosts?" she says.

"Oh, dozens. And if we're really lucky we can completely upend the balance of power in this city."

"Mmm. You know just how to get me going."

I pull her in tighter. There's a knot in my gut that I realize is fear. Fear that what we're doing is too much. That it's not enough. It feels fragile, this connection. Saying or doing the wrong thing will shatter it like spun glass.

Fuck it.

"I love you," I say. Gabriela stiffens against me and doesn't say anything for a long time. Slowly she pulls away and looks up at me, an expression on her face I can't read.

"Don't get killed tonight," she says, then turns stiffly away from me and leaves me there in the hall.

That went well.

Chapter 4

My phone rings on my way out of the shelter. Danny.

"Where you at?" he says.

"Just leaving Gabriela's."

"Awesome. That lead you gave me panned out. I'm just down the street. Meet me outside the Harrison. Fifth and Wall." He sounds pissed.

"The hell you doing over there?"

"I think I actually got her this time," he says.

"Seriously?"

"Yeah. Your dead merc friend wasn't lying. His boss had a meeting at this murder hotel Downtown two nights ago for the retrieval job on you. The client was shrouded by a spell but he was certain that it was a woman."

"And you think she's still there?"

"Yeah, because the best part is that he had to meet her in person at the same place this afternoon to tell her it had all gone tits up."

"You know how Jimmy works," I say.

"Yeah, well, fuck him. It. Whatever. Just get over here."

"Don't go in without me."

"No promises."

I meet Danny outside the Harrison Hotel, an old SRO hotel built in the early twenties Downtown. SROs used to be real popular around these parts. The Harrison took the Single Room bit a little too literally. Closet? Please. Bathroom? Go down the hall.

The Harrison is what we call a murder hotel. Sketchy history, soaked in blood, etc. Another perfect example of a murder hotel is the Cecil. Ridiculous number of murders, weird crimes, suicides, serial killers. At least two active ones lived there within six years of each other in the eighties.

If anything the Harrison's history is weirder. No serial killers I'm aware of, but at least as many murders, suicides, assaults . . .

Plus they had Satanists. There was a raid in the twenties on a group that had rented out an entire floor for their—I can't say this with a straight face—"Black Magick Rituals." There were rumors of Aleister Crowley's Thelema religion being involved. Everybody loves sex magic, after all. But Crowley didn't have much presence here until the mid-thirties.

Something like a dozen people died, though all the reports I've seen have been light on details. All I know is that it freaked out enough people that they didn't want to write it down and felt it was easier to just throw it under the Satanism bus and call it a day.

Kind of funny how the eighties' Satanic panic had people freaking out when there weren't even any blood-soaked sex rituals. It was all cocaine-fueled orgies with prostitutes and bankers, a couple priests, at least one mayoral candidate. The only person I know of who died during one of those was a stockbroker with a heart condition.

The sad thing is that like a lot of these buildings the Harrison used to be a shining jewel in an up-and-coming city. Now it's a dilapidated husk that fits in just fine with the street stink of car exhaust, sidewalk piss, and dead things in the gutter.

Danny's leaning against a Jeep Wrangler parked across the street, glaring at the hotel. He's wearing a long coat. It's not cold out, but he's hiding a shotgun.

"The fuck's wrong with you?" he says.

"What do you mean?"

"I dunno. You look . . . off."

"Enh, it's nothing," I say. "The Harrison, huh? Surprised she picked this place. She's not a slumming-it kinda gal."

"Maybe Jimmy picked it," Danny says.

"That doesn't make me feel any better," I say. "But yeah, probably."

Last I saw Nicole I was ready to kill her. Wanted to. And that was before she went on her murder spree.

I didn't, but not because I was being merciful. She was firmly ground under Jimmy's influence. I didn't see them together much, but I don't think I've seen a more dysfunctional, abusive relationship. Killing her would have been kinder. So, I didn't.

You look back sometimes on the mistakes that you make and wish you could just erase them. Take a different path, go left instead of right. Walk away instead of sticking around.

After Jimmy got caught cheating in Vegas I was about to throw him to the wolves and skip town. And then Nicole and her boyfriend Sebastian asked me if I wanted to kill a guy and then bring him back to life so he could live forever. I'm a necromancer. How do I pass that shit up?

They'd gotten hold of a medieval book of necromancy spells. Trouble was, they couldn't understand it. They could read the words just fine. The problem was more that the writer assumed you already knew what you were doing. Like trying to follow your grandmother's recipes when half the steps are missing.

For me, it was easy. I knew most of the spells already, and I could see ways to streamline the others. But there was one in particular I'd never seen before. Didn't even realize it was a necromancy spell. It was the only one they cared about. Making an Oracle.

I stand in front of the Harrison's heavy iron-and-glass door looking for wards, trip wires, pressure plates, flying darts, giant boulders, or anything else that might get me killed with a lack of discretion and an abundance of stupidity. Narrowly avoiding multiple recent attempts at murder and/or kidnapping can make a guy cautious. Don't say I can't be taught.

"I don't think they booby-trapped the front door," Danny says.

"You're the one who said you'd set a bomb off if you were trying to take me down."

"Yeah, I would," he says. "But it wouldn't be on this door. That thing's gotta weigh half a ton. You'd see any bomb or wards strong enough to take it out. So just fuckin' open it." I flip him off and go inside.

In its heyday, the Harrison must have been beautiful. Before the fires there were a lot of old L.A. hotels like this. Complete shitholes with faint signs of what they used to be.

I can see stained glass so filthy only a hint of its original color survives, most of the panes broken and covered by cheap plywood. Art Deco flourishes along the ceiling and at the base of the banister, with chunks of plaster chipped or missing altogether. The most banal things—doorknobs, light switches—crafted with all the care of intricate art pieces, then ignored like poorly maintained plumbing.

"The Edgewood used to look like this," I say.

"I heard you burned that place down."

I first met Gabriela at her hotel, the Edgewood Arms. While I was there, they got a demon-and-crazy-Russian-mobster infestation, which, okay, sure, might have been partly my fault.

"I'm not the one who set it on fire."

"Not how I heard it," Danny says.

"Blow me," I say.

"No thanks," he says. "I mean, you're cute and all, but you're really not my type."

A number of things are called oracles, but an Oracle-with-a-capital-O takes the idea to stupid new heights. An oracle tells you what the future will be. An Oracle tells the future what it will be.

That's what was in this spellbook. Basically, you take a particular type of demon, slam it into a human soul like a high-speed car crash and—this is where the necromancy comes in—trap the results inside said human's head, then cut it off.

I had an Oracle described to me recently as what you'd get

if a monkey's paw fucked a hand grenade. In a lot of ways, Oracles can grant wishes. They just tweak a little bit here and a little bit there, and the person using them gets the result they want. Problem is, those tweaks have side effects.

For example, someone once asked Jimmy to ensure they won a particular bet. Jimmy made some changes and made it happen. It also "inadvertently" crashed an airplane. Jimmy knew that was going to happen. It did it anyway.

We head toward the front desk, which has a cage surrounding it that looks strong enough to stop rhinos. It's been painted over multiple times in thick layers of black paint, the original brass peeking through in worn-down patches.

A gawky Asian kid sits inside the cage doing his homework. He jumps when I ring the bell.

"Dude," he says. "Scared the shit outta me."

"Not a lot of people ring the bell?" Danny says.

"Not in the last five years they haven't. At least not while I've been on duty."

"LAPD," I say, showing him a sticker in a badge holder where I've written "I'M THE POLICE. I'M HERE TO HELP YOU."

I had to pump a lot of power into that one, because these days nobody in L.A. but rich white people actually believes the police are there to help them.

"We're looking for a woman who checked in recently," I say. "Would have paid cash."

"Dude, look around," he says. "Everybody pays cash. Shit, half of 'em pay in nickels."

"She wouldn't have fit in," Danny says. "At all." The kid's eyes pop.

"Oh. Her." Jackpot. "Knew she was gonna be trouble. She checked out a couple hours ago."

Of course she did. Dammit. "We're gonna need to see that room," I say.

The kid reaches over to a peg board for a key and slides it through a slot in the cage. No argument.

"You want 3C. Nobody's been in there since she checked out."

I take the key. "Thanks."

"No, thank you. You're making my life easier. People see cops running around the hotel, they stay in their goddamn rooms. Cuts the hassle of cleaning the place in half."

We head to the elevator and the kid stops us. "That thing hasn't worked in the entire time I've been here. You'll have to take the stairs."

"At least it's not a tall building," I say.

"Hooray for small favors," Danny says, putting his hand over his nose. The staircase is more rank than the bottom floor. Dark stains on the steps that could be years of urine, blood, who knows what else. It smells like we're walking through a latrine.

Floor three is surprisingly busy for this time of night. But then none of these people are nine-to-fivers. The rooms are tiny, perfect for poor single people living on a fixed income. Well, "perfect" is relative, I suppose. There's a pervasive stink of rancid garlic and liver.

Two old men wearing pants that might have been fashionable fifty years ago and sweat-stained undershirts are having some sort of argument in what I think is Hungarian. Down the hall people are standing in their doorways talking to their neighbors, smoking cigarettes, drinking cheap liquor. Everyone stops talking, their heads swiveling toward us as we step off the stairs. It's like time has stopped.

Then it snaps into fast forward. In a blink everyone has disappeared into their rooms.

"I don't think they like us," Danny says.

"Nobody ever likes us," I say.

"No, nobody ever likes *you*."

"Fair," I say.

We take up positions on either side of the door to 3C with our guns out. One of the small benefits of these old hotels is bullets have a harder time punching through six inches of lath and plaster than they do through drywall.

Nobody will care about gunfire here, but magic in Skid Row might turn some heads. Neither one of us really wants that. At least not until we know what the hell is going on.

"You feel that?" Danny says. It takes me a second, but there it is, a faint touch of magic.

"Barely," I say. "A ward?"

"Silence spell. Nothing strong."

"You can tell?"

"Half my work is sneaking up on people," he says. "You pick up a few things." I slot the key into the knob. It's unnaturally quiet.

"Yeah, it extends to just this side of the door," Danny says. Well, I don't have to worry about being heard. I push the door open, expecting the hinges to creak like it's a set from a Hammer horror movie. But there's no sound at all.

There are also no bullets or spells. Nothing. Danny ducks his head in and out of the doorway to see what's there without hopefully getting it shot off.

"Oh, fuck me," he says, holstering his gun. I take a look into the room and say the same thing, only louder.

"Were you expecting this?" Danny says. "I wasn't expecting this."

I holster my gun and step into the room. The silence spell isn't like the one I used in Long Beach. This is just a shell to block sound from inside. Somebody wanted to work in peace.

I step into the room—it really is tiny—and flick on the overhead light. Yeah, it's what I thought. I go over to the window, crouch down to get a better look.

"Hi, Nicole," I say to the corpse sitting on the floor against the wall. "Fancy meeting you here."

Chapter 5

"Dude, what the fuck?" Danny says. He's staying to the side of the window and looking through it like he did with the door. I appreciate a good dose of paranoia, but if there was a sniper, they'd have shot us already. A room this small, only way you could miss is if you couldn't hit the window.

Nicole's body is a mess. Throat slit. That's what did her in. The rest of the wounds look like they're post-mortem. There's plenty of blood spray on the walls and ceiling, but there's not enough at the right angles for anything else.

She was plenty dead before whoever did her in went to town on her. A crude Y incision like a drunk med student might use on a cadaver goes across her chest and down to her belly button. Her guts have been pulled out. They're sitting on her lap.

"I get the throat," Danny says. "Why the rest?" He's stepping carefully, trying to avoid the blood. I don't even bother. There's just too much of it.

"I can think of a few reasons," I say. "Like I can make her stand up and dance a rumba, but with that sort of damage I can't make her talk. She doesn't have anything left to talk with."

Whoever did this was thorough. Not only did they slice into her, they punctured the lungs and—I take a quick look in her mouth—cut out her tongue.

"You sure this was because of you?" Danny says. "Maybe she pissed off one of the residents?"

"Please," I say. "No offense, Danny, but that's stupid."

"It's wishful thinking. I do not like this."

"Neither do I. You need to walk, walk. This isn't your problem."

"If you were me, would you?" he says.

"In a heartbeat."

"Yeah, well. She fucking made me kill kids."

I get it. Neither one of us is happy about that situation, but Danny's the one who pulled the trigger. I'm focusing a little more on the fact that they literally did not know what hit them. They were dead before they could be surprised by it. Small mercy, I know, but it's something.

"All right, but know that if you need out, no harm, no foul," I say.

"Can you get anything out of her?" he says, totally ignoring what I just said.

"Can't talk to the corpse, left no ghost. No. Nothing I can think of."

"How about writing?"

"Fine motor control is iffy at best. Hell, getting a corpse to formulate an intelligible thought in the first place is a big ask."

"So what the hell happened?" Danny says.

"I think Jimmy might have some new friends."

"That doesn't sound good."

"It isn't. But it shouldn't surprise me. Anybody who knows about Jimmy is going to piece together what happened in Vegas and know it's in the wind. There's gonna be a lot of competition to find it. Plenty of people it can manipulate."

"If I understand how he works I see a problem with that," Danny says.

"Yeah," I say. "If it happened, Jimmy wanted it to happen."

Danny looks around the tiny room. "Where's her luggage?"

Good question. There isn't so much as a purse in here. There is, however, an empty square space in the middle of the blood, where it likely pooled against something heavy enough to keep it from flowing underneath. It coagulated enough that when the object was picked up, the floor stayed clear.

"That look about the right size for a case to fit a bowling ball?" I say. "Or a head?" Last time I saw Jimmy it was sitting in a wooden case that opened at the front like a cabinet.

"Bespoke head luggage," Danny says. "For all your skull transportation needs."

The single bed has a thin mattress and a bent metal bedframe that's more prison chic than flophouse fashion. The frame is light enough that Danny can lift it to look underneath.

"Check this out," he says, picking up a bloodstained hardback book.

"*The Divine Order of the Royal Arms of the Great Eleven*,'" Danny says. "The fuck is the Great Eleven?"

It takes me a second to remember where I've seen this book before. "Rachel had a copy of this," I say.

"Rachel?"

"McManus. Ran a prepper school out in the desert outside Vegas."

"Oh yeah, I know her. Think I know her. Redhead, right? Built like an Amazon? Did mercenary work with her dad a while back?"

"Yeah. Nicole killed her along with a bunch of other people I knew in Vegas after we got Jimmy for her. I found her with her throat slit like this, and the top of her head blown off with a shotgun."

"That seems . . . excessive," Danny says.

"I thought so, too. Especially because the other guy in the room was shot with a pistol." That's been bugging me since I saw it. I just don't know what it means.

"So why is there a copy here?" he says. I take the book from him. The bloodstain on it is a handprint. I look at Nicole and back at the book.

"I think Nicole was holding it and then tossed it under the bed," I say. "I think she left it for me."

"You mean Jimmy did," Danny says.

"Maybe. But maybe Nicole. Jimmy couldn't perceive her very well. It knew where she was but not necessarily what she was doing."

"Like with you?"

"Yeah, except that Jimmy can't see me at all." Or affect me, apparently, except indirectly. I flip through some of the pages.

"This isn't just a copy. I think it's Rachel's copy," I say. "She had a few other books with this one. Parsons, Crowley. That sort of thing."

"Isn't Parsons the rocket scientist who went out to the desert and jizzed all over some rocks trying to do magic?"

"Tried to summon a goddess, yeah," I say. Jack Parsons was a genius who was a rocket scientist before there was rocket science. He was also a crackpot who bought into Aleister Crowley's occult garbage. Mostly because it let him attend a bunch of orgies.

Most occult writers don't actually know what the fuck they're talking about. Crowley and Parsons are perfect examples. They crossed paths at some point. Parsons started up a Thelemic church under Crowley's tutelage out in Pasadena. Thelema's a weird mix of beliefs that all seem to funnel down into one thing, lots of fucking. I understand it attracts a fair number of erotimancers. But Thelema itself was all horseshit. Not a bit of magic in any of it.

When I saw the book at Rachel's, the Great Eleven sounded familiar but I couldn't place it. This time it comes to me and it just makes this whole scene weirder.

"The Blackburn cult," I say.

"Never heard of them," Danny says.

"Back in the twenties. What the hell was her name? May . . . May Otis Blackburn. Ran a scam with her daughter, bilked a lot of people out of money, maybe killed a few. Tried resurrecting a girl in Venice. Weird scene. Not sure if either of them were mages, though."

"Big?"

"Not especially," I say. "I don't know much about them. Animal sacrifices, illegal burials, killed a couple people, cooked some woman in an oven."

"They cooked somebody in an oven?"

"That's the story," I say. "The fuck does a hundred-year-old cult have to do with Jimmy?"

"And why is Rachel's copy here?" That's an even better question. Shit. I think I have the answer. I really hope I'm wrong.

"The kid downstairs," I say. "He said Nicole checked out earlier today."

"Clearly made a mistake," Danny says.

"I'm not so sure," I say. "Let's go find out."

When I got the spell book from Nicole and Sebastian I was horrified and intrigued. Well, probably more intrigued than anything else. This was magic that was right in my wheelhouse and fuck if I wasn't going to learn it.

I got everything together, minus one important piece: the head donor. Now, I had no intention of going through with the whole spell. My plan was to bail before it reached that point.

Then I screwed up and tried a dry run of the ritual, because nobody ever said I was smart, and accidentally summoned the demon. Without an appropriate sacrifice. I managed to stall it to keep it from trying to eat me, but that meant if I didn't find a head to cut off soon, I might as well volunteer my own.

Then three options appeared out of nowhere. Two I should have seen coming. Sebastian tried to convince me it should be Nicole. Nicole tried to convince me it should be Sebastian.

And then Jimmy suggested it should be him.

Doors crack open as we pass, stares following us down the hall. Once we're out of sight they'll crowd around the room arguing about what to do. Eventually, they'll leave it to the management. It's not like seeing a corpse in one of these rooms is all that uncommon.

The kid's still doing his homework when we get down to the lobby. He's so focused he doesn't see us coming up. I ring the bell again just to see if I get the same result as last time. I'm not disappointed.

"Jesus, dude," he says. "Oh, it's you. You get what you need?"

"Not quite. You said the woman in that room checked out earlier?"

"Yeah."

"What'd she look like?"

"Tall," he says. "Bright red hair. Looked like she wanted to get into a fight. Oh, and she was Irish, maybe? She had an accent."

Motherfucker. "Rachel," I say.

"No idea what her name was. Like I said, we're a cash only establishment," the kid says, like he's talking about a five star hotel and not a rat-infested, urine-soaked flophouse.

"I thought Rachel was dead," Danny says as we walk to the other side of the room. The kid doesn't need to hear this.

"So did I," I say.

"Doppelgänger?"

One of the best ways to make people think you're dead is to be dead. That's where a doppelgänger comes in handy. It's a constructed mimic that matches you down to the genes. But it's only alive enough for you to kill it.

Say you get one, stick it in your car, and light the whole thing on fire. Next day the cops are running your dental records and you're down in Belize drinking margaritas. They are ridiculously expensive.

"Easier than that," I say. "I met her ex-husband's girlfriend in Vegas. Guy's got a type. They could be sisters. Wouldn't be tough to enchant the body to make a medical examiner think it's Rachel's."

Dammit. I let who I thought Rachel was get in the way of realizing who she is. Were the signs there and I just missed them? Maybe. Was I so focused on watching my back around Nicole I didn't see what was standing in front of me?

"You think Rachel and Nicole were working together?" Danny says.

"If they were, the relationship soured at the end there. If they weren't . . . I don't even know what to make of that."

Some things are starting to make sense. Rachel's prepper school was attacked by a bunch of hired thugs when I showed up and helped take them out. Then another group came after me and Nicole at her home.

I couldn't figure out who'd hired them. They didn't even know who'd hired them. I found the guy who brokered the deal and before I could find out who his client was, Rachel put a bullet in his head.

At the time I thought she might have been the one behind the attacks. But she said it was revenge for all the people who got slaughtered at her school. I didn't really buy it then but there were more important things happening at the time.

Now I'm sure at least one of those attacks was Rachel. Probably both. Did she kill everyone else, too? Lucas? The Twins? Everybody at Candyland? She would have had to. Maybe Nicole helped.

And the Gold Rush casino where I'd met with Jimmy and Nicole after we sprang it out of a vault. When I went back looking for them I found the place wired to explode. Almost didn't make it out. Rachel certainly had the skills to do that.

I can see how it played out. She kills her ex's girlfriend. Maybe the body's already in the hotel room at Caesar's when she and Lucas get there. She kills Lucas and stages the two corpses.

The explosives at the Gold Rush would have already been in place. That blast took the building down. Not something you throw together in half an hour.

Then it's off to Candyland where she murders everyone there. By that time, I'm already on the road to L.A. Then she calls me on the Twins' phone and bails. That brings me back to find the bodies. I of course assume Nicole did it.

Fuck. Fuck fuck fuck. This whole time I'm hunting down Nicole when I should have been looking for Rachel.

So why the redirect? Did Rachel want to do something without me getting in the way? Was it even to distract me? Or someone else? Both? Neither?

"The Oracle would have seen this coming," Danny says. "Wouldn't it have told Nicole?"

"What?" I say. I'm having trouble focusing.

"Dude, you okay?"

I can't get the scene at Candyland out of my head. It was a massacre. All the people Rachel was able to murder so easily because they thought they knew her. She just waltzed in and started killing everyone.

Except for the Twins. Near as I've been able to tell, the Twins—Ken and Kendra, though they've had other names—weren't exactly human. They'd finish each other's sentences, sometimes talking at the same time as if they were one person, which I think they might have been.

Two of the most powerful erotimancers I've ever met. They ran Candyland, a strip bar / sex club / safe haven for their people. Erotimancers are unusual among mages in that they need to make connections with other people. They're hardwired for empathy. That's not necessarily a good thing. If you really want to manipulate somebody, first you have to be able to put yourself in their shoes.

Mages by and large are a guarded, paranoid lot. We don't have friendships so much as alliances of convenience. But erotimancers need relationships with other mages. It's how their magic works. Some of their most powerful spells come out of ritualistic orgies.

Or so I've been told. Nobody ever invites the necromancer to the orgies.

When I got to Candyland after Rachel had gone through and murdered everyone, I found one of the Twins dead. They'd been shot in places intended to wound and hurt, legs, ankles, hands, before they were killed.

But the other Twin, Rachel left alive, if you can call it that. Imagine having half of your brain blown out of your skull with a twelve-gauge. They couldn't stand up or talk, just twitched on the floor. The most they could communicate was to grab my hand and press my gun into their chest. I did the only thing I could for them and shot them through the heart.

Keeping that Twin alive was cruel. I don't know why she did it. I'll be sure to ask her before I skin her.

"No," I say. "I don't think I'm anywhere near okay."

Chapter 6

I shove down my rage as well as I can and focus. Danny's got a point. Jimmy would have been aware that it was going to happen. So why didn't it tell Nicole?

"Maybe it didn't know?" I say as we step outside onto the sidewalk. "Its inability to see either of us is sort of a cloud, I think. Me having you looking for Nicole might have been enough cover to keep Jimmy in the dark? I don't know enough about how it works."

"Then Rachel might not know we've found Nicole's body?" Danny says.

"Maybe. Though that seems a little doubtful." Another possibility comes to mind. "Unless killing her was part of the plan."

"How so?"

"She outlived her usefulness," I say.

"I don't buy it," Danny says. "A mage willing to do whatever he wanted her to do? You don't throw something like that away. It was something else." That's a good point. But what else could it be?

"Maybe she was a threat," I say. "Jimmy couldn't completely control or even see Nicole, but it doesn't have that problem with Rachel." Did Nicole figure out a way to destroy Jimmy? Or was she close enough that Jimmy was just playing the odds?

"How would she be a threat?"

"No fucking idea. Everything I've seen says Jimmy can't be destroyed. But that's like eight-hundred-year-old information. But if she could—"

"Then you can, too," Danny says.

"Best news I've heard all week," I say. "I just don't know how."

Jimmy couldn't see Nicole very well, but it can't see me at all. I turn Rachel's book over in my hands. There's nothing special about it other than the fact that it's a ridiculously niche subject.

It's not very large. A couple hundred pages at most. The cover has a black-and-white photo of two women sitting next to each other, neither looking at the camera. They're clearly related. The older—May, I assume—sits hunched in on herself in a heavy long coat closed tight. She has a sour look on her face like she's barely tolerating being there.

The other, her daughter? I don't remember her name. She's the polar opposite. The word "vivacious" comes to mind. Arm around her mother's shoulders, smiling, coat as open as her body language. I get the feeling she'd be fun to party with, right up to the point she stuck a knife in your back.

"Nicole thought the book was important," I say. "She tossed it under the bed knowing that Jimmy probably wouldn't be able to see that she'd done so. Or it's a plant and we're just playing into Jimmy's plans. Fuck." I'm overthinking everything.

Did Nicole leave me a clue to . . . something? Or was it dropped there by Rachel after killing her? I'm not sorry to see Nicole's dead. But I am sorry that she spent the last thirty years under Jimmy's thumb. Of course, I'm pretty much the one who put her there.

There's nothing left for us here. I step through the hotel doors, Danny close behind me.

"Now what?" Danny says.

I see something out of the corner of my eye, but when I turn to look it's gone.

"Now we keep hunting," I say. "Rachel and Jimmy will show themselves soon enough, but I'd really rather find them first."

"I'll start digging," Danny says.

"Watch yourself. Whatever the fuck is going on, I think it just leveled up."

Again, I see something out of the corner of my eye. I feel a weird buzzing underneath my skin, like static made flesh. This time, though, when I turn to look it's not nothing.

"Do you see this?"

"See wha—Holy shit. Where did that come from?" Danny shoves the palms of his hands against his eyes.

The hotel is wrong. The sidewalk we're standing on is normal, cracked, stained, covered in chewed gum and trash. There's a homeless guy nearby who's built a tent out of a plastic tarp and two shopping carts. Everything is as it should be. Except for the Harrison.

"I'll take that as a yes."

The squalid SRO that stank of urine and onions is gone. This hotel's clean, exterior bright with fresh white paint, no boards covering broken windows. The stained glass is clear and new. It's a gorgeous building. And it hasn't looked like this in over fifty years.

"Stay here," I say, and before he can try to stop me, I pull open the door and step inside.

The foyer is just as new as the outside. It's quiet. Through the door I can see that it's night outside. I can barely hear any traffic. Almost as if there was no traffic to hear.

A doorman in a clean red uniform apologizes to me for not getting the door. There's a bellhop standing at attention next to the front desk. The cage around the front desk is gone, as is the kid, who's been replaced with a pudgy, middle-aged white man in a three-piece suit.

The Harrison hasn't looked like this in decades. The floors are polished, the lights are bright, the chandeliers dusted. An enormous Christmas tree stands in one corner of the lobby.

This is all bizarrely familiar. It reminds me of the ghost of the Ambassador Hotel, but where all of the people there are merely puppets, extensions of the Ambassador itself, I think these might be the real deal.

I reach out and poke the doorman in the shoulder. He looks at me like I'm the weird one and takes a step back. "Sorry," I say. "Just, uh. Just making sure."

I can feel a couple Wanderers outside that I hadn't felt

before I walked through the door. Another point in favor of "We're Not in Kansas Anymore, Toto."

I head up to the desk with the concierge. Cravat and gold pocket watch chain to go with the suit. He's a little plump, a little bald. But he's full of warm smiles and, from the smell, quite a lot of liquor.

"Good evening, sir," he says. "What can we at the Harrison Hotel do for you?"

Am I hallucinating? I doubt it. Danny saw it, too. I don't feel any magic, but that doesn't mean much. Lots of things don't trip that particular sense. But there is something. That buzzing just under my skin, like my body's too big for the skin it's in, has gotten more intense. Everything tightening, hands clenching.

"Sorry to bother," I say. I smile as best I can and hope it doesn't come across as some kind of Joker rictus. "I was wondering if you knew the date."

At this point all three of them are looking at me funny. I'm wearing a suit, but compared to them it's decades out of place. Although the issue might also be all the blood on it.

"December twenty-second," the concierge says. He and the bellhop exchange worried glances.

"Odd question, I know, but what year?"

"I'm sorry?"

"The year," I say. "What is it?"

"Uh . . . nineteen-twenty-four," he says.

"Thanks."

I turn around and let the doorman open the door for me. I stop at the threshold. The street looks blurry with occasional flashes of movement. I see an SUV go by, and just as it's moving out of sight it turns into what looks like an old Packard.

A few years ago, I think I'd have been freaking out at all of this. But I've been dead, sacrificed myself, destroyed pocket universes, and built a god. This feels oddly normal.

Let's see if outside is just as 1924 as the inside. I step through the door and, from one step to the next, modern-day L.A. greets me with the comforting scents of smog and urine.

When I slide over to the dead side of things, where the ghosts will eat you and the very environment will try to kill you, I can feel it. There's a burst of noise, a feeling less like walking through a door and more like ripping a hole in a wall.

But this doesn't feel like that at all. This doesn't feel like anything. That tension I was feeling disappears, like when your ears clear from pressure and suddenly you can hear everything again.

I turn around to look at the hotel. The Harrison is back to all its squalid splendor. But Danny's gone. Something else is missing. Traffic noise. It's there, but it's not as loud as it was. I was only in the hotel for a minute or two. How long has it been out here? A few hours? A few days?

"Dude," Danny yells from across the street. He's over by a taco truck I swear wasn't there when I went inside. "Wasn't sure you were gonna come back out again."

"How long have I been in there?"

"Almost five hours. I tried to follow you, but when I opened the door it was the same shithole hotel and you were gone. I waited a bit and then went and got something to eat. I didn't want to call your girlfriend and let her know I lost you until I was sure of it. She'd come down here with a fucking wrecking crew and take the hotel apart."

"She's not—"

"Don't say it," Danny says. "We both know it's bullshit. So, what happened?"

"I was in there maybe two or three minutes," I say. "It was 1924."

"Seriously? Okay, what the fuck?"

"I don't know," I say. "But there's an awful lot of time fuckery going on and I don't like it."

The hotel, the adobe house in Simi. What the hell is happening? Are they connected? Are they connected to Jimmy? My gut says the answer to both is yes.

My phone buzzes. I take a look and see multiple calls from Gabriela, Amanda, and Letitia. Letitia's an LAPD detective.

More accurately, she's a mage who's slumming as an LAPD detective.

She's part of a collective of mages called the Cleanup Crew. Most big cities have them. People believe in magic. There's just too much out there not to. Most normals never notice the real deal, though. It's not always obvious.

I've seen wizard fights that to normals would just look like two guys staring at each other for twenty minutes until one of them dies of a heart attack. Mages, though, we can sense the magic, see effects normals wouldn't see.

Sometimes, though, somebody does something that gets out of hand. That's when the Cleanup Crew, sometimes more than one group, work together to shunt attention away from whatever weird shit happened.

"Gets out of hand" should really be the motto of mages everywhere. Case in point is the L.A. Firestorm. Half the city burned in a single night and about a hundred thousand people died, not to mention the thousands of others who kicked from injuries over the next few weeks.

I get blamed for that a lot. Hell, even I blame me for that. I'm the one who pissed off the Aztec god Quetzalcoatl. He'd wanted me to burn down Mictlan for him with the fires of Xiuhtecuhtli, one of the gods he'd helped kill five hundred years ago.

I said no. So he burned down L.A. instead.

The damage is still being dealt with. Keeping the public in the dark as to the actual cause is a full-time job for some mages all across the fucking planet.

Gabriela calling me more than once is a little concerning. Same with Amanda. But seeing so many calls from Letitia is really worrying. She doesn't want to talk to me at the best of times.

"About fucking time," Letitia says when my phone connects. "I've been calling for hours. Where the hell have you been?"

"1924," I say. "What the hell's going on?"

"Forget I asked. I got a bunch of corpses down at a club off Hollywood Boulevard." A club. Fuck.

"Is Gabriela one of them?"

"She's here, but no. And the Werther kid. They really an item?" she says.

"Yeah."

"I thought you and Gabriela were an item."

"We are," I say. At least I think we are.

"Huh. Anyway, they're wandering around here looking over bodies. Gabriela said to tell you she thinks it's related to the adobe house? I don't know what that means."

"It means I should get my ass down there. Text me the address."

Chapter 7

This club on Cherokee near Hollywood Boulevard is built like a warehouse. Danny drops me off nearby. There's nowhere to park and he's got other things to do. People have lives. Who knew?

I've been here before, but it's never been like this. Cherokee is filled with LAPD cars spilling out onto Hollywood Boulevard, lights flashing, crime scene tape marking off a chunk of the street. I don't bother with Sharpie magic. Probably should have, though. A cop stops me at the tape.

"You'll have to move along, sir," she says. "Nobody's allowed in."

"I got a call from Letitia Watson," I say.

"Oh." She looks me up and down. "You're the consultant?" I feel a slight flare of magic from her but nothing seems to be happening.

"That a problem?"

"Is that blood on your shirt?"

"A little," I say. "Occupational hazard."

"The fuck kind of occupation—"

"He's with me, Janna." Letitia walks up. Letitia's a tall black woman wearing a gray pantsuit with an LAPD badge hanging from a chain around her neck. "Don't give my officers a hard time. I'll have them shoot you."

"At least this time I won't be surprised when it happens."

"Come on," she says. "Janna, get Parker to relieve you and meet us inside."

"Yes, ma'am," Janna says.

"She's a mage?" I say, following Letitia to the entrance.

"Yeah," she says. "Needs training. Like a lot. Figured out

she could do shit about a year ago when it spontaneously manifested. Now it just sort of leaks out."

When children learn they're mages, others try to take advantage of the situation. Sometimes good, sometimes bad. They either get trained or get used. A lot of baby mages don't make it to toddler mages, if you catch my drift.

"Bad?" I say. When a mage comes into their power in adulthood it can get messy fast. Better than when they're teens, though, believe me. Magic and hormones are a deadly combination.

"Could have been worse." For mages, "could have been worse" can cover consequences up to and including leaving a crater where a house used to be.

"What's her knack?" I say.

"No idea. She doesn't seem to have an affinity for anything in particular. Or a lot of control. I found her—Are you all right?"

I'm not. I double over and fall to my knees the second I cross the threshold. I feel like I've been punched in the gut. There's that buzzing under my skin like at the Harrison, but more. A lot more.

At first I think a bunch of people have just died, but when that happens it's over fast. This just keeps going.

I feel someone grab me, drag me back outside. Sounds are distant, my vision is nothing but a blur of color. The pain subsides, but now I feel like I've just done a bunch of cocaine and stuck my tongue in a light socket.

"What happened?" I hear. Gabriela? Maybe Amanda. Sounds still all garbled.

"The fuck if I know," Letitia says.

"I'm okay," I say, vision clearing.

"You're shaking," Gabriela says.

"Fuck, I said I'm okay." I sit up, wave them off. "I'm fine."

"What the hell was that?"

"How many corpses are in there?" I say.

"Forty-eight," Letitia says. "Pretty sure we found them all.

Three of them were embedded in a wall. If we hadn't seen a hand sticking out we never would have found them."

"And they're all dead?"

"I sure as hell hope so," Letitia says. "We're still chipping out the three in the wall. And that one in the bathroom. Jesus."

"What happened in the bathroom?"

"There was someone in a bathroom stall in the men's restroom when it happened," Gabriela says. "And then suddenly there was someone else in there with them."

It takes me a second to parse that out. "Jesus. That must have been messy."

"Not as much as you'd think," Gabriela says. "It killed them, but there wasn't any blood or direct trauma that I could see. They just merged."

"Now what the hell just happened with you?" Letitia says.

"I had the same feeling I get when I'm around a lot of people dying at the same time," I say. "Only it isn't stopping."

"Can you still feel it?" Gabriela says.

"A little. Not as strongly out here. Mostly it just caught me by surprise." It feels as though the moment of their death is being stretched out like taffy. I get to my feet. "I'm okay. Let's try this again."

"You sure?" Letitia says, but I'm already stepping through the door before she can finish the sentence.

I'm ready for it this time and it doesn't take me by surprise. It's no less unpleasant, but at least it doesn't knock me on my ass. It's like having the sort of headache that's just this side of a migraine and lets you know you're about to have a really shitty evening.

"You look a little green," Gabriela says. "And covered in blood. You have a party and I wasn't invited?"

"Feel a little green," I say. "No, not even so much as a shindig. Found Nicole. She's dead. Turns out Rachel isn't. Jimmy's fuck knows where."

"Sounds like you've had quite the evening," she says.

"I'll tell you all about it. Think it might be related to this, too."

"Fuck."

"I felt pretty much the same way," I say. "You look nice, though. The little-black-dress look suits you. What the hell happened?"

"Thanks. We'll need more excuses for me to wear it," she says. "There was a flare of magic and then everything changed."

"Changed how?" I say, stepping through a blackout curtain into the club proper. "Oh."

The last time I remember being here, the walls were all painted black. There was a stage in the middle of the main room and a dance floor in another. Three bars were spaced around the venue and a metal staircase at one end led up to an office with wraparound windows overlooking the entire space.

The layout's the same, but now half of it is painted off-white, and there are white booths with red leather seats mixed in among the ones painted black and upholstered in pleather.

A stage in the first room has a bizarre mix of musical instruments, trombones, trumpets, a stand-up bass, and . . .

"Is that bondage gear?"

"Yes," says a gravelly voice I wasn't expecting. Joe Sunday, Gabriela's undead friend with one of the opals in his chest keeping him alive and moving, comes down the stairs from the office. "We're a BDSM club on Tuesdays."

"And you keep the giant wooden cross out all the time?"

"It's bolted to the floor," he says. "And the goths on Thursdays like it."

"Wait a minute. We?"

"I own the place," he says. "Sorta inherited it."

I don't really like Sunday. Aside from the fact that he's dead and I don't understand how he's still moving around, he's just unnerving to be in the same room with. And coming from me that's saying something.

He only breathes when he talks and I don't think I've ever seen him blink. If he runs this place, he's gotta spend a lot of time upstairs in that office to avoid scaring the straights.

"He worked for a guy who left it to him when he died," Gabriela says.

"He was eaten," Sunday says. "I was actually the second choice. The other guy got eaten, too."

"Lotta people get eaten around you?" I say.

He taps his chest where the opal keeping him upright is sitting behind his sternum. "Not anymore."

"All the instruments are new?" I say.

"I don't know about new, but not here before," Gabriela says. I pick up a trumpet. I see what she means. It's been polished, but it's obvious it's gotten a lot of use.

"Come on," Gabriela says. "This part's weird, but the rest is weirder." I follow her to the other room.

Of all the people in there, only Kyle and Amanda are alive. Whether Kyle's here from the coroner's office at the request of Gabriela or the LAPD, it's good to see him. He's checking out the corpses and Amanda seems to be asking him questions, though I can't hear either one of them.

Dozens of bodies are laid out on the dance floor. They're all dressed in tuxes and cocktail gowns, as wait and kitchen staff. The death feeling intensifies. My eyes are getting a little blurry. Then I realize what's going on. Sort of.

"They're not dead," I say.

"What?" Letitia says. "Sure as hell look dead."

"No, they're all still dying." The reason it feels like their moment of death has been stretched out is because it has been.

But the intensity doesn't make sense. If it were just slowed down, wouldn't I feel less of it? But this has the same intensity as if it had happened all at once, except that it's going on and on.

I crouch down next to one of the people in tuxedos to get a better look. "His clothes are out of date," I say.

"Last year's fashions?" Letitia says.

"Sure, if by last year you mean the 1920s. This guy's wearing a paper collar." All of his clothes look vintage except for the fact that they're new.

"You an expert in 1920s men's fashion?"

"I used to buy a lot of clothes at estate sales," I say. "Yes, I know it sounds weird. Fuck off."

There was a time I found it easier to get close to the dead by surrounding myself with things owned by the dead. Pretty much all the men's clothes you find at estate sales are old suits. I don't need a dead man's clothes anymore, but I kind of got in the habit of wearing suits.

"I don't criticize somebody else's style choices," Letitia says. "I lived through the nineties, after all."

"You got IDs for any of these people?"

"Some," she says. "The rest don't seem to have anything on them."

"Coat check room?" I say.

"Not that we've found," Letitia says.

"That's because it was walled up," Sunday says. "There's a hidden door behind the bar that'll get you into it. My old boss Simon used to store shit in it he didn't want people to see."

"And now?" Letitia says, narrowing her eyes. She might be a mage, but she's just as much a cop.

"Cleared it out years ago," Sunday says. "That's where we keep the bar snacks. You want a box of pretzels, knock yourself out. Latch behind an old bottle of Jägermeister on the bar over there."

"Betting you'll find some more clues in there," I say. "And probably a dead coat-check girl."

"Jesus Christ," Letitia says. "Janna, get on that, would ya?"

"Yes, ma'am." The rookie heads over to the bar and starts rummaging behind bottles.

"Don't you have enough people to boss around?" I say.

"She's an apprentice," Gabriela says. "That's what apprentices are for."

"She is not—You know, fuck both of you," Letitia says.

"I don't see any wounds on them. They just showed up and hit the floor?" I say.

"Pretty much, yeah," Gabriela says.

I'm really having a hard time getting a good read on the energy coming off these people. I'm dreading getting slammed by it like when I walked in the door if I look too closely. But if I want to get a better idea of what the hell happened here I can't think of any other way to do it.

"Okay, I think this is gonna suck," I say. "If I start screaming and trying to claw my eyes out, hit me really hard in the head until I pass out."

"Why wait?" Letitia says.

"Funny." I close my eyes and concentrate on the bodies. I get a sense of inertia, momentum. Like a car rolling down a steep hill and gaining speed as it goes. Or a rubber band being stretched to breaking.

Whatever is happening to them isn't just that their deaths are being drawn out, it's almost like they're alive and dead at the same time. I reach out with my mind until I can feel the energy of the body lying in front of me. I try to grab hold of it. See what happens.

And boy fuckin' howdy does something happen.

The body jackknifes to a sitting position, milky eyes snapping open. His arms reach out to either side and start to windmill, his legs kicking wildly. He tries to get up but he can't get his feet under him.

"North Star," he says. "Willa. Tree of life. North star." His voice sounds like a whisper through ground glass, a wheeze from lungs without enough air in them.

"Okay, what the fuck did you do?" Kyle says. He and Amanda run over from where they were checking out bodies.

"Not much of anything," I say. Though I think I might start throwing up. I thought I was peeking under the hood. Didn't think I was slamming my foot on the gas. "Hey, Sparky," I say to the body, putting some magic behind my words. "Why don't ya slow down a bit."

There's a difference between a corpse and meat. I can

animate a body, but I can't do anything to a steak, for instance. Sometimes it's hard to gauge where the cutoff is. It's time, how much energy is left over, how much I push my magic.

There have been three-week-old corpses embalmed and lying in caskets I've been able to animate, and a few fresh corpses I couldn't do anything with. But I've never seen one sit up and just start talking.

Another corpse sits up and starts talking in sync with the first. "She's coming," they say. "North Star. Tree of Life. Willa. Willanorthstarwillawillawilla." The words blur together until there's nothing but a weird, droning noise coming from the two of them.

I throw a command at him to stand the fuck down, but instead, two more get into the act, then another five, another ten. Soon they're all babbling the same thing over and over again like a monastery of monks who just can't stop chanting. And not a goddamn one of them is listening to me.

Then they figure out how to stand up.

"Oh, fuck this," Letitia says. She draws her service weapon and shoots one of them in the head. It drops and at the same time a searing pain shoots through my eyes like a hot poker. Another gunshot and I'm on the floor, the pain blinding me.

"Eric?" Gabriela.

"Stop—" I say. More gunshots. Trigger-happy cops getting in on the action. More pain. I can't even speak.

"Stop fucking shooting," Gabriela yells. The gunshots stop and I can focus enough through the pain to see that about a dozen of the bodies have been gunned down. The rest are still not listening to my commands, like an alarm clock that won't shut up no matter how many times you hit it.

Which gives me an idea. If the off switch doesn't stop the clock, yank the damn thing out of the wall. I feel around for all that energy, find all the bits and edges. Pull.

I've taken in souls before, ghost energy. It's never fun. Fucking agonizing, in fact. Some necromancers get off on it. Me, it's like gargling with razor blades. That's got nothing on this. I feel the energy slam into me like a freight train. My mind and body feel like they're being crushed and lit on fire at the same time. Like I'm being torn apart and put back together over and over again.

It feels like it goes on forever. I can't think straight. Words and phrases rip through my mind so fast they're nothing but an ear-splitting whine of noise amid the agony. Then a snap in my mind like something important has broken and everything changes.

Chapter 8

I'm on my hands and knees in the dirt trying not to throw up. I can smell wildflowers, manzanita. I look up and see the adobe house. It's daytime.

Smoke drifts out of a chimney. There's a wagon, a couple horses out front. I get to my feet.

The whine in my ears begins to fade and then sound picks up again. Only now it's not nonsense loud enough to blow out my eardrums, it's crying. Children, an adult. A few seconds later it turns into screaming.

Then I feel the magic. A lot of it.

There are raised voices all talking at once. I can't make out what they're actually saying.

I stagger to the door, but before I can push it open it silently swings in on its own. Inside is a small room with a fireplace, a couple chairs, a table. All the furniture is ornately carved and not a single piece has been mass produced. I really do not like where this is headed.

The yelling is in Spanish. Someone calling someone else a murderer.

And then a woman's voice in English. "Oh, will you just shut her up, already?"

"We need her," says another voice. Similar but older. I can make out the sounds of splashing.

"I don't mean kill her," says the first voice. "Just shut her up."

"I'll get to it. You start a baptism, you fucking finish it. Fuck, did I teach you nothing? So hold your horses, the brat'll be dead in a minute."

The crying abruptly stops.

I don't know what the fuck is going on, but this shit is ending now. I run toward the voices, but just as I reach the door that feeling of being torn apart hits me again. My knees buckle and I hit the ground.

Only there isn't any ground. There's no up or down. It's all just a void. There's nothing. Until.

"Oh, hello."

I . . . turn? Shift? Suddenly there's a floor, space, light, gravity. I'm in a mausoleum built not of stone but wood, poorly constructed, creaking, water dripping down the walls, icebox-cold. Two metal cases lie on the dirt floor. No. They're caskets.

A girl—fifteen or sixteen, maybe, barefoot, wearing a long white nightgown, flowers braided into her thick hair—sits on the longer of the two cases. She's holding a puppy. At her feet, six more are playing, tumbling over each other, nipping at each others' butts.

"You're not supposed to be here," she says. "Not yet, at least."

"Where the fuck is here?"

She laughs. "Mother never allowed me to swear. And Aunt May was very strict about it. But you don't have that problem, do you?"

"Who are you?" I say.

"I'm the Tree of Life," she says. "And you're Eric Carter."

"You know who I am?" Who names their kid Tree of Life? Then I remember I live in L.A. and honestly that's almost normal. But why is that phrase ringing a big fucking church bell in my head?

"Of course, silly. I—" The puppy in her arms makes a quiet yip and she raises it to her ear. "Oh, that's right." A pause. "I'm sorry. We haven't met yet." The puppy yips again and she lifts it back up to her ear.

"Yes, I know you like him. And yes, killing him would be kinder, too. But you know we can't do that." There's a pause as she listens to her pup. I can't hear a damn thing.

"Of course, there will be consequences," she says to the pup. "No matter what he does there will be consequences."

"You, uh, have conversations with your dog often?" I say, trying to ignore the fact that she's talking about my being better off dead. Not that I necessarily disagree. "I mean, where they talk back?"

As if in answer, all seven puppies start barking at me, a bunch of adorable, yet really fucking creepy, high-pitched yips.

"Hush," the girl says, and all the dogs go quiet. "I'm sorry. They're all very opinionated."

"I can see that," I say.

"You need to go now," the Tree of Life says. "But don't worry. We'll see each other soon. Or a long time ago. It can be very confusing."

"Wait, what?"

"Goodbye, Eric."

Pain rips through me again and I hope maybe this is over and done with and if it's not, then yeah, it would be kinder to kill me.

I'm behind the wheel of a red Cadillac Eldorado that I haven't seen in years, driving down a road made of ground-up bone, wheels kicking up white dust. Outside I can see a wide expanse of desert made up of cracked femurs, shattered skulls. Crude approximations of plants, leaves and fronds made of desiccated skin, wave in the breeze.

This is Mictlan. Or at least the way Mictlan was before I took over the top spot and started to fix the place up. Without a Mictlantecuhtli for five hundred years, the landscape shifted from green and vibrant to this nightmare of skin and bone. I've only been gone a few months. How did it get this bad so quickly?

"Hello, Eric." I turn to see a young Asian woman in the passenger seat. Her skin goes translucent for the briefest moment and beneath her skin I can see her bones.

"Tabitha?"

"Even when you were here you didn't call me that. Things really have changed."

Mictecacihuatl. Aztec death goddess. Amalgam of Santa

Muerte and Tabitha Cheung, a woman sacrificed to a goddess because I couldn't move fast enough to save her.

My ex-wife.

I stop the car, bone dust spraying out behind it. I throw open the door and get out. The sky is the color of an angry bruise, a swirl of purple and green. What the fuck am I doing here?

"Am I dead again?" I say. "Tell me I'm not dead again. It shouldn't fucking hurt this much if I'm dead."

"Technically, yes," she says, stepping out of the car. "You're dead. But it won't last. Not this time, at least."

Her skin melts into bone as she grows taller, her blue flannel shirt and jeans shifting to a red wedding dress. "So, as far as I'm concerned, no, you're not dead."

"The fuck am I doing here? And the fuck is all this doing here? We cleared this shit out years ago." The red dress is confusing. Muerte's dress changes color based on mood and for what she's being called on.

Santa Muerte is a hell of a lot more than death. In the white she's purification and innocence, black for revenge and protection. In the red she's love. Seriously.

"This is a stubborn patch of Mictlan. Up until a moment ago it wasn't very large."

"This isn't large?"

"I said 'up until a moment ago,'" she says. "It spread like water out of a burst dam. I've been able to slow the worst of it, but it's still creeping out."

Time moves differently for gods. Whatever happened could have felt like a dozen years here just as easily as it could have been the blink of an eye.

I don't understand what's happening, whether it's a vision, a hallucination, or I'm really in Mictlan, but I have a very bad feeling about it. The last time I saw Mictlan it was through the eyes of my other half, when he told me Mictlan was confused about which one of us to listen to.

"What the hell happened?"

"You did," she says.

"The fuck did I do now?"

Last time this happened I was having a crisis of, I dunno, existence? Once I accepted that I'd been separated from Mictlantecuhtli and was alive and human, it stopped. But now?

"I was hoping you could tell me," she says.

"That why you brought me here?"

"You did that on your own," she says. It takes me a second to process that and when it clicks my blood goes cold.

"That shouldn't be possible," I say. "I'm not Mictlantecuhtli anymore. I gave up any connection I had to this place months ago."

She fixes me with an accusatory glare. Impressive, considering her face is just a skull. "It gets better. Mictlantecuhtli's Asleep." I can hear the capital letter in Asleep.

I know what she means. I remember being Asleep for five hundred years trapped in jade until some dipshit necromancer came by and killed me.

Her form shifts, grows taller, her dress turning black. Shit. I know that look.

"What the fuck did you do, Eric?"

"The corpses in the club," I say. "Has to be."

"Tell me."

"Not much to tell," I say. But the more I tell the more I realize that's not true. The corpses, the hotel, the adobe, Nicole, Rachel, Jimmy, Vegas today, Vegas thirty years ago. Then the adobe house just now and the void. The Tree of Life and her adorable yet creepy puppies. Mictecacihuatl listens patiently like only a skeleton can.

"And then I woke up here in the Cadillac. Wait. Why is the Caddy here? It wasn't here before I left. And this isn't a dream. Is it?"

"Not entirely," she says. "You're not here physically, but you're here. Mictlantecuhtli liked the car," she says. "So, he recreated it."

I have a sudden flare of anger. That was my goddamn Cadillac. Then I realize how stupid that sounds since we were the same person up to a few months ago, and I feel like an idiot. Add it to the pile of stupid shit I'm jealous at my other half for.

"Can't fault his taste. What do you make of all this?"

"I think you somehow tipped the power scales between the two of you."

"What does that mean?"

"It means you're currently more Mictlantecuhtli than he is."

"We're swapping places?" I say. "Like last time?" Fuck me. As the man says, déjà vu all over again.

"I don't think so. I think it's more that you've gotten a jolt and it was strong enough that Mictlan sort of—"

"Got confused?" I say. "Happens a lot, doesn't it?"

"Only since you moved in," she says. "Mictlan's never had to deal with this sort of situation. You might have renounced any claim to the throne, but the land still knows you."

The land still knows me. That's a good point. Mictlan is more than a place. It's a concept, an identity, a breathing, knowing thing.

I close my eyes. I can feel it. I think she's right. It is confused. It knows me and it doesn't at the same time. And this is why we're standing in this landscape of bones.

"It's going to be fine," I say. "We'll get this solved."

"Damn right you will," Muerte says.

"I wasn't talking to you."

I feel an ease in the world around me, like a breath that's been held for far too long finally being let go. There's a sliding sensation under my feet. Green shoots burst up through the bone. They're fast. In seconds there's already a thin covering of grasses, the beginnings of trees, bone sloughing off the land to expose soil and rock underneath.

Muerte looks around, and if she wasn't just a fleshless, eyeless skull, I know I'd see shock on her face.

"What did you do?"

"Next time just give it a little encouragement," I say.

It's hard to gauge what a skeleton is looking at, what with

the lack of eyes and all, but I know Muerte in whatever form she takes.

"What?" I say.

"You sounded like you were talking to a baby," she says. "Or a spooked pet. Are you going soft?"

"When have I ever gone soft around you?" I say.

"Hah. Funny."

"Now what—Did you feel that?" A low thrumming like being too close to a speaker at a Metallica concert. Shit. It's happening again. Only this time there's something more to the buzzing under my skin.

A high-pitched shriek builds in my ears and the feeling of being torn apart starts to spread from my core. I push against it as hard as I can, but it's like something trying to rip out through my body.

Mictlan disappears in a wave of agony.

Chapter 9

"You died three times," Gabriela says.

Gabriela, Amanda and I are in the office overlooking the club. The décor strikes me as very unlike Sunday, kind of a Ye Olde Britain vibe. Oxblood leather club chairs and sofa, a desk that looks like it was carved out of a solid piece of oak adorned with nothing but a leather desk pad, a black wing-back office chair behind it. There's a faint scent of old pipe tobacco and cigars in the air. Whoever smoked in here hasn't for a very long time.

We've been up here for about half an hour. I was able to give them both a rundown of what happened at the Harrison and when I pulled that energy out of the corpses. Gabriela takes the book on the Royal Arms of the Great Eleven. She has a college student on staff doing work study she can have summarize it.

"We'd get your heart beating and ten seconds later you'd die again. And then you were fine. Stood up like nothing had happened." Gabriela's speaking matter-of-factly but she's pacing and there's a tension in her voice I don't hear very often.

It wasn't quite that simple. Last time I keeled over Amanda was able to repeatedly reshape my heart to pump until it started on its own. This time her magic didn't take. We don't know why and it's one of several elephants in the room.

My chest hurts from the repeated efforts of CPR and a defibrillator. Breathing isn't fun. I think one of my ribs might be bruised and my guts don't like the fact that a lot of air was forcibly shoved into them during the process.

I glance over at Amanda and she gives a tiny shrug. She hears it in Gabriela's voice, too.

"I saw that," Gabriela says.

"Good," Amanda says. "Then maybe you'll get that we can tell you're freaked out."

Amanda's sitting in the office chair behind the desk. Like Gabriela, she's dressed for a night out, in a striking, backless blue mini dress that I have to say really works for her.

And then of course there's me, in a rumpled, blood-spattered suit and tie. The shirt buttons are torn off so they could get the defibrillator on me. Maybe I should up my wardrobe. Or stop splashing around in blood and dying. The wardrobe change sounds easier.

"I don't think I was actually dead," I say. "Well, not dead dead."

"And how the fuck was I supposed to know that?" Gabriela says.

"I'd have texted, but funny thing, there's no signal in the void," I say. Now I'm starting to get annoyed. "This is me. Shit like this happens. Hell, shit like this happens to all three of us. You know that."

Amanda gets up from behind the desk, goes to Gabriela, and puts her hand on her shoulder. The instant she touches her all Gabriela's tension drains away. She closes her eyes, drops her shoulders, and lets out a deep breath.

"Yes," she says. "I know that. And—and I don't know why this is bothering me so much."

"Yes, you do," Amanda says, her voice quiet.

"Don't," Gabriela says. "Not right now."

I know there's a whole other conversation going on here, and I'm not so stupid that I can't follow along. I get up from my chair to stand on the other side of Gabriela with my hand on her other shoulder, Amanda and I holding her up like flying buttresses.

I should say something. I even know what I should say. So, of course, I don't say it.

Instead: "It's been a really long night. I know I have a lot of shit to process and I can tell you do, too. I promise I will try really hard to not die again. Tonight."

Gabriela lets a laugh slip out. "How fucked up is it for us that we have to throw that many conditionals onto 'I'll be careful.'"

"I could just say, 'I'll be careful.'"

"Except that your idea of careful usually involves you dying."

"Hey, it gets you run through with a fucking samurai sword," I say.

"That was one time," Gabriela says.

"And the shotgun blast in that other skin?"

Long time back she had access to an Aztec relic, the obsidian blade of Xipe Totec, the Flayed God. Walked around with his skin hanging off him. One of those blood-soaked Rites of Spring sorts of gods.

"That was years ago." The thing about the blade is you could steal a person's skin with it. And by skin, I mean everything. Memories, abilities, personality. Once you have it you can call it to you whenever you want.

She'd used it to take some La Eme fucker's identity and got in a firefight while in it. Shotgun to the gut. It almost died. She changed back before it did. Now she has it but doesn't use it. She figures the second she calls it back, it'll die, and we don't know what that will do to her.

"My point is that we get into these scrapes whether we want to or not," I say. "And it's not like we go looking for them either."

"Much as I love watching this back and forth," Amanda says, "Eric's right. It's been a really long night. There's not much else we can do here. And we all need some sleep."

"Yeah," Gabriela says. "I'm—I'm gonna go home. Alone."

"Okay," Amanda says. "Do you need a port?"

"Yeah, thanks."

"Of course." Amanda gives her a quick kiss and lets her go.

"Hey, I really will be careful," I say.

Gabriela smiles at me like she's indulging an idiot child. "No, you won't," she says. There's a flare of magic and a hole opens up in the air, with the receiving room of Gabriela's shelter visible on the other side.

I start to lean in to kiss her, but she moves before I can shift so much as an inch. She steps through the portal and Amanda closes it.

"That could have gone better," Amanda says. "You can be a real idiot, sometimes."

"Only sometimes?" I say.

"Do you love her?" Amanda says.

We had this conversation over the phone a few months ago when I was in Vegas. We were both trying to sort out how we felt about Gabriela while trying to get her soul back from Jimmy.

"Do you?"

"I asked first," Amanda says. She walks over to a fully stocked bar in the room, grabs a bottle of something that's no doubt expensive, and pours us both a glass.

"Yes," I say, taking an experimental sip from my glass. Good whisky. I notice the bottle's almost full. Figures Sunday wouldn't drink.

"That came out faster than I expected," Amanda says. "What changed?"

"I don't know when it happened," I say. "Maybe a long time ago and I didn't realize. I know I've been fighting it. Even when I knew it's what I wanted. And I don't really know what to do with it."

"And you haven't told her."

"I told her," I say. "Earlier today."

"Oh."

"Yeah," I say. "How about you? You were on the fence a few months ago."

"Still am," she says. "But if anything, I've learned you have to grab on to some kind of happiness and hold on tight while you still can."

"I wonder if there's much point," I say. "It's all going away anyway."

"Maybe there isn't," she says. "I don't know. You ever been happy?" she says.

"Yeah," I say. For five years being Mictlantecuhtli. Ushering souls through their final ordeals. Growing into my power with Mictecacihuatl at my side. Having a purpose.

"And?"

"I was dead at the time."

"Right," she says. "I forgot. You know, I'm just as scared I'm going to lose her. You're right. This shit happens to us. This is our normal. People try to kill me all the time. You keep dying all the time."

"And Gabriela?"

"She keeps having to watch it. She doesn't do damsel-in-distress well and she can't play white knight if she can't find a dragon to kill. She gets into fights with whole drug cartels. Sometimes she's the one who starts it."

"Everyone wants a piece of us," I say. "They want a piece of La Bruja, they want a piece of the Queen of Los Angeles. Are they really calling you that?"

"Just as much as they're calling you King of the Dead," she says.

"I hate that," I say.

"Welcome to the club. You know the three of us have at least one thing in common."

"That we like dancing in mine fields?"

"That we're all afraid we're going to lose each other."

"Maybe it means we need to let go of each other," I say.

"No," she says. "It means we need to hold on that much harder. I don't know what's going on between the two of you. That's your relationship, not mine. It affects mine and vice versa, but I can't tell either one of you what to do."

I let out a laugh. "Jesus, how old are you? Twenty-three? I should be the one spouting out wisdom. I've got thousands of years of Mictlantecuhtli in my head." I pause. "Scratch that. He was never what you'd call emotionally stable."

"Hey, I'm almost twenty-four," she says. She pours herself another drink and refills my glass. "And I read a lot of poly fanfic."

"Well then. To poly fanfic, I guess," I say. We clink our glasses and slam our drinks back.

She glances at a clock on the wall. "It is officially tomorrow. And I need sleep. You need a port?"

Four in the morning is probably the only time driving from Hollywood to Venice is remotely pleasant. But I'm gonna fall over soon and with two drinks in me that's probably not the best move. Plus I'd have to go to the trouble of stealing another car.

"That would be great," I say. "Thanks." The portal opens to the front of the Venice house.

"Goodnight, King of the Dead," she says.

"Goodnight, Queen of Los Angeles," I say, and step through. A sudden snap of cold air, the smell of the ocean nearby, sound of water in the canals lapping against the dock. The portal closes behind me.

Venice is a weird place. Long time back a guy named Abbot Kinney built a series of canals to drain what was essentially a swamp so he could build a resort.

Not a man to let anything go to waste, he set up the canals to mimic Venice, Italy, which fit into his vision of the resort. It worked surprisingly well. People would come in on the Red Car from all over L.A. At one point they were pulling in something like 150,000 tourists on the weekends.

Like everything else in this fucked-up town, it didn't last. The only things remaining are the canals lined with overpriced houses, a pier that's been rebuilt multiple times, and the shell of an arcade that burned down during the firestorm.

This is my sister's house. Was my sister's house. She was murdered here, and though I've exorcised her Echo it feels like she still haunts the place, a woman I never knew grown from a little girl I ran away from.

I wonder sometimes how things would have turned out if I hadn't left, if I hadn't hunted down and killed the man who murdered our parents. What if I'd just never been born? Would she still be alive? Would L.A. have burned down? Would Jimmy have existed?

"You know," I say as I unlock the front door with a spell, "you might be good at killing people, but you really suck at sneaking up on them."

"And I was trying so hard."

I turn around. If the slight Scottish lilt hadn't given her away, the flaming red hair would have.

"Rachel. How are things?"

She's wearing jeans, a t-shirt with a Universal Studios logo on it—conclusively proving that she's not from here—a gray hooded jacket, and a blue baseball hat.

Oh yeah, and there's the gun she's pointing at me.

"Busy," she says. "Little bit of this, little bit of that. You know how it is. You don't seem surprised to see me."

"Saw Nicole tonight," I say.

There's a flicker on her face of something I can't quite make out before it's gone. Surprise? Concern? Joy that I took her bait?

"Did you now? Would have happened, eventually."

"I'm just not sure why."

"Dunno," she says. "I'm just following orders."

"Oh, I know that. And that's the thing I don't understand. Why are you following orders? What's Jimmy got on you or doing for you that you're willing to slaughter a couple dozen people and torture the Twins? Christ, I thought you and Lucas were friends."

Her eyes go hard. "I have my reasons and I'm not here to discuss them."

"You're looking for the opal," I say.

"And they said you were stupid. Where is it?"

"No idea," I say.

"Don't dick me around, Eric."

"I'm not. I honestly don't know where it is. On a mountain, bottom of the ocean, butt-crack of some unfortunate hobo riding the rails. I got a friend to open a portal without bothering to think about where it might lead and I dropped it in."

One of the things about the opals I found out in Vegas is that Jimmy can't see them either. They're not just a blind spot for it, they actively keep its magic from fucking with them. It only found this one by having Nicole do the research until she tracked down someone who had one.

"You're fucking joking," Rachel says.

"Nope. I mean, you're welcome to toss the house. Believe me, it's seen worse."

"How about I shoot you in the knees and you tell me the truth?"

I can't help but laugh at that. "Jesus, Rachel. I thought you were good at this. You don't threaten to shoot somebody's kneecaps, you threaten to shoot one at a time. That way you've got more leverage."

"Fine, I'll shoot them one at a time," she says.

"You sure about that?"

"I—" She lets loose a startled cry as wet, rotting arms wrap around her ankles and pull. The gun goes off, but the angle's wrong and all it does is dig a hole in my front door. She hits the ground hard, her jaw smacking the cement with a cracking sound. The gun skitters toward me. I pick it up.

"What the fuck is this?" she says. The bloated, rotting corpse I had hidden in the canal in front of the house and covered in masking spells starts pulling her back toward the canal while climbing up her legs.

"Archie," I say. "Not his real name, I'm sure. But that's what it said on his driver's license. Did you know that was Cary Grant's original name? Really. Archibald Leach.

"Anyway, Archie tried to assassinate me a few months ago. I dropped him in the drink to float away. But after I got back from Vegas, nobody'd found him. So hey, waste not, want not."

She manages to get one of her feet free and kicks the dripping corpse in the face, dislodging its jaw. It hangs by a tendon before slipping out of what's left of its shredded skin and into the canal with a wet plop.

"How about you and I go to my office and have a chat," I say. I'm not stupid enough to get close to Rachel. She doesn't need a gun to kill me. Luckily, I don't have to.

I cast a spell I can do in my sleep at this point. A rush of jet-engine noise, all the colors around us wash out into muted blues and grays, and we slide over to the dead side. The canal is here, most of the buildings, some of them even though they burned down on the live side years ago.

And the entropy of the place immediately starts to eat at Rachel. She clutches at her throat. She can breathe, but her brain doesn't really know how to process the environment and the closest it can come up with is the sensation of drowning.

Another spell, and a shimmering bubble, a barrier from the entropy of this place, forms around her. She gasps in big lungfuls of air, the spell temporarily shielding her from the worst of the place.

"I think we got off on the wrong foot," I say. "Let's start over. Where's Jimmy?"

Chapter 10

"Fuck you think I'm gonna tell you?" Her breathing is still ragged, but she's weathered the worst of it. "Where the fuck are we?"

"This is where all the ghosts are," I say. "Not a lot of them around at the moment. That'll change soon, so we're on a bit of a clock. Where's Jimmy?"

"Fuck you, I—" She freezes as the bubble noticeably shrinks.

"Oh yeah, this is a place for dead things," I say. "Seeing as you're not dead, it's sucking everything out of you. Energy, power . . . hell, maybe even your soul. I'm really not sure. I should get a better understanding of how this place works.

"It's still leeching your life out, but it'll take a lot longer because of the shield. Of course, I drop that and you won't last very long at all."

"I'll last long enough to kill you," she says.

"Maybe," I say. "Where's Jimmy?"

"Fuck—" The bubble shrinks another few inches.

"Oh hey," I say. "You see that over there? Those are Wanderers. You've seen them before. Remember the watchdogs when we were kids in Vegas? Those ghosts I let you see?" Her face pales. "Yeah, you remember."

"The fuck do you want, Eric."

"I want answers. I want to know what the fuck Jimmy's trying to manipulate me into doing. I want to know what it's giving you that you'd so casually murder everybody. But most of all, I just want Jimmy."

"I don't know what he wants. I'm just here to get back the opal. He needed someone he could trust more than Nicole to handle his shit. He promised me . . . something, and fuck you if you think I'm gonna tell you what it is."

"Someone it could trust more than Nicole," I say. "You mean somebody it could completely manipulate by screwing with your future to keep you in line."

"Nicole was gonna betray him. She already had."

"Uh huh. Try again. No way Jimmy could know that. It could barely see her, much less what she was going to do or what she was thinking. You know that."

"So fucking what?"

"Nicole and me. We made it. Jimmy's our pride and joy. Our sweet little bundle of horror. And it can't sense us like it can everything else. It could get a read on some of what Nicole was doing, but I'm a big ol' blind spot. And when I say blind, I mean blind."

"It's not absolute. It can't be."

"Okay, don't believe me. Let's say I'm lying. How was she going to betray it? How was she going to do anything to it that it wouldn't see?"

"I don't know," she says. The shell shrinks some more. "Goddammit, Eric. I don't know."

"Why now? Why not have her killed thirty years ago? Conventional wisdom is that Jimmy can't be destroyed. No reason to kill her because there's no way she could hurt it. So why do it at all and why do it now?"

"I'm telling you, I don't fucking know."

"Then tell me where Jimmy is and I'll ask it myself."

"He's going to change things so that I get out of here, you know."

"Oh, I'm sorry, that was the wrong answer. I think the studio audience doesn't like your game show performance, Rachel. In fact, they're looking kind of feral. And closer.

"See, one of the offshoots of this whole invisibility thing is that it's not just me it can't see. It can't see much of the futures of the situations I'm involved in, either. I'd say I'm pretty involved in this situation right here, wouldn't you?"

"The fuck are you saying?"

"That Jimmy won't find you. It can't see you. It won't even know where to look. I'll ask again, where's Jimmy?"

Rachel glares at me before finally saying, "Storer House."

"Come again?"

"It's a Frank Lloyd Wright in the Hollywood Hills."

"Why?"

"What?"

"Why there? Seems kind of a specific location, don't you think?"

I don't know anything about this 'Storer House.' The name sounds a little familiar. Wright was commissioned for three or four homes in Hollywood and Pasadena in the twenties. Most of them have fallen into disrepair over the years.

Being L.A., where we tear down anything that doesn't smack of whatever's the fad of the last twenty minutes, it's kind of surprising they haven't been hauled off into a landfill. Pretty sure they're considered national landmarks. No doubt there are real estate developers trying to build megamalls who are shaking their fists.

"I like Wright," she says. "It was available. He said to find something, he didn't care where. So I did."

"No, you didn't," I say.

"I'm telling you the truth."

"I know you are. But I guarantee you Jimmy arranged it before you even picked up a phone."

"Sure. Fine. You got your answer. Get me the fuck out of here."

"Oh, look. They've noticed us. You know Wanderers can move pretty fast when they want to. See? They're making good time."

"Eric."

"Look at 'em go. Like horses coming to the finish line. Or maybe starving hyenas to a crippled gazelle."

"Eric, you said if I gave you where Jimmy was, you'd get me out of here. I kept my end. Now it's your turn."

"Oh yeah, that. I lied. I'd say to tell the Twins hi for me, but you're not going where they went. You're not going anywhere at all."

"Eric. No. Fuck, no." Rachel stands up to attack and discovers that it wasn't just a bubble of breathable air I conjured. She hits the shield hard and lands on her ass.

"I'd stay and watch, but I am just beat. Gonna go take a nap. I'd suggest tossing spells at the ghosts. You'll drain faster that way and might actually kick before they get their claws into you. Trust me, hurts like the dickens. Goodbye, Rachel."

I slide back over to the living side as the first Wanderers close in, Rachel's pissed-off screams drowned out by the jet-engine noise of the transition.

From this side I can see the Wanderers clearly. Rachel is a human-shaped blob of light that thrashes around as the Wanderers jump her. It doesn't take long before she stops thrashing and her light disappears.

I stand there watching the Wanderers go at each other like sharks at a feeding frenzy until they slow down, forget what just happened, shuffle away.

Storer House, huh? Part of me wants to go running up there right now and break down the door. But I'm exhausted and if I tried it now I might not make it out again.

I'll take the chance that Jimmy's gone by the time I get there tomorrow. After all, I wasn't hunting him. I was hunting Rachel. Jimmy will come to me.

I just need to be ready for it.

There has never been a situation in all of history where waking up to someone beating on your front door and yelling your name is a positive development.

I grab my gun and stumble toward the door. I consider simply putting a few rounds through it, but it's poor manners to shoot a caller before knowing who they are.

I take a chance and look through the peephole. Letitia. Shit.

"Go away," I yell. "I'm naked and armed and I'm not afraid to use it."

"Use what exactly?"

"You really want to find out?"

"Just open the goddamn door."

I unlock the door and lower a security ward on it. Letitia pushes in past me.

"There's a—Oh, Jesus."

"I told you I was naked and armed."

"Put some goddamn pants on. I did not need to see that this early in the morning."

"No peeking," I say and head to the bedroom.

"Trust me, that won't be a problem."

"The fuck are you doing here?" I say a few minutes later after I've found a pair of jeans and a t-shirt. "I'm getting coffee. You want coffee?"

"I could use the caffeine, but I'd rather have bourbon. Especially after seeing your ass. Christ, do you have tats everywhere?"

Over the years I've had spells, sigils, and runes tattooed all over my body. Throat to wrist to ankles. Most are for protection. They used to be varying shades of black, but after I was brought back from Mictlan they've been bright red, green, blue, gold.

The strangest tat is on my chest and it's changed the most of any of them. It used to be a circle of ravens that would move around, which was really uncomfortable for anyone else to look at. I could let them loose and they'd try to fuck up whoever was trying to kill me.

But when I became Mictlantecuhtli, they changed. Now they're jade eagles and I have no control over them whatsoever. They only seem to come out to play when they want to.

"I can give you another look if you want. Give you a real reason for that bourbon. How about I put some in your coffee? I know you're here about last night. If you're not, then the world's more fucked than I thought it was. So what happened?"

"Tell you on the way?"

"Fuck, if you said you wanted me to head out with you I'd

have gotten dressed for real. Now ya gotta wait. Tell me what's happening. You'll have to be louder than the shower."

"Every time I think you can't be a bigger pain in the ass you exceed my expectations."

"Exponentially?"

"What?"

"Never mind. Talk." I close the door and start the shower, move under the spray.

When I finally got inside this morning, I crashed. Kind of surprised I made it to the bedroom. Hadn't realized I had so much blood on me. Now there's a metaphor for my life.

There's something about watching somebody else's blood go down a shower drain that hammers home how fucked up my world is. I murdered Rachel last night. And I don't feel a thing.

No regret, no sadness, no joy. Not even satisfaction. I killed her with no more regard than I would kill a rat. It does feel a little poetic that it's Nicole's blood going down the drain, though.

"You ever hear of the Pacific Electric Red Car?" Letitia shouts.

"Yeah. From back when L.A. actually had a real public transportation system. Wait. No."

"Yep. Middle of Culver Boulevard."

The Red Car was a series of connected rail lines for large red-and-orange trolleys that crisscrossed Los Angeles.

The freeways killed them, naturally. Worse, the freeways made L.A. even more racist and classist than it already was, if you can believe it.

All of a sudden you couldn't get anywhere without a car because the bus system was shit, the Red Car was gone, and nobody walks in L.A. The freeways might as well have been big concrete fences.

"Same situation as last night?"

She nods. "That one, we've got twelve bodies," she says. "Looks like a conductor and eleven passengers."

"Okay, so—Wait. *That* one? There's more than one?"

"Did you know the Valley used to be all orange groves?"

"You are fucking kidding me."

"Nope. A whole section of Victory turned into an orchard. During rush hour. Near the 405."

"Are the trees alive?"

"Nope," she says. "Some people who saw it happen say they showed up, looked as normal as a bunch of orange trees suddenly appearing in the middle of the street could, and then they turned black and withered."

"What about the cars? Any of the trees materialize in the middle of a Cadillac or something?"

"An F-150, actually. Dipshit was doing a hundred-and-ten in a forty-five when it showed up in the middle of his engine. Paramedics weren't sure if the driver was going to make it."

The adobe house, the Harrison, the club in Hollywood, and now a Red Car in Culver City and an orange grove in the Valley. Everything except the adobe house seem like they're from the same era.

The Harrison didn't appear the same way, though. It didn't displace anything, and I was able to walk into it. And when I left it was gone. So there's something different about the Harrison.

"What the fuck is going on?" I towel off, step into the attached bedroom, and get dressed.

"Kinda hoping you knew," she says.

"All right," I say, opening the bedroom door. "My shame is adequately covered. Happy now?"

"You have no idea."

"Yeah, that's a Red Car all right," I say. It's a long, closed, red-and-orange trolley car with folding doors at either end. Thing's built like a tank, rows of massive bolts holding it together. The electric poles at either end reach up to the sky, skeletal arms trying to pull the car out of the bureaucratic grave it was buried in seventy years ago.

I'm at a distance from the train where I'm close enough to

feel that buzz of energy under my skin but not so close that it's fucking with me.

The thing is, I want to get closer. Pulling in that energy last night hurt like a motherfucker, but there's something about it that makes me want to do it again, like one of those hook-ups you know you'll regret but go home with anyway.

"Yeah, got that," Letitia says. "The fuck's it doing here?" Letitia says. The train was moving when it appeared and the wheels have dug furrows into the pavement.

"Old rail line," I say. "They never pulled up most of the tracks in the city, just paved over them. You can see here where the wheels tore up the pavement."

"Oh Jesus," Letitia says. "Are we gonna see more of these things?"

"The trains? No idea. The other stuff? My money's on yes."

"Um," Letitia's not-an-apprentice rookie cop—Janna—says.

"What is it?" Letitia says.

"Last night we found these in some of the victims' pockets." She hands Letitia a plastic evidence bag holding a wide paper ticket. "And we found these here." The rookie hands Letitia another.

"Okay," she says. "They're Red Car tickets. Back then everybody was taking these things. What of it?"

"Can I see those?" I ask.

Letitia hands me the bags. I hold them up to the light to better see. "No shit. Oh, Tish, you gotta hang onto this one. She's a fucking treasure."

"What? What did I miss?"

"These little things people sometimes call clues," I say.

"I can still shoot you, you know," Letitia says.

"Tease. Look, you see how they're punched? Origination, destination, transfer, date."

"Okay."

"Should I be having this conversation with your apprentice?"

"Eric."

"Some of the ones from last night—How many?"

"Ten," Janna says.

"Same location?"

"No, but all the same route."

"Ten people got on the line going from West L.A. to Hollywood and Highland. Some of the people here were coming from Hollywood and Highland and heading to West L.A."

"I still don't get it."

"You want to tell her?" Janna blanches.

"I, uh. The ones we found last night are punched December twenty-second. The ones here are dated December twenty-third. There's no time-stamp, but everybody in there looks like they were on their way to work in the morning."

"They're not all coming from the same time," Letitia says.

"No," Janna says. "And they're not matching our time, either, not exactly. But their time is moving."

"How do you mean?" Letitia says.

"Most of the people on the train have a watch," Janna says. "They've all stopped. A couple of them had newspapers. They're dated December 23, 1924."

"But it's not December here."

"That's not the point," I say. "The point is that whatever the fuck is going on here, we have a connection. Something happened around the end of the year in 1924."

"Great," Letitia says. "What does it mean?"

"Fucked if I know," I say. "You're the detective. How long do you think you're gonna be able to keep a lid on this?"

"For the last five years we've kept a lid on a fucking toxic cloud over South L.A. that kills everything that goes into it," she says. "I think we can handle this."

"Sure," I say. "This one. And when another one hits? And another? Do you really think an orange grove in the fast lane on Victory is gonna be the last of it?"

"No," she says. "Can you take a little pressure off us and burn the city down again?"

"Funny," I say. "And fuck you. Have fun."

"The hell are you going?"

To get away from all these corpses. It's an effort to pull myself away from the train. There's something drawing me to them and it's hard to resist. But I don't need a repeat of last night.

"Gonna go immerse myself in architectural history," I say. "Why do I even ask?"

Chapter 11

I know this has to be related to Jimmy, but until I know how I'm better off just looking for the damn thing. Rachel's dead, thank fuck, and I have an address. If it's lost sight of her then it'll know we ran into each other. And if she hasn't checked in, it'll know what happened to her.

And what is it about the end of December in 1924? I don't know for sure that the orange grove is from then, but the Red Car, the club, and if the Harrison are. But then there's the adobe. That doesn't fit.

The Harrison is bugging me. It didn't show up like the others, and I could go inside but Danny couldn't. What if I'd stayed there? Would I have been able to come back?

"Excuse me." Woman's voice. Yelling behind me with the combined authority of a pissed-off mom and Satan. I turn on my heel, my shield ready to go, but it's Rookie Janna.

"Didn't recognize your voice there," I say. "You always get so quiet around Tish?" Her face scrunches up in embarrassment.

"It's that obvious?"

"She can be pretty intimidating," I say. "Hell, she stabbed me in high school."

Rookie Janna squints at me. "Like caught on school grounds and stabbed you?"

"What I like is that your instinct isn't to deny she might do something like that," I say. "No. High school. We went together."

"You don't look—"

"Oh. Right. I don't look old enough, do I? Trust me, I am. What can I do for you—I keep thinking of you as Rookie Janna and that's not working for me."

"Benson," she says. "Janna Benson." I feel sorry for the kid. She's working under a hardass like Letitia and trying to get a handle on her power and probably not able to tell anybody. It's got to be overwhelming.

"What can I do for you, Officer Benson?"

"Captain Watson wants me to go with you." I look past Officer Benson and see Letitia. She smiles and waves at me.

"No," I say, turn around and keep walking.

"Uh, Mister Carter? Eric? She really wants me to go with you."

"It's good to want things," I say. "Gives a person goals."

"She really—"

I stop dead and turn around to face her. "What has she told you about me?"

"That your magic is about ghosts."

"That's it?" She nods. "Jesus Christ, what the hell is Letitia thinking? She's either trying to get you killed or teach you some kind of object lesson that she doesn't realize is going to get you killed."

"She told me it'd be good to ride along."

"I can tell you with absolute conviction that it would not. Go back to your crime scene, Officer Benson. You're too good at your job to waste on me." I leave Officer Benson to decide her own fate.

I find a Lexus that's about as close as I'm going to get down here to inconspicuous for the Hollywood Hills. The houses up there start at five million bucks. Nobody's driving anything under $80k.

I know I won't find Jimmy at the house. Who knows, maybe we'll run into each other stuck in traffic on opposite sides of the 405. Statistically, everyone in Los Angeles will eventually get stuck in traffic next to everyone else.

"Wanna go toss a house?" I say when Danny picks up my call.

"Is there a special someone we might run into?"

"Sadly, no. One of them is in the wind and the other one is on the other side of the veil as ghost kibble."

"Dude. You could have called."

"She sorta dropped in on me. Anyway, Jimmy's on the move. But I have a last known address."

"Reliable?"

"Gonna find out. Care to join?"

"Fuck yes." I give him the address.

"A Frank Lloyd Wright house?" he says. "People actually live in those? I always thought they were like Bigfoot. Things you hear about but don't actually exist."

"If they don't, they're spending a lot of money on empty real estate," I say. "I'm not expecting anybody to actually be in there, but don't start the party without me."

"Oh, sure. You get to drop the house on the Wicked Witch and I gotta hang outside the Emerald City? Some friend you are. I'll see you there."

It takes me over an hour to crawl my way up to Hollywood. La Cienega is a mess, as always, but eventually I get onto Crescent Heights to head up into the hills. The second I hit Sunset the cops hit me.

A black and white is up my ass flashing its lights and bumping its siren. You've got to be kidding me. How did I not see it? It's not like those cars don't stand out.

It's easier to just deal with the cop than try to get away from them. Especially in this traffic. I pull over, grab a sticker and a Sharpie, and write "Nothing to see here. Have a nice day." I pump some magic into it.

I roll down the window and—"Officer Benson," I say. "Fancy meeting you here."

"Sir, will you please step out of the vehicle." It's not a request. She has very different energy from when she was around Tish or talking to me right before I left.

"See, this is how you should be around Letitia. Let yourself be a badass. It suits you."

"Sir, please grab your belongings and step out of the vehicle."

"You really want to do this?" She doesn't say anything but I notice she's had her hand on her sidearm the entire time. I wonder if Officer Benson is one of *those* cops. The ones who let their fear and bigotry out to play because they can.

No. That's not fair. Letitia wouldn't be working with her if she was. In fact, if she were a mage like that, Letitia would have killed her already.

"All right," I say. "I'll play along." I grab my messenger bag and do as she says.

Officer Benson is pure cop. She is not fucking around. I get the distinct vibe that if she needed to she would shoot me in an instant. Good instincts. She'll get along fine with Letitia.

"Get in the car." She throws open the passenger side of her black and white.

"But I just—" I stop at the look she gives me. I feel sorry for any kids she might have. I give her a quick salute. "Getting into the car, Officer."

I'm trying not to laugh. Partly because I'm curious to see where this goes and partly because it feels rude. Yeah, like that's ever stopped me.

She's taking it seriously. She's not a little girl playing cop. She is a hardass officer of the law and she will not be fucked with. And I can respect that. Mostly.

"I didn't notice your car," I say as she gets in. "You were behind me the entire time, weren't you?" I reach out and now I feel it. A faint trace of magic. This is subtle but powerful and well thought out. I seriously doubt I could do it.

"I'm impressed," I say. "Nicely done."

"What?"

"The spell you cast? Invisibility on the car?"

"I don't know what the hell you're talking about."

Oh, shit. No wonder Tish has taken her under her wing. This was a powerful, complicated spell with a lot of moving parts, and she cast it instinctively without even realizing she was doing it.

"Huh. Okay, well. Not my pig, not my farm."

"You know that car was reported stolen," she says as she gets into the driver's seat.

"Mercy me. Not stolen."

"Why?"

"You're gonna have to get a little more specific there."

"Why'd you steal the car?"

"Because I needed one."

"But you stole it."

"I think we've pretty much covered that ground." She chews on that for a second.

"What's with the sticker?"

"It's a sort of camouflage spell," I say. "Makes people see what I want them to. Compared to what you did with the car it's like trying to hide myself behind a daisy. You learn that from Letitia? What's she teaching you?"

"She's not teaching me a goddamn thing." Hardass Officer Benson is suddenly replaced with apprentice Janna Benson who's clearly overwhelmed by this crash course in magic.

"How long have you been with her?"

"A year and a half," she says. "I've been on the force for about three years now. I spent a year on administrative leave. She helped me get through that." I run through the math.

"LAPD academy takes, what, six months?"

"Nine," she says.

"So most of your time you've been in training or dealing with all this magic bullshit."

I'm curious to see how she reacts to that. Her face starts to get red, but I can see her tamp down on her emotions. Simple anger? Doubt it. Probably a lot of shame, self-recrimination, sense of failure.

Interesting. Something happened with her power on the job. Kill somebody? Probably. On purpose? Probably not. I don't think Letitia would be helping her out if she had.

But now either Officer Benson is so talented Letitia doesn't have anything to teach her other than how not to piss off other mages or she's an idiot who needs to be put down before she becomes a danger to others. But it's probably option three, Letitia is horrible with this sort of thing and is desperate to foist her onto somebody else. I am so not biting.

"Okay. Let's table that. I told you, you're not coming with me."

"You're right. I'm not," she says as she starts the car. "You're coming with me."

Compared to the rest of the homes along this stretch of Hollywood Boulevard, Storer House is tiny. It's a Mayan Revival style using Wright's concrete textile blocks. Gives it a look that's somehow both ancient and modern. Tall columns of sculpted concrete inside and out, narrow floor to ceiling windows. All acute angles, sharp corners.

It's only a short drive from Hollywood and Highland through a couple of twists on a narrow stretch of Hollywood. It stands out simply because it doesn't stand out.

"Go past the house," I say. "Don't slow down." As we go past I see a man in a suit on the front terrace brazenly holding a submachinegun.

"What are we doing here?" Janna says.

"Looking for a head," I say. To her credit she doesn't even blink.

"Like, in a jar, a grocery bag? What? I need a little more to go on."

"If it's there, which it probably isn't, it should be in a box. I need to ask it some questions."

"Ask it questions?"

"If we run into it, you'll see what I mean. Keep going and make a U back onto Hollywood. We're gonna loop around onto Crescent Heights and get up to the house behind it." Since Storer's at the bottom of the rise we should be able to get into the back easily enough.

"There are three guys we'll have to deal with," she says. "Armed."

"Three? Huh. I missed the other two. Where are they?"

"Inside," she says. "Wait. How do I know that? Fuck."

"Get used to it. Until you know more, your magic's gonna

leak out like that. Happens to all of us. Eventually you'll figure out your knack."

"My what?"

"Oh, fuck sake. We need to get somebody else to teach you some shit besides Tish. A knack is the one type of magic that we're ridiculously good at. Doesn't mean that's the only magic we can cast, but it's what we're best at."

"She never told me this," Janna says. "What's hers?"

"Finding the truth," I say. "If you lie to her, she'll know. In case you ever have to hide something from her, know that it's not infallible. She can't tell if you're leaving anything out or if you just believe that you're telling the truth. She's good at figuring that stuff out on her own. Try to avoid yes or no answers if you can."

We pull behind Danny's Jeep parked across the street from the house we're going to go through. He's sitting in his Jeep eating Cheetos and watching something on his phone. He doesn't notice us until we're out of the car.

"Where the fuck did you come from?" he says, stepping out of the Jeep.

"Danny Kwan, meet Officer Benson. She makes her car disappear."

"Sometimes," she says.

"Sometimes?" Danny says.

"She's new to magic and Letitia Watson has taken her on as an apprentice."

"Letitia. Isn't she the chick who tried to kill you in high school?"

"With a knife, yes," I say.

"She's not the one who threw the car at you?"

"No, that was . . . I wanna say Susan?"

"Is this normal for mages?" Janna says.

"Yeah," Danny says, "pretty typical."

"Mages are, by and large, not the most stable people," I say. "Imagine giving a bunch of emotionally stunted narcissists superpowers and letting them loose in public and the only thing keeping them in check is the fact that they tend to get themselves killed early on."

"That sounds like a disaster," she says.

"Usually is, yeah," Danny says.

"Why haven't I heard about any of this? I mean, the Captain told me stuff happens but wouldn't talk about what."

"You have," Danny says. "The fires, Vernon blowing up, toxic cloud? Any of that ring a bell?"

"Letitia told you about the Cleanup Crew, right?" I say, and she nods. "That exists because normals finding out about magic would be bad for everybody. And we don't exactly police each other. At least not until one of us goes completely off the rails and needs to be put down."

"You call us—We call them 'normals'? Captain didn't say anything about that." There's a look on her face that tells me something is about to click.

"That's because it's fucked up and she doesn't like it. It's like calling people peasants. But it's better than 'ordinary.' At least 'normals' implies that we're the abominations."

She looks around at all the houses, back at her car, touches her badge. She's thinking. She's thinking real hard.

"Mages have fights all the time," I say. "But mages and normals? People would die by the thousands. And have."

Danny points at me. "He'd know better than anybody."

"This is great and all," I say, hurrying to move on before she starts asking questions about that, "but I'm not the one who should be telling you this stuff and I got shit to do. Officer Benson, thank you very much for your assistance in getting me here. Your tenacity honors the badge."

"I'm not leaving," she says.

"There might be breaking," Danny says.

"Definitely entering," I say. "And a possibility of gunfire. Inside a historic landmark, even."

To make the point, Danny pulls an FN-P90 submachine gun and a belt loaded with mag holders out of his Jeep.

"Do you have a license for that?" she says.

Danny stops, cocks his head, and looks at her like a confused dog, then goes back to getting his gear on.

"Officer Benson," I say. "Janna. You look like you're about to have a stroke. I don't think Letitia meant for you to be a part of this."

"What exactly are you planning?" she says.

"There's an artifact," I say. "It's an undead talking head. It does stuff we don't need to get into right now. It was probably in that house. It most likely isn't anymore. There are at least three people in there that we'll have to deal with. Which is a good thing."

"Why?"

"Because if it's just sitting there on a table and nobody's around, that means it doesn't think it needs guarding and that shit's about to go sideways in ways that could take a long time to explain."

"Wait here," she says. She steps behind the car and I can't see what she's doing. God, I hope she doesn't try to arrest us.

"Where the fuck did you get Officer Obie here?" Danny says, failing to keep his voice down. He shrugs into a Kevlar vest.

"You think maybe you shouldn't be hauling all that military hardware out in the middle of the street?" I say.

"Oh, I got wards," he says. "Anybody comes around here, they're gonna see gardeners. Even if they look out their window." He nods toward his P-90. "This is a weed whacker."

Janna comes back carrying a Benelli M4 shotgun and her phone. She hands the latter to me. It's Letitia, of course.

"I'm not a babysitter," I say. Janna's face turns red.

"Not asking you to be one," she says.

"You didn't ask, period. The fuck are you playing at?"

"She needs to see the shit," Letitia says. "And the shit I can show her isn't close to what she needs."

"So, what, I'm the deep end you're throwing her into?"

"Yes," she says. "She sinks or swims. She lives or dies. You're not her babysitter. I'm not her mom."

I walk away from the two of them and lower my voice. "Jesus, Tish. This is cold even for you."

"She needs more mages to be around," she says. "She wants to be a cop. She isn't. Not anymore. I can't get that through to her."

"You are," I say.

"No, I'm not. Not first and foremost. I can quit the job. I can't stop my magic."

"What I'm doing right now could get her killed. This isn't the deep end you're throwing her into. It's a fucking shark tank."

"Then she learns how to swim with sharks. She's better off learning how from one of them. Otherwise, she's dangerous to herself and everybody around her."

"Dangerous how? I thought you said she was new?"

"New does not mean safe. Have you seen her cast yet?"

"No. Saw the effects of a camouflage spell she did, which was honestly pretty terrifying, but not her doing it. She says she didn't know how she did it."

"That's right," Letitia says. "That's the problem. She did it without even thinking about it. Or realizing she did it. Right now, everything's instinct. And she's fucking powerful. You know how that goes. Ask her how she and I connected and you'll see what I mean."

"You're right," I say. "She does need somebody. And I am not it. You threw her in my fucking lap, Tish."

"Yes, I did," Letitia says and hangs up.

I walk back to Janna and Danny. Danny is making a show of checking his gear and ignoring a seething Janna. I toss her phone back to her.

"Tell me how it happened." She doesn't need more than that.

"We were on a call. Domestic disturbance. Me and my partner. He . . . Anyway, we were on a domestic. We get there and there's a major fight going on. Yelling and screaming. We can hear furniture breaking. There are a couple blown out windows.

"So, we decide it's probable cause, call it in. Start banging on the door, yelling through the window. They're not paying attention. Door's unlocked. My partner's the first one through and barely gets out of the way of a thrown plate."

"Those are never fun," I say.

"Yeah, well, this one was less fun. Even before I get through the door I feel it. This—this buzzing. Not my ears. Not even in my body. Like my soul's been hit with a tuning fork. Does that make sense?"

"Never heard it put that way, but yeah. I'd say that's pretty accurate."

"We get inside and there are two women beating the shit out of each other. They're both bruised and cut up. One of them looks like she has a broken arm. Only they're not throwing anything. Just standing there staring at each other on opposite sides of the room, screaming shit. Crap's flying all over the place and they're not touching any of it.

"Then a side table hits my partner in the head. Hard. He goes down. I don't know exactly what happened next. I remember screaming for them to stop and then having this feeling like—I dunno, like a release that you can feel all over?"

"Kinda like cumming," Danny says, helpful as ever.

"Seriously?" I say.

"What?"

"No, he's right," she says. "I mean, he's wrong, but not entirely? I don't know how to describe it."

"Got it. You cast a spell. What happened?"

"I—I blew up the building."

"Whole thing?" I say.

She looks at me like she's expecting me to be shocked or horrified or something. Around these parts we call that Tuesday.

"No. Just that apartment. The one above it. Nobody was in that one."

"Anybody survive?"

Again the look. Probably only ever been asked if anybody died, like it wouldn't be a given.

"My partner's in a coma. I don't know if it was the table or the explosion, but he's got brain damage. The two women—they died on scene. Next thing I know, I'm standing in what's left of the doorway. Nothing touched me. It all went past me or around me. Same with my partner. Like everything bounced off him. Then I passed out.

"I woke up in the hospital with the Captain and some doctor, never got her name, hovering over my bed. Captain and I had a long conversation after that."

I'm beginning to see what Letitia was talking about. When that spell went off, Janna probably caught the attention of every mage in a five-mile radius.

"I've heard worse," I say. "Fuck, I've done worse. Here's the thing, Letitia is trying to get through to you that the life you had before is over and it's not getting through."

"I fucking get it," she says. "I feel like I'm constantly holding shit in. Like any second I'm about to explode and kill somebody."

"You will," I say.

"I—No. I fucking won't."

"Yes," I say. "You will. Guaranteed. Do you understand you are no longer a police officer?" I say.

She blinks. "What?"

"You can keep the job, but you're a mage. How you decide to live with that or what you do with it is up to you. Tell me, what are you? Start with the basics." She doesn't even need to think about it.

"A woman."

"Right. And you're white. And you're straight, gay, whatever. All these labels we go through to build our identities. Those are who you are. Somewhere after all that you're a cop. You're going to have to accept that mage is a hell of a lot higher on the totem pole than that. You can quit the job. You can't quit you."

"Captain—Letitia said she made it work," she says.

"Past tense. She made it work by lying to everybody, including her wife, who left her because of it."

"Are you trying to scare me?" she says, hunching up her shoulders like she's about to throw a punch.

"Yes," I say. "You should be. That said, and I can't believe I'm doing this, if you really want to go in there with us, fine. Tish wants to throw you into the shark tank. And she seems to think I can point out the sharks."

"What the hell are you?" she says.

"First good question you've asked," I say. "I'm one of the sharks. I'm a necromancer. I talk to ghosts. I make zombies. Occasionally I murder people and do both at the same time. I'm not the most dangerous mage out there, but I have a tendency to piss off a lot of them. Don't ask me what my body count is, I don't know, though I suspect it's somewhere in the low six figures."

"I—" Janna says, but can't seem to finish the sentence. She takes a step back, staring at me. "This is how the bodies started moving last night."

"It is."

"And Letitia sent me here with—"

"That's right, Officer, your boss just partnered you up with an admitted murderer and so many other things you have no idea about and would and should make you run screaming that make the whole Zombie Master thing look tame. Letitia, too. Only differences are motivation and magnitude. She actually tries to follow the law. But a lot of times, she can't."

"I just shoot people," Danny says. "Or stab. Punch, kick, you get the idea. That's how my magic comes out. Are we doing this? The bad guys probably want to break for lunch. I know I'm getting a little peckish."

"Well?" I say. "You ready?"

"No," she says. She unpins her badge and slides it into her pocket. Her face is a stone mask, but the eyes poking out of it look like she just heard her parents died. "But I'm going anyway."

"I like you, Officer Benson," I say. "I hope you don't die."

"Or worse," says Danny.

Chapter 12

"All right, Officer Obie, let's do this," Danny says. Janna's got maybe half a foot and twenty pounds on him. She gives me a look that says if this were anywhere else she'd deck him.

"He may not look it," I say, "but he really is very good."

"Yeah, I—Hey."

"How are we doing this?" Janna says.

"Preferably quietly," I say. "And without destroying a historic landmark."

"Why are you looking at me?" Danny says. "I hit what I aim at."

"More worried about the three guys inside. We're cutting through this yard over the fence and down to the rear terrace. There are five tall windows in the front and back. The bottom sections are doors. There's no cover once we get onto the property."

"Dude, how do you know all this?" Danny says.

"Google," I say. "How do you think?"

"This place looks like it's built out of Legos."

"It kind of was," Janna says. "Wright used textured cement blocks to—Uh. Sorry."

"I wouldn't bother," I say. "It'd all be wasted on Danny, anyway."

"So, what happens when we get to the house?" Janna says.

"Then we improvise. Let's go."

The mansion yard we're cutting through is easy to navigate. Janna's nervous the way a kid breaking into an abandoned church is nervous.

It occurs to me that she's an idealist. That can be a good

thing. But if the ideal is uphold the law at any costs, well, that gets ugly fast.

I get the feeling she's the sort who wants to do good and isn't there for a power trip, though. I think power might frighten her.

The LAPD needs more empathy, more compassion. But I don't know if the LAPD deserves her. It certainly isn't going to help her.

We clear the fence and stop behind some foliage just above the back. Through the windows I can see the other two guys inside. The three all look like professionals. Suit and tie and a relaxed stance. I'd prefer anxious and slightly paranoid. I suspect these guys won't make mistakes.

"All right," I say. "You're up." I pull the sticker off my jacket, wad it up, and stick it in my pocket.

"Sorry?" Janna says.

"Your invisibility thing. I don't think there are any mages in there. They don't look the type."

"Why would that matter?" she says.

"Because if you cast a spell, other mages can feel it," Danny says. "So does this invisibility make it so you're literally invisible, or do you just not get noticed?"

"I don't know," Janna says, clearly frustrated. Nobody likes being on the spot. "I don't know how to do it."

"Sure you do," I say. "Go on, give it a try."

The frustration on her face is starting to turn to anger. "I don't—" There's a flare of magic and . . . nothing's happened.

"You did something," Danny says. "I don't feel invisible."

"Hang on," I say. I pull out my phone and turn on its camera. I point it at Janna and Danny. "No shit. Take a look." I hand Janna the phone. She points it at us.

"You're not there. I—I did it. On purpose."

"Remember the feeling," I say. "Hang onto it. It'll get easier as you do it, but it'll be tough at the beginning. Recalling the feeling will help."

"Yay," Danny says, his voice flat. "Can we please go deal with whatever the talking head left us?"

"Sure," I say.

"Thank you," Danny says, stepping into the open and hopping down to the terrace.

"What the hell is his problem?" Janna says.

"He's itching for some payback. Someone who works for Jimmy—that's the talking head's name—they set us up and he ended up shooting four people yesterday who were just in the wrong place at the wrong time."

"Jesus. Wait. Yesterday? Was this Long Beach?"

"Yeah. And don't ask for details. They'll just upset you. Come on." By the time we get down, Danny's already gotten inside the house.

"You ever fire that gun in a real-world situation?" I whisper.

"Once," she says. Okay, good. She'd have gotten enough training to know that you don't shoot to wound because legs and arms are smaller targets and you'll probably miss. Always shoot center mass. Shoot to kill or don't shoot at all.

"Good to know. Let's go."

We crouch low and follow Danny inside. They might not be able to see us, but I don't know if they can hear us.

One of Jimmy's people is sitting on a leather-and-wood craftsman chair reading a book. Danny gets behind him and draws a wicked looking Gerber knife. Just as he's about to run it across the guy's throat, the guy is gone.

Fucker moves so fast I can't track him at first. Then I see him on the other side of the room across from his buddy. Janna and I hit the floor.

Danny jumps to the side as they open fire, bullets tearing into the concrete walls, disintegrating the furniture. Hundred-year-old tables and chairs turn to splinters in no time flat.

They're sweeping their fire from where Danny was a moment ago back and forth across the room. They can't see us.

"One of them's a mage," I mouth to Janna. They can't see

through the spell, but they know one was cast. And if it's just invisibility, then Danny making noise must have tipped them off. Which means they probably don't know Janna and I are here.

The guy from the front terrace comes running in, straight into Danny, who's crouched low. Danny takes advantage of the guy's momentum and flips him into the room, right into the line of fire.

Bullets tear into him as he sails through the air and lands a couple of feet from Janna and me. She starts to get up, but I wave her back down. They've already shifted fire toward Danny's location. He's put up a shield so, for the moment at least, he's good.

"Letitia wanted you to see the ugly side of this life," I say. "So, here's the ugly side."

I cast a spell at the dead shooter, which immediately grabs the attention of one of the live ones, who start firing in our direction. Then I feel a shield go up around us. A quick glance at Janna tells me she doesn't know she's casting that one either.

The dead shooter stands up, which has the effect of drawing more fire. That's fine. I don't actually need him, I just need his blood.

One of the tricks I picked up from Mictlantecuhtli is manipulating blood. I've gotten better at it over the last months and I'm pretty sure I can do this.

I concentrate on drawing all of the blood left in his body and collecting it behind his ribcage. Then I push it out through his chest.

But not like a hose. More like a needle and thread. A long line of blood terminating in a sharp, solidified arrow shoots across the room and spears the normal gunman through the left eye, exiting the back of his skull.

It's so fast the mage doesn't seem to have noticed it's happened. He has a shield, but he's only got it up in front of him. He's a few feet away from the wall, after all. Why waste the energy?

I zip the arrow of blood into a sharp turn toward his unprotected flank and shoot it into the base of his skull. It bursts out through his left eye, jumps back through his right. I run it through his skull like an in-the-shell egg scrambler.

Both men are very dead and hanging limply by this blood rope. I drop the spell and they hit the floor, along with the splash of this long, thick line of blood. I'd love to see what the forensics guys make of this.

"Jesus fucking Christ," Danny says. "You didn't even break a sweat doing that, did you?"

"There's some effort, but yeah, it was a lot easier than I expected." I turn at a noise to find Janna throwing up in a corner. I suppose police training doesn't really cover this sort of thing.

"You doin' all right, there, Officer?" Danny says. She gives us a thumbs-up, spits a couple of times and wipes her mouth on her sleeve.

"You really made a zombie," she says. "Like last night. But worse."

"I really made a zombie," I say. "And yet, worse. Come on, let's go see what they were guarding. And watch your step. There's a lot of blood and . . . stuff."

"I—I have to call this in."

"Whoa there," Danny says. "That would be a real bad idea."

"Trust me, it'll make Tish's life a lot more difficult," I say. "Yours, too."

Janna takes a deep breath, nods. "Yeah. Thanks. Now what?"

We don't run into anyone else. We clear most of the house quickly. It's a small place and mostly open-plan. I don't feel any wards, any spells, nothing. I didn't think there'd be much in here, but I figured there'd be something besides guys with guns.

There's a bedroom to one side. Danny pops his head around to see if anybody's going to try to shoot it off.

He pulls back, a puzzled look on his face. "You ever see Charlie's Angels?" he says.

"Uh, seventies show?" I say. "Three women spies or something. Get orders from some guy through a speaker on a desk?"

"Yeah," he says, and steps into the room. I follow him and stop the second I see it. It's a small room with a queen-sized bed. In the center of the bed sits a square white speaker plugged into the wall.

There's a pop and a burst of static, then: "Hello, Eric. Mister Kwan. Officer Benson." I see Janna looking around for cameras.

"Don't bother," I say. "It's not looking at us that way. In fact, it might not be able to see us that way at all. Hey, Jimmy. I assume you already know about Rachel."

"In the 18,435 scenarios I saw, she was only successful in 3,672."

"And you let her go?"

"She made a choice to find you," Jimmy says. "You're difficult to pin down."

"Right. Choice. That's a good one. Ya know, I'd be happy to make this easy. Tell me where you're at. I'll swing by."

"You know you can't hurt me," it says.

"Then there's no reason not to have a tête-à-tête, as it were." Pause. "Nothin'? I worked on that one for hours. You see, because tête means head, and—"

"I understood the joke," Jimmy says.

"Who are we talking to?" Janna asks.

"My apologies. Officer Benson, this is Jimmy. Seems Jimmy already knows you."

"I've been watching you for some time, Officer Benson. It's nice to finally meet you," Jimmy says, his voice flat and monotone. And too late, I see the trap. "How's your father? I understand they're very good at Cedars Sinai."

"Oh, you sonofabitch," I say. "Janna, you need to leave now. This is a bad play, Jimmy."

"What?" Janna says. "How does he know my father's at Cedars?"

"I have good news," Jimmy says. "There's a donor liver available and they've matched it to your father. It's being couriered down from Bakersfield as we speak. It should be reaching him in about four hours. Motorcycle accident."

"Don't fucking do this, Jimmy."

"All right, stop," Janna says. "What the fuck is going on?"

"The TL;DR version is that Jimmy is a thing called an Oracle. It sees multiple futures, picks the one it wants, and then manipulates events so that it'll get it."

"It sees the future?"

"It makes the future," I say.

"Eric is being too kind," Jimmy says. "He is a particular blind spot for me. In order to manipulate his future I have to do it indirectly. I have to extrapolate. For example, out of the 37,643 different scenarios I could see this conversation happening today in 36,973 of them. Of those Officer Benson was present in 28,237, Mister Kwan 18,922, Miz Cortez 6,923. So I focused my efforts on Officer Benson."

"You played the odds."

"Yes."

"Wait," Janna says. "You made it so my dad would have a donor liver just because I might have come here with Eric?"

"Yes," Jimmy says.

"And if you hadn't," I say, "you'd get what felt like a lucky break."

"I—Why?"

"Because he's going to ask me for something and if I don't give it to him, that liver won't make it to your dad in time, or at all. Or something else will happen. Isn't that right, Jimmy?"

"But why me?" Janna says.

"Because you're here," I say. "That's all. It's meaningless and stupid but sometimes that's just how the world works."

"It's not a very large ask," Jimmy says. "And it's not like it didn't belong to me already."

"Right. Stole it fair and square."

"As did you."

"Even if I still had the opal, and I don't, you really think this would make me hand it over? You know me, Jimmy. I let a couple thousand people die because Darius didn't think I had the balls to let him kill them. What makes you think this will work?"

"As you say, I do know you," he says. "This isn't to sway you, Eric. It's to remind you what I can do. If I want, I can hurt you by hurting the people around you. And in that way I can hurt you over and over again. Miz Cortez has a number of people she cares about enough that she very well might betray you just to save them. Mister Kwan certainly does. His brother in Portland, for example."

"Oh, don't even fucking go there," Danny says.

"I hope not to," Jimmy says. "And as a show of good faith, Officer Benson, rest assured that your father will get the liver, everything will go perfectly, and he will live for many more years. Regardless of what Eric decides to do. Consider it a gift."

"You really are a fucking monster, you know that?"

"I am my father's son," Jimmy says. "Oh, when you see her next, say hello to the Tree of Life. I'll be in touch." There's a click and the speaker goes silent.

Before I know it I'm shaking the small speaker, screaming at it. But there's not even static.

"Motherfucker. God fucking dammit fuck!" I hurl the speaker against the wall and it shatters into a hundred plastic shards. "I knew it. I knew that sonofabitch was behind it."

"Hey man," Danny says. "What's going on?"

"That motherfucker. You know what I should have done years ago? Nothing. Not a goddamn thing. Then I wouldn't be in this fucking hole."

"Is he all right?" Janna says.

"Probably not," Danny says.

I pick a lamp up off the side table and throw it against the wall, too.

"Okay, definitely not."

I stop. I have an idea. It should work. Probably won't learn anything, but doesn't mean I can't try. I march into the foyer, Danny and Janna on my heels.

I stand over the one corpse with an intact brain and scream

at it, "Get the fuck up." Its milky eyes snap open and it sits up. I hear Janna swear behind me, but I'm not really paying attention.

"Where is it?" I say. "Where is Jimmy? And so fucking help me, if you dick me around I will hunt down your soul and shove it into this slab of rotting meat so fast you won't even get a chance to see what Hell looks like."

"I don't know."

"That was informative," Danny says.

"Why did I expect anything more out of a corpse?" I say. Fuck. Twenty questions time. "When did it leave?"

"A few hours ago."

"How did it leave?"

"On a truck."

"Where was the truck going?"

"I don't know."

"Then what the fuck do you know?"

It starts to sing. "A B C D E F G—" Of course. It's going to tell me everything it knows. Starting, apparently, with the fucking alphabet.

"Stop. Who took it on the truck?"

"Woman."

"Name?"

"Didn't say."

"What did she look like?"

"Jeans, blue hoodie, motorcycle helmet."

"Come again?"

"Jeans—"

"Why was she wearing a motorcycle helmet?"

"I can answer that one," Janna says. "She didn't want these guys to see her face. Means she knew you were going to be here and that you'd ask them about her."

"If Tish doesn't make you a detective by this weekend, she's an idiot," I say. I pull back my energy and the corpse falls back to the floor.

"All right, you want to tell us what the fuck that was all about?" Danny says.

"I'm not entirely sure," I say. "It's a girl. Looks to be about sixteen. Has a bunch of talking dogs."

"Did you say 'dogs'?" Janna says.

"Puppies, yeah. You had to be there. Point is, Jimmy knew I'd talked to her. I don't know how, though. I don't even know how I was talking to her."

"When was—" Janna starts, before her phone rings. She ignores it.

"You're gonna want to get that," I say. "It's the hospital."

She doesn't believe me until she sees the caller ID. She answers, they talk for a bit, she hangs up.

"They have a donor liver," she says. "Coming down from Bakersfield. Motorcycle accident. It's real. Excuse me." Her voice is very distant. She turns on her heel and walks out of the house, back the way we came.

"She's good," Danny says. "I've seen newbies piss themselves and run screaming when shit like that happens. That woman's a fuckin' rock. All she's doing is dissociating." I can't disagree.

"She'll get used to it," I say. "Probably not soon, but she will."

"So what now?"

"Nothing," I say. "We've been played. I've been played."

Jimmy might not be able to see me, but it can see other people. Though as soon as they come into my orbit they should get shrouded as well.

Unless it looks at where they've been and goes from there. How far back would it have to have started this just to set up that conversation we just had?

It told me in Vegas that it could see me a little bit the further into the future it looked. If it can see the possibilities, guess the different places I might end up and know where I've been, it can connect the dots.

But if there isn't anyone else for it to look at, I'm effectively invisible. I'm thinking the only way to do this is if I do it alone.

"Nothing? Why?"

"It knew we were coming," I say. "It was ready for us and

knew we were going to be here before we knew we were going to be here. There's no way we're sneaking up on it. Even though it can't see me, it's figuring out the likely possibilities and preparing for them."

"Looking for him just plays into his plans?"

"Exactly. So, I keep an ear to the ground. When it wants to see me, it'll let me know."

"You mean we," Danny says.

"No. Jimmy can't see me, but it can see everyone else. Maybe not well, since I'm involved, but I think it can use other people to extrapolate what I'm going to do next."

"What was this about, then?"

"I think Jimmy was reestablishing my position. It's got a new start point to track me from. And knowing that you and Janna were with me, that's going to help him narrow down the possibilities."

"Jesus. How the hell do you even counter that?" Danny says.

"I just gotta ask, 'What would Eric Carter do?' and not do it."

"Do you realize how stupid that sounds?"

"Look, I'm tryin' to make lemonade out of a lemon party here. It's what I got."

"Why the fuck did you make this thing?"

I don't say anything. I don't have an answer.

Chapter 13

Danny heads out after Janna. I stay behind for a moment. There's something I'm missing. Why here? Why the Storer House? I don't buy for a second that Rachel picked this place. It was picked for a reason.

Come to think of it, why the Harrison? I can't think of any benefit Jimmy would have gotten from being in that shithole hotel.

There's something I'm remembering from my search on this place, but I'm not sure I have it right. I pull out my phone and check online. The place was built in 1923. Okay. Right time frame. I look up the owner. Nothing special. Check a couple pages and something jumps out at me. A name. Clifford Dabney. Why do I know that name? He was some rich-kid nephew of a local oil magnate, I know that much. They seem to have had some connection, but what it is I can't find.

I get pulled out of the rabbit hole I'm rapidly falling down by a text from Danny.

> Dude, your girl is messed up. You need to talk to her.
>
> What's she doing?
>
> Nothing. Just sitting in her car.
>
> OMW

When I get up the hill to the street I see what Danny's worried about. Janna's sitting in her car with a thousand-yard stare. I tap on the window. She slowly turns her head, nods, and the passenger door unlocks. I slide in next to her.

Cop cars have a certain smell. Bleach trying to cover up the urine and vomit inevitably left in the back seat. It doesn't really work.

"That was really somethin' back there, wasn't it?" I say.

"I should arrest you," she says. "Or shoot you. But I don't know what I would charge you with and I don't think I'd be able to kill you. But it'd be easier than having to think about what just happened."

"Pretty sure this is what Tish wanted to get through to you," I say. "Everything's different now. Your professional life, your personal life. All of it."

"Must be what turning into a vampire is like."

"I hear the transition's not that bad." She turns toward me and locks my eyes with that thousand-yard stare.

"No," she says.

"No?"

"Don't tell me vampires are real."

"All right, I won't tell you vampires are real. But you just saw zombies. Vampires are a bridge too far?"

"What do I do?" she says. "You're right. I don't think I can be a cop anymore. Knowing that there's shit in every fucking shadow that might jump out at me? Seeing what I just saw? I watched you murder three people."

"Technically, I only murdered two," I say. "Danny sort of took down the first one."

"Not funny," she says.

"I'm not laughing. Look, right now you don't need to figure anything out. You're not going to anyway. Go to your dad. He's about to go through some major surgery and you should probably be there for him."

"Yeah. But what about all this?"

"This is not your problem," I say. "Probably the biggest lesson you're going to need to learn is to walk away. Shit seems huge, earth-shattering. Like having to rescue a busload of burning nuns or some shit and it's all on you. But it's not your problem."

"But it is," she says. "I'm involved. I'm here. I have to do something."

"No," I say. "You choose to do something. That's important. That's something 90% of these fucks don't get. We choose. Every ritual, every spell, every demon summoned or ward raised."

"Demons?"

"Just go with it," I say. "My point is that if you don't understand that you make your own choices, good or bad, you're gonna do a hell of a lot of damage. Own up to the things you do, even if to no one but yourself."

She laughs. "Great, now I'm Spiderman. 'With great power comes great responsibility.'"

"You're missing my point," I say. "Nobody's making your choices for you. Be responsible, don't be responsible. Ultimately, nobody cares but you.

"You're gonna see some shit. And sometimes you're gonna think, 'I have to fix that.' And sometimes you will, sometimes you won't. Sometimes you'll realize that the best thing you can do is not be a part of the problem. You're gonna have to make a lot of hard choices. If you have the option to walk away, trust me, you'll want to take it."

"This is fucked up," she says. "I don't know how to do magic. How is this even a thing? Jesus fucking Christ. My life really is over, isn't it?"

"No," I say. "It's different. You'll know when it's over, trust me. Talk to Tish. Have her introduce you to some of the Cleanup Crew if she hasn't already. From what I understand, one or two of them are pretty decent for mages. Have her show you the upside of this nightmare."

"You don't have a very positive outlook on mages, do you?" she says.

"Do you?"

"No, I guess not." Janna's phone rings. "It's the captain."

I pop the door open and step out of the car. "Talk to her," I say. "Let her know what happened. And when you see her, punch her in the face for me."

"I'll punch her in the face for both of us."

I steal a Mercedes out of somebody's garage and head down toward Hollywood Boulevard. I have questions. Questions and no answers. Jimmy's got someone else working with it. The one that bothers me the most, though, is Rachel. Why did it sacrifice her? There's no way it didn't know that my killing her was a possibility. So why let her go?

I feel stupid for even going to look for Jimmy now. I've given it a new start point for my movements. It knows what to look for, the sort of wake I might leave as I pass through the day. I'll be easier to predict now.

And I'm pissed off at Letitia for getting Janna into this mess, too. The woman's got enough on her plate without this shit. I'll need to call Letitia later and yell at her some more.

Jimmy knew about the Tree of Life. The hell kind of name is that?

It's not. It's a title. What the hell were all the corpses saying? North Star? And Willa. That sounds like a name from the 19th century.

Or the early twentieth. Things from the early twenties keep popping up. What was happening in the twenties in L.A.? Lots of stuff. A lot of people were moving to California for a new start, for an escape, to figure out who the hell they actually were.

Religion took off like whoa. Pentecostalism was born here at the turn of the century, but Aimee Semple McPherson refined it in the twenties, inventing the megachurch in Echo Park. Theosophy was huge. Basically, we had cults coming out our assholes.

Cults. Like the Blackburn Cult.

I call Gabriela.

"Hey," I say.

"Wow, that was enthusiastic," she says. "Long morning?"

"You could say it was eventful."

"Bad eventful or good eventful?"

"Let's go with 'Could have gone better' eventful," I say. "About last night. And yesterday. I realize I caught you off guard with what I said. I'm sorry."

"It did catch me a little off guard, yeah," she says. "Not that I didn't like hearing it. I just—I dunno. There's nothing to apologize for at the club. You did what you thought you had to do. Between the two, I just needed time to think."

That sounds a little ominous. "Come to any conclusions?" There's a long pause. Do I really want an answer to that question?

"Not yet," she says.

"Okay. Well, let me know what you come up with." I don't want to push. It's a combination of feeling like I don't have a right to and being scared what will happen if I do.

"I will," she says. "So, what was so eventful?"

"You hear from Letitia?"

"No," she says, "but I heard about the Red Car. I think they're bringing the bodies down to Mission." Of course. The county coroner. Where else would you take them?

"You know if Kyle's on duty?"

"Maybe, why?" I give her the highlights. She stops me halfway through.

"She dropped her apprentice in your lap?"

"Yeah. Tenacious woman," I say. "Holds her shit together remarkably well. And more powerful than she knows. I thought I'd given her the slip and it turned out she was riding my ass the whole time in a black and white. Never noticed her."

"That part of her knack?"

"No idea, but she didn't know she was doing it."

"That's not good. What the hell was Letitia thinking?"

"She wanted to throw her into the shark tank and figured the best way to do that would be to have her hang around a shark."

"I can't fault the logic, but it sounds a little extreme."

"I think she was trying to get across to her that the life she's known up to this point is over. I'd say she got the message."

"That bad?"

"Worse. But hey, her dad's getting a new liver."

". . . what?" I rant some more about what happened in the house before she stops me again. "It knew about this Tree of Life person?"

"Yeah. I don't know how. But then, I don't know how I ran into her, or how I could talk to her again. I'd have to—Oh, wait a minute."

There's a pause and then she catches up. "No. Fuck no," she says.

"I didn't get close enough to the Red Car to know if they're exactly like the bodies in the club, but I definitely felt a similar energy. If they are . . ."

"Eric, you died three times. I almost didn't get you back."

"Because it took us by surprise," I say. "We can create a controlled environment. Then I animate one, it does its chanting schtick, and I pull the energy out of it."

"And die."

"We'll have a defibrillator on hand. That and some epinephrine and I'll be fine."

"No, you fucking won't," she says. She's pissed but holding herself back. "I know death isn't something that bugs you a whole lot, but the rest of us really have a problem with it."

I think about that for a second. Even before Mictlan I wasn't overly concerned about death, and since then, knowing what I know, am I taking it less seriously?

I think over the last few months. Risks I've taken. Beatings I've taken. How close I got to dying again—and in a couple instances, how I died.

"Have I gotten that blasé?" I say.

"Yes," she says. "You already were before the first time you died. First time you died permanently."

"Semi-permanently," I say.

"You know what I mean. This is not a joke."

"I know it isn't a joke," I say. "Do you really think I see it as one?"

"Sometimes, yeah."

"Something for me to work on, then. Okay. No dying."

"Thank you."

"On purpose," I say.

"That kind of goes without saying," she says.

"You know this applies to you, too. No more getting run through with swords."

"That happened one time."

"Shotgun blast to the stomach."

"That wasn't me. Okay, that was me but I was wearing somebody else's skin. And also, one time. Christ, I need to find better ways to get grievously wounded just so you have something else to throw at me, don't I?"

"Maybe even things out a little."

"So, what's next?" she says.

"Venice," I say. "Home, sleep, thinking." Home? When did I start thinking of that place as home?

"If you need a nap," she says, "I'm closer and have lots of beds. Or just one big one, slightly occupied."

"Yeah, but would I sleep?"

"Eventually."

"You sure you don't need some alone time?"

"No," she says. "Come over."

"Don't need to tell me twice. I'll see you soon. Oh, the Blackburn cult book. You have a chance to look at it?"

"No," she says. "I got this kid from USC on work study. He's taking notes. I'm training up the next generation."

"God help us all."

"Uh huh. What do you want to know?"

"Between the Red Car and what happened at the club last night, there seems to be a connection to the twenties. The Blackburns were active then. There's gotta be something there."

"Okay. I'll have a copy of the notes by the time you get here. You can help me grade it."

"Another euphemism?"

"No, but it can be. See you soon?"

"Traffic willing."

Traffic isn't as willing as I'd hoped. Gives me plenty of time to think, which isn't always a good thing. I feel like I'm waiting for another shoe to drop. Lots of shoes. The Red Car feels like a harbinger. At least the club was self-contained. What happens when it's something bigger?

I click on the radio, tune it to an AM news station. The Red Car story is there, but it's being spun as a movie set accident with injuries but no deaths. I'm not sure how they're justifying that, but hey people still seem to be buying Los Angeles burning down and the Toxic Zone as simply Shit Happens.

As if to underscore that point, as I'm going through the intersection at Hollywood and Fairfax I hear car horns, screaming, explosions. A herd of cars appear in the middle of the road and a 1920s Buick convertible slams into me.

Chapter 14

I've stolen a late model Mercedes, built like a tank, airbags in places you didn't think they could fit airbags.

Good thing, because when the Buick hits, it shoves the Mercedes into the next lane. More cars hit, bouncing me around this new wave of traffic like a fucking pinball. I hear a tire go out, then the grinding of metal. I come to a stop when I hit a lamppost, snapping it at the base.

I feel a burst in my head from dozens of deaths all happening at the same time as if a bomb had just gone off. I black out for what I hope is a quick second and not half an hour. It's hard to gauge these things sometimes. When I come to, it takes a bit to get my bearings. My ears are ringing, but I don't seem to have any broken bones or cuts. I'll take that.

I untangle myself from the seatbelt and deflated airbags, grab my messenger bag, kick at the driver's side door. It doesn't budge, so I hit it with a push spell hard enough to blow it off its hinges.

I get out, steady myself on the car, and take a look around. It isn't good. About thirty cars appeared literally out of nowhere. The road was narrower in the twenties, so half the cars appeared coming toward me and the rest coming up behind.

Top speeds back then were maybe twenty-five miles an hour. With how fast today's cars were moving they all might as well have been brick walls.

Cars on fire, people screaming, a few walking wounded too dazed to do more than stand there and blink. And that's just the standard collisions. Then there are the cars that suddenly occupied the same physical space and somehow merged.

I see two of them, a Prius and what looks like a black Model

T, fused together in a way that I can't tell where one ends and the other begins. A glance through a window is all I need to know there are no survivors. There are two people in there but only room for one.

I'm getting that same feeling of death in a slow buzz like at the club, punctuated by a bunch of fast deaths all around me as people succumb to their injuries.

I limp over to the Buick that plowed into me. Top down, two women, two men, fairly young, all dressed like they're from the same era as the car. All four dead, of course. The impact killed the driver. He's impaled on the steering column. The other three don't look like they've taken any damage at all, but they're just as dead.

The two in the back seat snap up, spines going straight. Eyes staring into nothing. "She's coming," they say. Well, fuck.

The adults sit ramrod straight in their seats, the driver ripping himself off the steering column with a wet squelch. "North Star. Tree of Life. Seven trumpets. North Star. Tree of Life. Seven trumpets." He's chanting, and the chant gets louder as the rest of the corpses join in the fun.

I didn't do anything this time. What the hell triggered it? Was it going to happen anyway and I just pushed the button early back at the club?

The feeling is getting overwhelming. My vision's getting blurry and my head feels like it's going to pop. I need to get out of here. I don't know what will happen if I stay too long with this sensation, but I really don't want to find out.

Then the fuckers start to get out of their cars. At first it's no big deal. The people who run to help are leading them out of the pile-up, thinking they're just dazed and not dead. Confused about what all the chanting is, maybe, but they can chalk that up to shock.

Until one of them turns to a guy helping him across the street and tears his throat out with his teeth. The other corpses get in on the action. I see three more people go down. And all the while the chanting keeps going.

Someone grabs my shoulder, pulls me back hard. It's one of

the walking dead. He's missing his entire lower jaw but that doesn't seem to make him want to chew my face off any less. I slam him into a car on its side with a push spell then pull the car down on top of him.

"Seven trumpets May May May North Star Tree of Life," and so on. I pull out my phone and send a quick text to Gabriela.

Sorry

For what?

Zmbs Hwd Ffx

She'll figure out pretty quickly I meant zombies at Hollywood and Fairfax and that I'm probably dead like at the club. But this is getting bad and I can't let that happen. The necromancer in the middle of a zombie apocalypse and he didn't make it happen? I have a professional reputation to uphold.

I reach out, feel for that energy surrounding them all like a net and pull it in. I barely register the corpses falling to the ground as I'm freezing and burning and dissolving into nothing all at the same time. I feel like I'm being ripped apart, a tiny moon between two angry stars.

My vision narrows, the pain reaches a point that I can't handle, and everything goes black.

Except this isn't me passing out. This is the black of the void. I'm in nothing. I feel nothing. The pain is gone. I wonder how the Tree of Life made us a floor to stand on when I was here last.

I wonder if it works like in Mictlan. There, I'd tell the world there was a floor and there'd be a floor. I made whole landscapes that way. It feels like forever ago.

What the hell. Let's give it a shot. I decide there's a floor. Suddenly there's a floor. How about some furniture? Maybe some walls. Voila, chairs and a table and four blank white walls.

"Oh, very good," the Tree of Life says, sitting cross-legged on the table with her seven puppies crawling over her. She looks around the room. "It took me ages just to make a floor."

"I've had practice," I say. "Nice to see you again."

"Oh, have we met? No. You must have met me later." One of her puppies yips and she brings it up to her ear. "Oh, it's him? That makes sense. I'm surprised he didn't come here sooner." Pause. "That's right. Well, then I'm surprised I didn't come sooner. And yes, I know I don't have any control over that."

The Tree of Life looks up from her puppy and says, "Hello Eric. It's nice to meet you. What can I do for you?"

"I dunno. Maybe tell me what the fuck is going on?"

"The Two Witnesses will complete the Seven Trumpets of Gabriel and usher in the Apocalypse," she says like it's the most natural thing. And who knows, maybe it is.

"I have no idea what any of that means."

She laughs. "I don't either," she says. "I'm supposed to, but it's never made much sense to me. I know that Auntie May has a plan for me to be one of the Eleven Queens but—" She frowns. "Something happened. Is happening? I don't know what. So, I'm here. Waiting."

"Whatever it is, I think they're a little late," I say. "Pretty sure it was supposed to happen almost a hundred years ago."

"It was," she says. "And it will. It just needs some momentum. Auntie May explained it like a rubber band that needs to stretch for a long time before it snaps, taking things back to the beginning."

"So it stretches and stretches and then snaps. Back to the 1920s?"

"It's supposed to. But it never does. It just goes back and forth over and over again. Except for now. I think it might be because of you. You and the lady. She's very smart. But very afraid. You should tell her it will be all right. She's doing what she's meant to."

"What's this lady's name?"

"She won't tell me."

This is getting me nowhere. I decide to change tacks. "How do you know Jimmy?"

"Who?"

"Jimmy Freeburg. Talking head?"

"Oh, him," she says. "I don't like him. He wants to break everything. But then, you know that." Do I? Uh, okay.

"You've met it?"

"Not yet, no. Soon. You called him a talking head? I don't remember that he'll look like that. I'm not looking forward to meeting him. He's trying to make a mess of everything."

"Happen to know why?"

She laughs. "You told me—will tell me? It's because, how did you say it? Right. 'Because he's a dick.'"

"That sounds like me."

"Whether you decide to let it happen or not," she says, "it's going to have consequences."

"Most things do," I say.

"You can't keep it from happening. But you might be able to change what those consequences are."

"Why can't I keep it from happening?"

"Because you broke it all a long time ago. If you mend a cracked cup, you'll still see the cracks."

"What am I supposed to do? You're not actually telling me much."

"Because I don't know," she says. "You haven't done it yet." The dog she's holding yips. "Oh. Ray thinks you'll make everything worse."

Smart dog. "Ray?"

"Mmhmm." She points at each of the puppies in turn. "Do, Re, Mi, Fa, So, La, and Ti."

"Got it. Scales. I've heard worse."

"I think it will hurt," she says. "A lot is going to be lost. Or it was lost. But that's okay. It wasn't supposed to be there anyway."

This is what happens when you stick your dick in time magic. Cause and effect go out the window and what has, hasn't, will, and won't happen blur into some kind of temporal paste.

If I'm reading the half-answers she's giving me correctly, Auntie May did something that's supposed to bring about the Apocalypse but it's needed time to build up a head of steam. And when it does, what then?

What the hell is this Apocalypse she's talking about? I've seen at least a dozen different situations people called an Apocalypse and not a goddamn one of them panned out.

"What can you tell me about the Blackburn cult?" I say.

"It's no cult, silly! Auntie May and Ruthie are the Two Witnesses. They want to make the world better for everyone."

"Auntie May's May Blackburn, isn't she? And her daughter is Ruth Blackburn?"

"Rizzio," she says. "She's married to Sam Rizzio. Well, she was. I think Auntie May killed him. Or Ruthie did. I'm not sure."

"You don't seem to be very concerned about that."

"They did what they had to do," she says. "You know what that's like."

"I do."

"Oh," she says. "It's time for you to go. Goodbye."

I'm about to ask her what she means when pain tears through my body and my eyes snap open to the hazy L.A. sky. A paramedic is hovering over me with a defibrillator.

"We got him," he says.

"I thought we agreed you weren't going to do this again," Gabriela says.

"Believe me, I didn't want to," I say. I try to sit up but my body isn't listening to me at the moment. She looks around the intersection strewn with bodies, not all of them anachronisms.

"I believe you."

Chapter 15

"Your boy needs sleep," Doctor Hilliard says, putting his stethoscope into his bag. "And a brain. The fuck were you thinking? Don't answer that. It was rhetorical and I really don't want to know."

I've dealt with Hilliard before. He occasionally works for the Werthers. He's good, but he's also kind of a dick. With Attila out of the picture he works for Amanda now.

"Thanks, Walter," Amanda says, holding the door open for him. "I'll be in touch."

"How are you feeling?" Gabriela says.

"I wasn't dead long."

"Long enough." I can hear the irritation in her voice.

"Yeah, well, next time fuckin' leave me that way."

Amanda, Gabriela, and I are back at the shelter in one of the exam rooms in the supernatural wing. It looks more like a vet's exam room at a zoo than anything I'm used to. Yeah, it's sterile with cupboards, cabinets, the usual medical equipment you'd expect. But everything else is just bigger.

The exam table, for instance. It's almost the size of a queen bed, mounted to an electric scissor jack lift so it can be lowered almost all the way to the floor, with fold-out sections to accommodate whatever appendages you're dealing with.

It never occurred to me that different supernaturals would have different needs. I mean, it makes sense. You get an aswang in here, you're gonna need a lot of room to unroll those tongues of theirs. Fuckers can be almost ten feet long. And a rock troll? You better have something that can hold a couple of tons at least.

Not sure how the paramedics got to me as quickly as they

did. Gabriela told me they had to shock me a couple times to get me back. A few more and maybe I'll get used to it.

"Hey," Amanda says. "Stop it, both of you. Jesus. I can't believe I'm the adult in the room."

"Sorry. Dying makes me cranky."

"Seriously, how are you feeling?" Amanda says.

"I'm okay," I say, even though I am very far from okay. I'm not sure how to express it in a way that they'll understand and not freak out over. The buzzing I was feeling under my skin is constant now. Easy to ignore but definitely there.

"Your eyes are black," Gabriela says.

"Still?" I will them to change back, but it doesn't feel right. "Anything?"

"Nope," Amanda says.

"Last night they changed back pretty quickly," Gabriela says. "What's different?"

"Exposure?" Amanda says. "You said you were pulling energy into yourself. Might be building up."

"I don't like that idea," I say. "But I think you might be right. Raising that body at the Storer house was like nothing."

"Not just practice?" Amanda says.

"Some, yeah. It's definitely been getting easier, but today was a *lot* easier. Same with knocking out the zombies at the car crash."

"I really don't like that," Gabriela says. Shit.

"I hadn't wanted to say anything, but, well, I can feel them all the time, now."

"What do you mean?"

"It's like there's this buzzing under my skin. That slow dying sensation. Not like I'm dying. It's like pinpricks. I'm not making any sense."

"So not an Obi-Wan sort of 'billions cried out and were suddenly silenced'?" Amanda says.

Hang on. I think she might be onto something. I close my eyes, focus on the feeling. "Yeah, actually. That's almost exactly what this feels like," I say. "But more that these people are all dying a tiny bit at a time and I'm feeling each bit."

"Does it hurt?" Gabriela says.

"No. It's just there. When I'm close enough it's uncomfortable. The time I got hit with it at the club was more surprising than anything else. It doesn't really hurt until I pull all that energy in."

"That worries me a little," Amanda says. "Where does it go?"

"I think it becomes part of me," I say. "Something Mictecacihuatl mentioned. Mictlan was seeing me as more Mictlantecuhtli than it should have. She thought I had somehow tipped the scales so that I was more him than he was. This whole thing has to be related to whatever it is the Blackburns did. A spell that's stretching to some sort of breaking point."

"How so?" Amanda says.

"Not sure, just something the Tree of Life told me. I need to get her name. I think it's Willa. It's one of the things the corpses at the club were chanting."

"Willa Rhoades," Gabriela says.

"How'd you get that?"

"I told you," she says, "I have a kid on work study." She picks up a tablet and the book from the counter, and tosses the tablet to me. "The Divine Order of the Royal Arms of the Great Eleven" is at the top of the screen in large bold letters.

"Jesus, how many names does this cult have?"

"At least half a dozen," Gabriela says. "The Great Eleven, Royal Arms of the Great Eleven. Mix and match.

"May Blackburn got hold of a kid who was supposed to be the next big thing. Willa Rhoades. She was sixteen. Came down from Portland with her adoptive parents."

"She told me she was going to be one of the Eleven Queens," I say. "I don't know what that means, though."

"After the Apocalypse, Eleven Queens will be raised up as rulers and have all of the gold and jewels in the world," Gabriela says. "And they'll live in mansions in Hollywood."

"Hollywood?" I say.

"I think that was the closest thing to paradise her followers could grasp. Wealth, glamour, comfort."

"That has got to be the most L.A. cult ever," Amanda says.

"Definitely up there," I say. I read a little ahead. "They'll each have a harem of twelve men at their disposal."

"I'm starting to like these guys," Amanda says. "They say anything about spa days and Rolfing?"

"Like most cults, it was more fucked up than it might look on the surface," Gabriela says. "And that's saying something."

"Animal sacrifices," I say. "People going missing, possible murders. And it was all centered around May Blackburn and her daughter Ruth."

"Who's the author?" Amanda says. "A descendant? One of her followers?"

"There isn't one listed," Gabriela says. "Looks like it was done by a vanity press. No publishing date, binding's falling apart. Can't even find any mentions of it online."

Things are starting to click. The adobe house, Willa, what she told me about how things will stretch out like a rubber band and then snap back and it'll be 1924 all over again. It's like I can see that they're connected and almost how, but something's missing. The more I think about it the less I like it.

"Seems May ruled her followers with an iron fist," Gabriela says. "Between her and Ruth, none of them were allowed to do anything they weren't explicitly told to do. Any money they earned they gave to May. All told, she bilked her followers out of a few million dollars in today's money."

"How?" Amanda says. She picks up the book and looks at the cover. "May looks like a pissed-off sea lion and Ruth's got an expression like a Barbie doll."

"Yeah, and you could pass for sixteen," I say. "It's not about looks. It's not even about power. It's about presence. They were really good con artists."

"And they had the perfect marks," Gabriela says. "I recognize the names of some of her followers. More than a few mages. You convince a mage about something, they'll take it to the grave before admitting they're wrong."

Cue uncomfortable silence.

"Lot of normals, too," Gabriela says. "Big money for the time. Some trust fund kid named Dabney funded a lot of it. Looks like oil money. Interesting. More than a few socialites here. Some of these names are the same as girls I knew in the sorority."

"Wait. That name. Dabney. Clifford Dabney?"

"Yeah, why?"

"I saw some sort of connection between him and the Storer house but couldn't find any details. The house was completed in 1923."

"You think that might be why Jimmy was there?" Amanda says.

"The Harrison Hotel," I say. "There was that whole weird Satanist shit where they rented an entire floor. You ever hear about that?"

"My dad told me about that," Amanda says. "Pretty sure it was in the twenties. I remember him saying it wasn't long after World War I."

"That would fit the timeline," Gabriela says. "I'll have the intern look into it."

"Anyway," Amanda says, "what does that have to do with this Tree of Life?"

"May liked giving everybody fancy titles," Gabriela says. "Willa got The Tree of Life. May was The North Star, though her weird, pervy husband got North Star of the Whole World."

"Weird, pervy—Jesus Christ." There's a photo of Ward Blackburn and a whole paragraph on him being a suspected pedophile. And he looks it. Creepy eyes, weird slouch, a mustache that looks like you pulled it out of a bear's asshole.

"I think she was high when she thought some of these up," I say, scrolling past. "*The Four Winds of the Whirlwind God*? *The Gravitation Upwards*? *Queen of the Skilling Breath on the Inside of the Body*? The fuck does that even mean?"

"It gets weirder," Gabriela says. "May and Ruth were supposedly writing a book. It's how they pulled in their marks."

"The Seven Trumpets of Gabriel?" I say, thinking back to something Willa said.

"That's the one. It was supposedly being dictated to them by the Angel Gabriel. They were known as—"

"The Two Witnesses."

"Witnesses to what?" Amanda says.

"The Apocalypse," Gabriela says. "They're from Revelation 11:1-13. They kept saying the book was going to be done by the end of 1924 and in 1925 everything was going to change. Only there was no book. A handful of typewritten pages and a bunch of blank paper underneath that they kept locked in a trunk. They'd pull it out only to convince marks it existed."

"Then what did they need Willa for?" Amanda says.

"Book says she was the key," Gabriela says. "The key to what, I don't know."

"Only she didn't live long enough," I say. "She got sick at the end of 1924 and died on New Year's Day. That's either very convenient or really horrible timing."

"Looks like they gave her seven puppies as some sort of goddess gift and when she died they killed the puppies, too," Gabriela says.

"Jesus. That explains why they're still with her. Did they stick them in her coffin?" Amanda says.

"They had their own," I say. "One for her and one for them. Custom-made out of iron and copper. And—am I reading this right? They kept them on ice?"

"For like six months, yeah," Gabriela says. "They had her stashed under the floorboards in a house in Venice and every day they'd truck in a few hundred pounds of ice."

"So that's what that was. The first time I met her we were in what looked like a mausoleum if you made it out of an old sailing ship. Water dripping everywhere. Cold."

"May kept telling everyone that Willa was going to come

back to life," Gabriela says. "Pushed it as far as she could. Eventually Willa's adoptive parents couldn't deal anymore. They were sleeping right over her grave, after all. They called the cops and everything started to unravel."

"What's the connection to the adobe?" I say.

"I had one of my people dig deeper into the land records," Gabriela says. "Nobody owned that particular plot, but May Blackburn purchased one nearby in 1923, less than a mile away."

"The location was important, then," Amanda says.

"I think it has something to do with the story that the mother tried to resurrect her sons," I say. "When I popped back to the adobe house I heard two women speaking English. I was pretty sure that was May and Ruth and now I'm certain."

"They had some way to go back in time and were kicking things off by murdering the family?" Gabriela says. "Okay. I can go with that."

"Why them?" Amanda says.

"The story goes that the mother tried to resurrect her children," Gabriela says. "Maybe they needed something only she knew how to do?"

"Whatever they wanted her to do, it was under duress," I say. "Sounded like they were killing her kids right in front of her. Called it a baptism."

"So, it starts then," Gabriela says. "Something's supposed to happen in 1925 with Willa but she dies before it can."

"After it fell apart it looks like May did some time for fraud," I say. "Judge wouldn't allow any of the cult activities to be brought into the case, saying they were irrelevant. Real progressive ideas on religion for the time, I guess. And nobody could prove the allegations of murder."

"Sounds like magic," Gabriela says.

"I don't know about that," Amanda says. "If that were the case I doubt she'd have gotten arrested in the first place. Something happened to them. Burnout, maybe."

"That tracks," I say. "Ruth dropped off the radar. May died sometime in the fifties, I think."

"That's it?" Amanda says. "All that trouble and they just fizzled out?"

"Seems that way," I say. "They, or at least one of them, was a mage. Something happened. But I don't know who we would even talk to about it. I don't know anyone who was in town in the twenties."

"My dad was," Amanda says. "He would have known."

Huh. The vague outlines of an idea are starting to form.

"Did you ever find out what year his soul was sent to?" I ask.

When Amanda's uncle Liam assassinated her father, he threw Attila's soul out of his body. It's still connected, though, and Amanda's holding the body inside a time-frozen room to keep it from rotting. We've narrowed the soul's location to Union Station. But we haven't found any trace of it.

The reason for that is because it wasn't just sent out of his body and parked in a specific location, but sent to the past, to some date that only Liam knew.

Once I told Amanda, she decided it was time to have another conversation with her uncle. She's been working on him since I got back from Vegas. I don't know if he's told her anything. Maybe he's harder to break than I thought. Or maybe she just really enjoys torturing the fucker. God knows he deserves it.

"1948," Amanda says. "April 18th. That's when Dad basically kicked my aunt Helga out of the States. I don't know the details but I know it was really painful for him. Liam says he's stuck in some sort of loop so he keeps reliving that event over and over again."

"Your uncle's an asshole," Gabriela says.

"Yeah. I pull him out of stasis every once in a while to remind him of that, and of who's in charge, in very painful ways."

"I have a really dumb idea," I say. "This spell the Blackburns threw together. Whatever it is they did, I think it's been active since they started it. Now it's coming to an end. And whatever it's supposed to do has something to do with resurrection and something to do with time."

"Not sounding dumb so far," Gabriela says.

"That's because the dumb part is that I think we can use this to pull Amanda's dad out of the hole he's in."

"How?"

"Still working that out, but the two things that aren't following the pattern are the adobe house and the Harrison. Both of those are locations we know can be physically entered."

"You want to do that again," Gabriela says. "But in 1948."

"Want to try, yeah. Willa seemed pretty certain that it was according to plan. That the amount of time it was taking was by design. It had to build momentum. When I tapped into the power of those corpses from the twenties I think I sort of rode the spell."

"What, like surfing a wave?" Amanda says.

"Maybe?" I say. "Willa said the spell was like a rubber band that needed time to stretch until it broke. And she was expecting me. I'm connected to it somehow."

"How would you control the date? That's a twenty-four-year difference. I don't think you're talking about hanging out in old L.A. until after World War II," Gabriela says.

"How would you come back?" Amanda says.

"Don't know yet. But these, I dunno, incursions of the 1920s aren't all the same," I say. "The Harrison's somehow important. So is the adobe. And I wouldn't be surprised if the Storer house is the same thing."

"It's leaking," Amanda says.

"Come again?" I say.

"The spell. It's leaking. That's why today and yesterday are being thrown together," she says. "Most of the time, things and people from the past show up and everything dies. Other times there's a crack connecting the two."

"So it's not just going to be the Harrison," Gabriela says. "There might be other leaks."

"I'm following you," I say.

"If the Storer House was involved with the Blackburns," Amanda says, "there might be a leak there, too."

"Don't get how we would manipulate any of these leaks, though," Gabriela says.

"Got an idea about that," I say. I grab my messenger bag and pull my pocket watch out.

"Watch where you're pointing that thing," Gabriela says.

"A pocket watch?" Amanda says.

"A 1919 railroad grade Sangamo Special," I say. "And one of the scariest things I've ever dealt with. You can instantly age something by pointing the face at it, winding the crown, and pressing it. I think it can do a lot more, though."

"Yeah, but you said you can't control it," Gabriela says.

"That's where these cracks come in. What if I fiddle with the watch at one of the cracks?"

"That sounds dirty," Gabriela says.

"What, make time move forward?" Amanda says.

"Something like that. I mean, I'm pulling this stuff out of my ass here."

"Something to look into," Gabriela says, voice hesitant. "But I really don't like it. Especially since it keeps killing you."

Gabriela seems really stuck on the whole me-dying thing. I think about that for a second and realize just how weird that sentence is.

"Much as I like that there's a possibility to get my dad back," Amanda says, "I'm with Gabriela. How many more times can you do this? You've already died multiple times in the last couple days."

"I didn't have to die to get to the Harrison," I say. I don't see what the big deal is. "Maybe if I went to where we want to go and tried to will it into being."

"But no pulling energy from corpses," Gabriela says.

"No pulling energy from time-traveling corpses, no," I say. "Amanda? You okay with giving that a shot?"

She thinks about it for a second, then slowly nods. "Yeah." A few months ago she would have dropped everything and gone running. But now it's a different world. "Let me wring some more information out of Liam. I'll let you know when I have something." She stands and stretches, vertebrae popping.

"I'll come with," Gabriela says.

"No," Amanda says. "You're going to stay here and talk to your man and tell him what the fuck is going on."

"I can see who's the top in this relationship," I say.

"And you," Amanda says, "are going to do the same. What you two have is your business. I love you both, but it's starting to piss me off."

A flare of magic as she opens a portal to her home. She's got it decked out to look like some Neuschwanstein Castle in the clouds. One of the benefits of having a pocket universe that changes based on your mood.

"Figure your shit out," Amanda says. She steps through the portal, and it closes with a sound like a slamming door.

"Well, that's us told," I say. "Look, I'm sorry about dying, okay? Christ, normal people never have to deal with conversations like this."

"I know that," she says. "That's not the problem. Not all of the problem."

"Okay. So, what is?"

"I—" She doesn't get any further because a massive explosion rocks the building, throwing both of us to the floor. Gabriela pulls out her phone.

"What the fuck was that?" She listens for a second. "That's insane. There's no way that'll work."

"What's going on?" I say. I'm not feeling any deaths, but with a blast like that it's just a matter of time.

"Some fucker drove a van through the concrete barrier to the entrance and opened up with a rocket launcher."

She's right, there's no way that will work. When she built this place, she designed it like a fortress with no blind spots or cover and a series of doors that act like airlocks. They can't fire enough rockets to take out the doors before they get gunned down from above. So why—

"Which side?" I say. "Human or supernatural?"

"Supernatural," Gabriela says. "This is bad." She bolts out of the room. I'm right behind her.

The wing for the supernaturals is heavily warded and covered in enough redirection spells that even mages'll have a hard time finding the doors. If they know where the doors are, then they know they're not getting through them. So why try?

I hear gunfire outside, yelling, feel a few deaths. What the hell are they trying to do? Then it comes to me.

"It's a diversion," I say.

"Fuck," Gabriela says. "Nobody's getting in here by busting down the front door. But the roof isn't as well defended. But why?"

Right on cue, I hear a helicopter. Too loud to be one of those dinky traffic copters. Whatever the hell it is, it's big. Big enough to hold a lot of people.

Only one thing I can think of. "Is Sunday here?"

"Shit," she says. "The opal."

I hope we're not too late.

Chapter 16

A series of explosions shake the building like an earthquake. This time they're above us. Whoever the hell this is isn't fucking around.

"Jimmy got some new friends," I say.

"Well, he's gonna have some dead ones in a minute," Gabriela says. We round a corner and the feeling of death hits me just as the sound of gunfire reaches us.

"Fuck," Gabriela says as she sees me stagger. "How many?"

"A dozen dead at least," I say. Mowed down with machine-gun fire.

Gabriela runs over to a firehose mounted inside a recess in the wall. She pulls on a hidden latch and the whole assembly pops open to reveal a deeper space behind it. Inside are a pair of Benelli M4s, bandoleers of shotgun shells, and gas masks.

When you're running a shelter for some of the most dangerous creatures in the world, it doesn't matter how nice and reasonable they are. At some point somebody's going to snap, and you better be prepared for it. Gabriela has stashes like this scattered throughout the entire facility.

"All I have in here are beanbag rounds." She pulls a shotgun out and slings a bandoleer over her shoulder. "But they pack enough of a punch they should drop anything we have here."

I grab one of the shotguns. She keeps these things loaded with one in the pipe. Dangerous? Irresponsible? Absolutely. Necessary when you've got three seconds to take down a pissed-off Manananggal? Fuck yes.

"How about the fentanyl?" I say. In addition to the guns, she's got her sprinkler system set up to switch from water to aerosolized fentanyl to knock everybody out if things really get out of hand. We had to use it a little while back to root out a shapeshifter. The shapeshifter didn't need to breathe, but once we took everybody else down, we could shoot the one left standing.

Gabriela shakes her head. "Back ordered. Guy I got it from was picked up by Interpol in Thailand a month ago. Got another supplier but we need more than just fentanyl. Alone that shit's more useless than pepper spray against most of the residents."

"I think they're in the cafeteria," I say. "I felt the deaths around there." A lot of the residents were probably in there when Jimmy's people blew through the roof. I'm feeling more dying, doing my best to ignore them all.

Why is it hitting me so hard? Because of that buzzing under my skin?

Gabriela puts her hand up as we come to a corner. I stop. I hear it too. People are running. People wearing boots. And carrying heavy, metal equipment from the sound of it.

I don't feel any magic nearby. Are these normals? I don't want to take the chance to find out.

I pull a thin, brittle disc out of my messenger bag, tap Gabriela on the shoulder, hand it to her. I mime what I want her to do.

She nods, then snaps the disc in half, tosses the pieces around the corner, and covers her eyes.

We look away and I snap a silence spell around us at the last second. I can see the flash through closed eyes but I don't hear anything.

A second later we're around the corner, the silence spell dropped. It doesn't take long to see that these aren't the good guys. Gas masks, black BDUs, submachine guns.

Apparently, they weren't expecting resistance. Whoever hired them did not brief them on the situation. Behind them I can see bodies in the corridor. Some residents, some mercenaries.

Gabriela gets one in the face, dropping him, and another

takes the butt of her gun in his stomach, doubling him over. She brings the shotgun up to his face and pulls the trigger. Bean bag or not, at that range he doesn't have a head left.

I try to get a blast in but my shotgun jams, so instead I swing it overhead like I'm throwing an axe. It doesn't hit anybody but I didn't expect it to. I just needed the distraction.

By the time the last two recover I've manifested my straight razor in my hand and I'm on top of them. The blade catches one of them under the jaw, slicing all the way back to his spine.

The second one tries to get his gun around, but I take it off just behind the barrel. He's quick, though. Has a Ka-Bar out of a sheath on his belt before I have time to recover from my swing. The blade slices into my arm before I can block him with the razor. The magic in my tats kicks in, but they can only do so much. The damage is reduced, but it's still a deep cut and it hurts like a motherfucker.

He goes in for strike but this time I'm ready for him. He jabs out with the blade. Instead of blocking it, I slash down with the razor, slicing the his knife straight down the middle, all the way through the blade and into his hand. The razor's well past his wrist before he feels it, but he has to realize something's wrong when he sees his hand flopping about like a banana peel.

That takes a lot of the fight out of him and he doesn't even try to block me as I slash at his belly, opening him up from one side to the other. Loops of intestines spill onto the floor.

He falls to his knees, tries scooping them back in. That shit never works. Especially not when he's bleeding out all over the place. But it gives him something to do for his last moments, I guess.

"Don't go anywhere," I say. He stares up at me through pinprick pupils. "You and I are gonna have a talk." I watch the life fade from his eyes, feel his death in my gut.

Gabriela runs over to a couple of the residents who are struggling to stand up. I go help another one. These are vampires, probably—they're ridiculously hard to kill.

"Can you do this without me?" Gabriela says. "These people need help."

"I want to say no," I say. "But yeah, I got this. Stay safe."

"Wait," she says. She pulls me closer, kisses me hard. "We'll talk."

"Hopefully after we can do more than talk," I say. She smiles.

"Nobody saying what order these things need to happen."

"Knew I loved you for a reason." Shit. I freeze for a second. Did I just fuck this all up again? Fuck. Fuck fuck fuck.

She answers by kissing me again. "I love you, too," she whispers. "Go."

"See you soon." I grab a machine gun and a couple magazines off one of the corpses and head down the hall to a T-junction, then turn toward the cafeteria. Doesn't take long before I'm close enough to hear gunfire, screams, roars, feel the gut-punch of deaths inside.

Fuck me. I don't know how long it takes for Sunday to go feral once he loses the opal, but from the sounds, I'm thinking not long.

And there's this sense of something off about them. A little like when I animate a corpse, but somehow different? What the hell is going on in there?

Bullets do fuck-all to Sunday. Shooting him in the head isn't going to take him down. I have an idea, but I really don't like it. I suspect I'm not going to have a choice.

One more corner and the doors to the cafeteria are at the end of the hall. They kick open. A woman wearing black riot gear steps through holding a submachine gun.

This woman has seen some shit. She's tall, and her reddish-copper hair with streaks of white all through it is pulled back into a ponytail. Her face and arms are a mess of badly healed scars, wide white slashes. Her left eye is a desiccated orb with a slash right down the middle that continues down to the left side of her mouth, pulling it down into half a sneer. For some reason she's wearing a single black glove on her left hand that goes up to her elbow.

I don't recognize her at first and when I do I don't see how it's possible she's even standing there. The undamaged side of her mouth quirks up in a smile.

Rachel.

"Miss me, darling?" she says with a new lisp and lets loose with the machinegun. Seeing her threw me enough that I'm almost not fast enough with the shield. I'm already feeling the knife wound, I don't need to add bullet holes to the list.

Bullets ricochet off my shield, blowing chunks out of the cement walls, exploding light fixtures. She stops after a couple seconds. I fire a couple shots from my gun more as an obligatory dick-swinging that does nothing. It's a stalemate. For the moment, at least.

"I was hoping I'd run into you," Rachel says. Her voice is rougher than I remember and I figure out why when she shifts her weight and I catch sight of her throat. It's even more scarred-up than her face is.

"Hey, Rach. New look?" I have no idea how she survived the Wanderers. At least she paid a price for it. "Gotta say, this is a little unexpected."

"I told you Jimmy was going to get me out of there."

"Took its time, didn't it? You look like you fell into a combine thresher. How exactly?"

"No idea. Woke up alive. All my wounds healed."

"That's healed? I know a hobo down in Venice who does better work than that. I'd sue your doctor for malpractice."

With magic, who knows what the fuck she can actually see, but if she's got a blind spot, it'd be stupid not to exploit it. I shift over to my right.

"I see what you're doing," she says. "It won't work."

"And I thought my nefarious plans were so subtle. Speaking of nefarious plans, how's Jimmy?"

"Same old, same old," she says.

"You know I have a friend with a bone to pick with you."

"Do you now? This about those kids in Long Beach your friend popped like they were water balloons?"

"Yeah, he doesn't like being made to kill kids."

"Uh huh. I know your boy," she says. "Ask him about Ensenada in 2015. He's just fine with killing kids."

"That's his lookout," I say. "I only care about the bones I have to pick with you."

"Are you still hung up over Candyland? Really?"

"Mostly I'm curious why Jimmy wanted you to do it."

"No, that was all me," she says. "I pulled off the 'we're all friends' angle pretty well, didn't I?"

"I had my doubts. But then I found your body. Well, what I thought was your body."

"Whatever sells the bit."

I've been edging closer to her and as I do I notice that what I had thought was a long black glove is actually dripping black goop all the way up to her left forearm. It's like she dunked it in a vat of tar.

"Here for Sunday's opal," I say.

"Got it, too," Rachel says. "Can't you tell?"

That's what the black goop is. The only way anyone was going to get Sunday's opal would be to tear open his chest. And pull it out. Is that what passes for blood in his body?

But it's not just the black goop. I can feel people dying fast and . . . I'm still not sure but I can feel something in there that doesn't make sense.

"You know this is your fault, Eric," Rachel says. "You had to go and throw the other one away."

"I did," I say. "And I know Jimmy's got the same sort of blind spot with them that he has with me."

"Hey, that tip about the Storer House pan out for you?" she says. "I had a few guys hang around for when you got there."

"If you're telling me that was a set-up to get me there, I figured. Too bad you weren't in on the gag. You could have just called me up and gotten the same result without getting torn up by ghosts.

"But yeah, Jimmy and I had a lively discussion. Do you know it calculated all the different scenarios to see if you'd come back from your visit with me and a lot more of them ended with you dead than not? And it let you go anyway."

She bristles at that. "He didn't *let* me do anything. I did it. On my own. My choice."

I can't help but laugh at that. "Struck a nerve, I see. You really believe you've got choice in this situation? Come on, Rachel, you're not stupid. You know how this works."

"I'm not some mindless drone, Eric," she says.

"Uh huh, keep telling yourself that. The fuck kinda midnight crossroads deal did you make with it?"

"We've been over this, Eric. None of your fucking business."

A particularly high-pitched scream rends the air.

"That does not sound good," Rachel says. "Lotta people getting chewed up by the zombie in there. Too bad you can't actually kill him. But I bet a big, scary necromancer could handle him."

"Or I could feed you to him. I bet he'd love that."

"The longer we stand here the more people are dying," she says. "Now you and I can fight. I'd kick your ass. I've done it before. But that would take more time than I've really got."

"Just spit it out," I say.

"You and I pass like ships in the night. You go in and take care of your zombie problem in there, and I go on my merry way."

"And give you a chance to walk through this place killing anybody run into? Pass."

"I'm open to suggestions."

I have a ring that creates portals to anywhere nearby. It doesn't have a lot of range and it's got some limitations, but if I want I can open up a hole in a wall or a floor or just in empty air.

I'm tempted to open one underneath Rachel and snap it closed before she's all the way through. Did that to a demon once. Worked great. But I don't know that'll work. Rachel's fast and if she hasn't beefed up her arsenal to give her any advantage possible after our last run-in, I'd be shocked. I don't doubt that if she wants to move lightning-fast, she can.

"How about this?" I say. "Same deal. We go our separate ways. But instead of you running through the halls murdering everybody, I give you a better exit."

I trigger the ring and a portal to the street outside opens up. Through it I can see the burning ruin of the car Rachel's people rammed into the entrance. There's surprisingly little activity out there. A couple helicopters, an LAPD squad car at the end of the block with two officers looking appropriately freaked-out wondering where the fuck their backup is.

"You want me to walk through that?"

"Walk, run, hop, I don't care. I just want you gone. And you're wasting my time."

"See, now this is the sort of thing the Eric Carter I knew thirty years ago would do. So selfless."

"Push it and the Eric Carter you know today will rip out your fucking soul and shove it up your ass."

"No need to get nasty about it. I got what I came for." She steps backward through the portal.

I think about shutting it closed while she's halfway through, but no. She isn't the only piece Jimmy has in play, but she's the one I know.

"See ya soon, Eric," she says. I snap the portal closed and bolt for the doors.

Chapter 17

I shove open the doors and freeze. I knew it was going to be bad, but I didn't realize it was going to be this bad.

The smell I was expecting. I caught enough of it outside. And I knew there was going to be a lot of blood, bodies, sure.

But this looks like a tornado hit a slaughterhouse. Blood and meat everywhere, not all of it human. The blood coating the overhead lights has given the entire room a dim red glow.

Joe Sunday is standing on a table, roaring like a pissed-off lion. He's degenerated fast. He's lost so much meat that his clothes hang on him like a nightmare scarecrow. Most of his flesh has sloughed off his frame, exposing rotting, pitted muscle and organs. His face has turned into a sunken mask of pockmarked green rot. Bits of him fall off and land at his gore-covered feet.

There are at least thirty corpses in here. Quite a few of the non-humans are still alive, though plenty aren't. They've let their disguises slip or their true natures come out. Teeth, fangs, claws.

But the humans are little more than meat. They're easy to pick out; they're all wearing black BDUs like Rachel.

I see the bodies of ghouls, a couple kitsune—fox heads torn off their human bodies—and here and there the corpse of something so torn apart I can't quite identify it. All that would be bad enough, but there's an additional wrinkle. Looks like anything Sunday's killed that still has a head and a pair of legs is up and walking about.

A gore-covered woman in tattered jeans and a t-shirt absolutely drenched in blood runs past me. She's young. Blonde, blue eyes. She punches a zombie and crushes its head. Takes me a second to recognize her.

"Rosalie?" I say. Rosalie's a vampire who's been around since the old Rancho days. "Took advantage of the situation?"

Normally Rosalie looks to be about eighty years old. She's one of a group of vampires in the city who, for some reason, can't ingest blood—it has to go directly into a vein. With all this blood around I'd be surprised if she hadn't been tempted.

"Fuck you," she says. "I shot up before I came in here. You think I'd have time with all this shit goin' on? What the fuck is happening?"

"Him," I say. "Hey, Sunday." All of the corpses' attention turns to me. Heads swivel in my direction in perfect match with Sunday's as he looks at me.

"How ya doin'? Nobody told me you could make more of yourself. Nice work, by the way. I say that as a professional."

Sunday hunches over like he's about to jump at me from the table and his zombies do the same. Okay, I can work with this. What I don't get is why Sunday hasn't changed back. Eating someone's heart should restore him to a not-quite-so-heart-hungry zombie. And then I see it. There's a metal band around his throat, and when I stretch my senses out I can feel the magic around it.

Rachel somehow got that thing on him and yanked the stone out of his chest. He's probably eaten lots of hearts in the last ten minutes, but he can't swallow them. I either get that off him and force-feed him somebody's insides or I find another opal.

Good thing I'm a fuckin' liar.

I reach into my messenger bag and feel around for the opal I stole from Jimmy. The sheer amount of loose shit I have in this thing is always a little alarming when I'm trying to find something.

It doesn't take long. My hand grasps it and I can feel a buzzing in my skin as soon as my fingers brush it. I just hope this one works like the one Rachel took out of Sunday.

"Now before things go completely pear shaped," I say, "if you can hear me, know that I'm here to help." I can feel the zombies around me. They're similar to the ones I've made, but nothing like the ones in the club.

And they're nothing like Sunday. They're like cheap imitations. I doubt they'll even last for long. But considering the carnage, I'd say they've lasted long enough.

I really don't want to try the whole pulling-the-energy thing with them. The last thing I need is to drop while there are still face-eating zombies around.

I don't know if fixing Sunday will change things, but he's the first priority. Almost everybody in here is dead, so they can't do any more harm unless they get out. I throw a couple shield spells on the exits in the room to make sure of it.

Probably should have thrown one up on myself first. Half a dozen corpses in riot gear lunge at me and Rosalie, leaning in to bite chunks out of us. Fortunately, they're still wearing their helmets. Small favors and all that.

Rosalie tears the heads off two of them and punches through another's skull. I throw two off me with a push spell and grab a third, pulling it close before throwing up another shield in a globe around us. I must be getting old, because I figure trying what I'm about to do with just one seems like a smarter move than all of them at once.

The zombie is trying to grab my face and I throw some magic at it and say, "Cut it the fuck out." And it does, thank fucking Christ. Knowing that works on these fuckers should make this easier.

At least it would if Sunday hadn't picked that moment to throw a table at me. It hits the shield and bounces off, immediately followed by another. Then a third.

Normally it wouldn't be a problem, but aside from a zombie horde trying to eat my face I've got three shields up. With everything all together, my personal shield cracks under the fourth table. And the rest of the zombies swarm in. The human ones are annoying. The supernaturals are fucking terrifying.

One ghoul missing most of his insides grabs me, unhinges

his jaw, and opens his mouth wide. Row upon row of inward hooked teeth. Something goes in there, it's only coming out through the back end.

I throw him off with enough power to bounce him off the ceiling. I feel something grab the back of my collar and before I can react I'm yanked out from under the pile of zombies and sent skidding across the floor into one of the cafeteria tables.

"The fuck are you doing, man?" Rosalie says.

"Trying not to die."

"Picked a shitty place to do that."

"Noticed, thanks," I say. "What are—FUCK." I throw her aside with a push spell as Zombie Joe bears down on us, his horde of death monkeys behind him.

I can't control Joe as easily as I can another corpse, but I can slow him down some. I lock his legs in place and throw his arms back, overbalancing him. He falls backward into the front row of his zombies, knocking them over like tenpins.

This is bullshit and I am done with it. I throw a command and a buttload of power at them and tell them to get the fuck down. They do, but they don't stay there. Seems Sunday and I are in a bit of a contest for ownership.

You know what? Fuck him. Who's the fucking necromancer around here? I grab their energy like at the club and the car wreck. It feels different. They're dead, not slowly dying, and the hit from them is nothing in comparison. This is more like sticking a nine-volt battery on your tongue instead of shoving a cattle prod up your ass.

They all drop in their tracks. Except Joe, of course. It's not the opal that's powering him, it's whatever magic made him. Proximity to the stone was keeping him from getting to this stage.

I back up to give myself some breathing room and am suddenly reminded that fresh blood is only tacky after it dries a bit. Until then it's like walking on grease. I make a wrong move and my legs slide out from under me.

That's all he needs to slip my control. He leaps, slamming into me and bouncing my head against the floor. Now is not the best time for a concussion, but we're going there anyway. So I think I can be forgiven for not being at the top of my game. Sunday gets his hands around my throat and lifts me off the floor.

I can grab hold of his energy but I can't keep it. But then, I don't need very long, and he's actually doing me a favor in a painful, choking, roundabout way.

I use a spell to loosen his grip just enough that my vision stops blurring. I shove the opal into his open chest cavity with one hand and grab the metal collar with the other. Doesn't take much magic to snap the band, and as soon as that stone gets inside him he starts to reform. It's like watching a time-lapse film. His cheeks fill out, split skin knits, pus-filled blisters shrink to nothing.

All of his animated dead drop to the floor with a sound like thunder, a couple dozen corpses all hitting the floor at the same time.

Sunday drops me, staggers backward. A few seconds later he's back to normal, though he still looks like hell. He's covered in blood, green pus, and rotting pieces of himself.

He looks around at the carnage and, despite the fact that he's dead and about as readable as stone, I get the feeling he's ashamed and disgusted. Maybe some of these people were his friends. I wouldn't discount it.

"You good?" I say.

"Yeah," he says. "I won't try to eat you. Today, at least."

"Best I can hope for," I say.

He puts his hand to his chest and frowns. "This one feels different. Not sure how. I mean, it's doing the trick, but there's more to it than that."

"One mystery at a time," I say. "Come on. Let's see what we can salvage from this horror show."

I check on Rosalie first, help her up from the floor. "You good?"

"I will be. Might need another hit when I'm done, though." She looks up at me with wide, hopeful eyes. Even covered in gore I can see how she managed to charm the pants off men and women for the last couple hundred years, until she got sick.

"We'll get you fixed up."

Joe, Rosalie, and I go around picking up survivors, getting them out of the room to the hall outside. Most are unconscious, some are in really bad shape. The dead who were raised and then dropped when I got the opal into Sunday are reading as just meat. Seems to be a thing. Once an animated corpse goes down it stays down.

A few minutes later I hear running down the hall. Rosalie suddenly looks feral, fangs bared, ready to jump. Sunday's got his gun out and I'm considering half a dozen different spells all designed to fuck people up.

It's Gabriela and a small army behind her. The second she sees us she gets her people in gear. A couple have EMT kits, some more go running off for gurneys and stretchers. I point out the ones who are circling the drain and aren't going to last long enough to help, speeding up triage.

"You doing okay?" Gabriela says.

"Yeah. Hardly a scratch. Couple bruises. And no dying this time." I give her a run down on what happened. The more I talk the angrier she gets. By the time I'm done she's pacing the hallway and swearing in Spanish.

She stops, turns to me. "You let her go. You gave her a way out and you let her go."

"Yes," I say. "I—"

"Thank you."

"Uh, you're welcome?"

"She could have hurt a lot more people. Don't get me wrong, I wish the bitch were dead, but thank you for—"

"Not making things worse?"

"For caring enough to not make things worse."

"I'm not sure exactly how to take that," I say. "You sound surprised."

"No, I'm—That came out wrong. All of these people are

my priority. Not yours," she says. "I wouldn't blame you if you'd made a different choice. I'm not sure exactly what I'm trying to say. Just, thanks."

"Kinda expected you to be pissed," I say.

"Not too long ago I probably would have been. But then, not too long ago you wouldn't have let her go."

"Guess we're both growing up."

"Took us long enough," she says. "Come on, we need to hose you off and burn those clothes."

Chapter 18

"**On the plus side,** with all the bullshit going on right now, somebody shooting up a homeless shelter with a rocket launcher barely makes the news," Letitia says.

"How bad is it here?" Janna says. She's out of uniform and wearing jeans and a white button-down shirt with the sleeves rolled up. Her badge hangs from a lanyard around her neck and her sidearm sits in a holster at her hip.

"Twenty-two dead," Gabriela says. "All human. Thirty-five wounded. Eighteen of those were human, the rest ghouls, aswang, kitsune, jötnar, some others."

"No vampires?" Letitia says. I see Janna blanch. I guess she still has a problem with the idea. Wait until she runs into a ghoul. Gonna have to introduce her to Kyle. He's probably the safest-seeming one in the whole city.

"No," Gabriela says. "We only had a few in and only one in the cafeteria when everything went to shit."

"One of them helped clear things out," I say. "You know a vamp named Rosalie?"

Letitia's face goes sour. "Yeah, I know Rosalie. I've had to throw her in lockup a couple times. Nice enough for a vamp, I suppose. Still a pain in the ass."

It's been about four hours since the attack. Letitia arranged to have the place cordoned off without any awkward questions from the normals. Plenty of other awkward questions being asked out there right now. Gave us some room to get an accounting of the dead and the survivors moved somewhere they can get care.

We're all exhausted. None of us has stopped moving all day. After a firefight, a car crash, and two mobs of zombies, I feel like I'm about to fall over. Not an option, yet.

"How you holdin' up over there, Officer Benson?" I say.

"Detective," Letitia says before Janna can answer. "Provisional."

"I still have to take the test," she says.

"Don't worry about that," Letitia says.

"I . . . okay." Jesus Christ. The woman's already overwhelmed and Letitia's throwing shit like this at her. I don't think it even occurs to her that this might all be a bit much.

"How's your dad?"

"Good," she says, her energy shifting immediately. Circumstances notwithstanding, this is a topic she can deal with. It's grounded in a reality she understands. "Surgery went without a hitch. He's in recovery now. They say he'll be out until tomorrow morning some time."

"At least something good's coming out of this," I say. "Any new time travel shenanigans?"

"Enough that it's officially a full-blown crisis," Letitia says. "Every hour I'm getting calls about a building changing, corpses showing up all over the place. The goddamn governor is sending in the National Guard."

"And I thought the fires were bad," I say.

"They were. Notice a common denominator here?"

"Don't even start. When are they from?"

"What?"

"Buildings, people, whatever. What time period?" I say. "Twenties? Thirties? Sixties?"

"How the fuck should I know? I'm not up on my paper collar fashion."

"Gimme some highlights."

"The Hollywood sign says Hollywoodland now," Janna says. "And it's lit up with bulbs. That puts it between early twenties and early thirties."

"You sure?" Letitia says.

"Yeah," I say. "Sign went up in twenty-three and they pulled the lights out in—I want to say thirty-two? Thirty-three?"

"So it would have been around in nineteen-twenty-four," Gabriela says.

"The fuck was it for, anyway?" Letitia says.

"It was an ad for a new subdivision," Janna says. "It's big selling point was that it was racist as fuck. Whites only."

"Of course it was."

"What else?" Gabriela says.

"An entire strip mall on Wilshire is gone. There's a big fucking hat in its place."

". . . what?"

"You ever hear of some place called the Brown Derby? I guess it was a restaurant? Shaped like a hat? Why was that even a thing?"

"Oh. Yeah, it was kind of a big deal in its heyday," I say. "Hey, is City Hall still there?"

"Don't you dare tell me that's on the list."

"There are orange groves on fucking Victory Boulevard," I say. "Nothing is not on the list. What about Union Station?"

"I haven't heard anything," Letitia says. "You expecting something with that?"

"Expecting? No. Just hoping."

"What the hell is that supposed to mean?"

"Dunno yet," I say. Union Station was built in thirty-nine on the site of old Chinatown, the second old Chinatown. If it changes and things are keeping up with the twenties then it'll turn back into old Chinatown.

"What's with this Rachel chick?" Letitia says. "I thought you killed her."

"Last night," I say. "She ambushed me at home. More than a little surprised to see her here."

"All right," Letitia says. "Tell me about this head that's making all this happen."

"I don't know that it's making anything happen," I say. "I think it might be taking advantage of something that was set in motion a long time ago. A spell."

I always thought that Jimmy only operated by making things happen. But if it's using something that was already there, I'll need to rethink it.

It feels more like he's redirecting a river. Jimmy doesn't

make the river flow, it just points it in a new direction and lets it do its thing. Events play out on their own for the most part. It just has to course correct from time to time. With me involved, it probably has to do a lot more of that than it normally would.

I'm the wrench in its plan. And that worries me. If it knows I'm going to cause problems, why not build that into its plans? It can't see me but it can extrapolate just fine. The fact that it knew about Janna long before I did is proof positive of that.

"By who?"

"A pair of cult leaders," I say.

"Pretty sure they were mages," Gabriela says. "There are a couple things that don't add up, though."

"What's the spell supposed to do?" Janna says.

"We don't know for sure," I say. "Whatever it is, I've heard it described like a rubber band. Once it stretches enough, it'll snap—and something will happen in the past."

"I liked you a lot more when you were dead," Letitia says.

"I've been getting that a lot lately," I say.

"Okay. I can put an APB out on Rachel," Letitia says, "but I kinda doubt she's gonna surface."

"I can get that handled," Janna says.

"Nope. I want you here doing whatever it is they need you to," Letitia says. "If the two of you are okay with that."

"You actually asked this time," I say.

"I'm fine with it if you are," Gabriela says.

"That depends," I say. "How you feel about the idea, Janna?"

She looks a little shaken. She got a look at the cafeteria carnage and I can imagine she's not crazy about being around for that sort of thing.

"Hang on," Janna says. "I need a second to think about this? I just—I'll be right back." She turns on her heel and strides out the door.

"That was a dick move earlier," Gabriela says.

"What? Eric handled it fine."

"I'm not talking about Eric. Are you so dense you don't see

she's about to crack? I hope you know a good mage therapist because she's gonna need it."

"Okay," Janna says, stepping back into the room. "I'm in. What do you need me to do?"

"Don't know yet," I say.

"Let me introduce you to some of my people," Gabriela says. "You know not all of them are human, right?"

"I—did not, no," she says.

"Okay. I get that right now everything's a little overwhelming."

"Yeah," she says.

"So, let's talk. Come on."

"Hey," I say. "When you get back, before more shit happens, we really need to talk."

"Ya know, I could—" Janna says.

"No," I say. "You need a real crash course. Not whatever bullshit Letitia's been feeding you."

"Hey," Letitia says.

"Oh, okay, Sensei. You saying you got her all sorted out?"

"I—No. Gabriela can show you stuff I can't," Letitia says. "You're in good hands. Now, I need to get out there. Any new fuckery, gimme a call."

Once everyone leaves the room I feel like I can take a breath. I'm going about this whole thing the wrong way. Feels like all I'm doing is reacting. Like Jimmy's already seen every move I can make before I can make it.

Let's break this down. First thing, I need to get rid of Rachel. I don't know how Jimmy pulled her out with all those Wanderers tearing chunks out of her, and there's no reason to assume he can't do it again.

Killing her didn't take. I want to, that's for goddamn sure. Maybe there's another way. I dig out my phone and call Amanda.

"Hey," she says, sounding a little out of breath.

"You all right?"

"Yeah," she says. "Just torturing my uncle. Only thing he

had to add was that what happened at Union Station happened at night."

"But still don't know what it was that had Attila kick Helga out of the States?"

"Says he doesn't know. I actually believe him. If there's one thing my family does well, it's keep their own secrets. What do you need?"

"First, Gabriela fill you in on what happened?"

"Yeah," she says. "Sounds like a complete clusterfuck."

"And then some."

"How's Gabriela taking it?"

"Hard to tell," I say. "She's in Hyper-Competent mode at the moment." I think for a second. "Also, pretty sure if I asked her, she wouldn't tell me."

"You two didn't talk?"

"Didn't have time. I think I got two sentences in when the shit hit the fan."

"Christ, this life," she says. "I know updating me on our mutual girlfriend is not why you called."

"I wish that's all it was. I need to set up a call with someone in Vegas. She's a little hard to get hold of."

"Sure. I can connect with Diane. She can find pretty much anybody. Who is it?"

"I'd rather not say, because I don't know what Jimmy can and can't see of me. I don't need Diane to contact them exactly. I need a bunch of falcons."

"Falcons."

"Yeah," I say. "Trained would be great, but right now I'm not picky."

"Trained falcons."

"Honestly shouldn't matter. With what I have in mind I think if they're told what to do, they'll just do it."

"What do you want to do with the falcons?" I can hear her trying to figure out what the hell is going on and it's best I don't tell her. So how do I phrase this?

"I want Diane to tell them that I need to talk to their . . . Patron. And to have them call me."

". . . okay," she says. "How many falcons you need?"

"As many as you can get," I say. "Need to make sure the message gets through."

"When this is all over, I'd really love to hear what this is all about."

"And when this is all over I'll tell you."

"All right, falcons it is. I assume this is ASAP?"

"And then some. Much appreciated. Talk to you soon."

"What was that about falcons?"

I turn to see Gabriela standing in the doorway. I cross the room to her.

"I'm afraid saying anything might tip Jimmy off. Probably not, but . . . I just don't fucking know. How are you doing?"

Her guard slips for a moment and I can see how tired and crushed she is by what's happened. She can be solid as a rock when she needs to be, but any time one of her people gets hurt, it's a gut punch. The mask starts to go back up. I take her hand.

"Don't," I say. "Maybe not the time or the place. I get it. But please don't hide from me."

It's like I've given her permission to let go for a couple minutes. Her head drops and she leans into me.

"It never stops, does it?" she says. "There's always something."

She might not be thinking it, but I sure as hell am. This wouldn't be happening without me. If I hadn't done something stupid a long time ago we wouldn't be in this mess and a lot of people would still be alive.

I don't say it, though. I'm afraid she might agree with me.

"Yeah," I say.

"Aren't you supposed to say positive, supportive things to your girlfriend?" she says.

"Hey, you don't lie to me, I'm not gonna lie to you. Here's something true I know. Shit happens. Shit always happens. But I don't know a single person more capable of meeting it head-on than you."

"Capable or stubborn?"

"Hard to have one without the other."

"Oh, I don't know. I know a lot of very stubborn idiots."

"Not ones who lived very long." I wonder how high on the irony scale that sentence is.

"It seems every time I make some progress it all falls apart," she says. "I've closed down the shelter. Spinning it as a gas leak. Nothing happened over on the human side, thank fuck, but everybody's freaked out and I can't exactly hide the fact that shit blew up."

"They scatter?"

"All the humans, most of the supernaturals," she says. "I've been able to arrange getting most of them someplace to stay for the night. God, I miss the hotel."

"What do you want to do?"

"Kill Rachel," she says. "Get rid of this fucking talking head. I don't like being a pawn in somebody's game."

"I'm working on both," I say.

"I know it's probably better you don't tell me, but I really want to know."

"If it works, you'll know soon enough," I say. "What now?"

"We were talking before everything went sideways."

"You okay with continuing that conversation?"

"I can think of some things I'd rather be doing," she says.

"Do tell."

"How about I show you instead?"

Chapter 19

I don't want to know what time it is. If I don't know the time, this doesn't have to end. That's how it works, right?

Gabriela's loft at the top of the building has a large curving wall made of glass with a view that looks out across most of Downtown. The mix of old and new buildings, lights glittering in the night, gives it an odd, dissonant vibrancy.

From the bed I can see the Eastern Columbia building in the distance, its turquoise terra-cotta exterior a distinctive contrast to the rest of the buildings in the area, the EASTERN sign on the clock tower lit up like a beacon. And on the opposite side I can see City Hall.

It's always amazed me that City Hall, the Jewelry District, dozens of beautifully restored buildings housing multi-million dollar lofts are all only a few blocks from Skid Row.

It's like watching a really hot porn scene and then you notice a massive carbuncle on the end of somebody's cock. I'm not really sure which part of all this is the carbuncle.

Without the fires, this view would be very different. A lot of the taller buildings were destroyed, changing the skyline drastically.

I have a momentary thought—maybe the fires weren't so bad after all—and I can't tell if it's my own or the part of me that's Mictlantecuhtli, that doesn't really care about what the fires did, but does admire beauty.

"Hey, that tickles," Gabriela says as I run a finger along a tattoo that starts at the small of her back and wraps around her left leg. It's a vibrant purple-and-gold ribbon with runes all along it. I recognize some of them. I have the same ones somewhere in this mess of ink on my body. She has more scattered across her skin. I have most of those, too.

"And whose fault is that?" I say.

"Yours," she says. She rolls over to face me. I brush a strand of sweat-slick hair from her forehead. I lean in and blow on her like I'm cooling a cup of coffee.

"Okay, that's not much better," she says.

"Jesus, woman. There's no satisfying you."

"Well, duh," she says. "I thought you'd have figured that out by now." I lean in and kiss her neck just below her jaw. "Okay, that doesn't tickle. Keep that going, we're not going to get any sleep."

"I'm okay with that," I say. She puts her hand on my chest and gently pushes me away.

"Seriously. Besides, we need to talk."

"Now?" I say.

"Best time," she says. "That way everybody's relaxed and if it all goes to hell at least you got laid beforehand."

I can't really argue with that logic. And given the last twenty-four hours, I'm not sure we're going to have another chance for a while.

"Okay," I say. "I'll start. What the hell are we doing?"

She traces the jade eagles in the tattoo on my chest. Most of the time they fly around inside the circle, but at the moment they're still, calmed.

"Is this about labels? Because I'm fine being your 'girlfriend,'" she says.

"No, I get that. I've had it pointed out to me a couple times that it's pretty much the case already. Hell, from Danny. If he can see it, it's got to be pretty obvious."

"Danny is, uh, a very direct person," she says.

"That's one way to put it," I say. "I'm not asking what our label is, or where this is going. Haven't really gotten much practice thinking long term and all things considered I'm not sure I ever will."

"I know," she says. "I had long term plans. This place. This,

I dunno, this mission? To help and protect people. No matter what it took. And I mean all people, human or not. But then shit like today happens. Or shit like last night happens. And that all falls apart.

"I love you. That doesn't scare me. You dying scares me. But not exactly? I mean it does. I don't want to lose you because some asshole stuck a knife in your guts or you pulled in some weird arcane death energy off a hundred-year-old corpse."

"To be fair, that doesn't happen very often," I say.

"You honestly think it won't happen again?"

"Not disagreeing with you. Just pointing out the overall frequency."

"What scares me," she says, "is how much I don't want to lose you. I don't know that that's something I can live with."

I can understand that. An event is a lot easier to deal with sometimes than all the dread that it inspires. That shit can be debilitating. But I'm not going to say it. When somebody's making break-up noises it's not the time to start agreeing with them.

"Okay," I say. "Counterpoint, you went to a lot of trouble to bring me back."

"I know," she says. "You don't know the half of it. I—I missed you. You and your acerbic bullshit. Of everyone I've ever known, normals, mages, supernaturals, you are the only one who I haven't felt judged by."

"I wasn't crazy about you going into that factory in Vernon," I say. She almost died in there with a sword through her guts.

"There's a difference between judging and disagreeing," she says. "You disagreed with me, but you came in and had my back, anyway."

"You don't have that with Amanda?"

"What I have with her is different," she says. "She has a different sort of, I'm not sure, ferocity? She feels like a kindred spirit in a lot of ways. She's trying to build an empire. Or at least keep her existing one intact. I understand that and what it takes.

"She's not judging, but she's constantly evaluating. Not looking for fault. Looking for what does and doesn't work and seeing if she can apply it to her own situation."

"Sort of a mentor-mentee kind of thing?"

"Oh, don't say that," she says. "That makes it sound creepy. But a little? She doesn't have a lot of models for what she's trying to do. Point is, what I have with you, what I've always had with you, is the feeling you might give me shit over something I need to do, but you'll understand that I need to do it and be there to help when I do."

"Like murder," I say.

"Murder, arson, theft, caring about vampires, the whole thing. Even when we met, you treated me like an equal. Or did you? Did you hold back at all?"

We first met at her hotel, the Edgewood Arms. She thought I was somebody else and tried to kill me. It was quite a fight. We destroyed most of the floor. Eventually called it a draw and went to her office to drink tequila. How's that for a meet cute?

"Only insomuch that I tried not to kill you. At first. You had information I needed. Near the end, though, I just said fuck it. You were more trouble than you were worth."

She laughs. "And now? Am I more trouble than I'm worth?"

"Not even a little bit," I say. "And besides, you're the kind of trouble I like."

"Likewise," she says. "But this still scares me. And it's really fucking me up. I have to make decisions that can't necessarily take you into account. I can't have that get in my way. Do you understand?"

"Oh yeah," I say. "The situation with Darius felt like that. He thought I'd balk knowing that I'd kill a couple thousand people if I tried to take him down."

"He was wrong," she says.

"Yeah. Doesn't mean I don't question if it was the right

thing all the time. When that was over, you reminded me that we're the ones who have to make hard decisions, not because we're special, or chosen ones, but because we're there.

"Death isn't simple and it's not necessarily the end. But at the same time, I felt every single one of those people die. And I knew I would. And I did it anyway."

"I know it was hard."

"Sure, it was. But that's nothing compared to what you're dealing with. You have, Christ, I don't even know how many people depending on you. Sometimes their lives are in your hands and not just in a 'the monsters are coming to eat them' way. Hell, most of them are the monsters. I can't do anything but admire that. I don't know if I ever really understood it until I died."

"Mictlan was like that?"

"A lot, yeah. Every soul in there was my responsibility. Sometimes it was easy, ushering souls to Chicunamictlan. Or making sure they never made it, which I technically wasn't supposed to do. And sometimes it was really fucking hard."

"Children?"

"They could be rough, but they usually just took it in stride and followed me as I guided them through. No, maybe the worst were the domestic violence victims. So many of them kept clinging to this idea that the person who'd killed them actually loved them and just did what they had to do."

"Jesus."

"Yeah. That was all sorts of not fun. I wanted to leave Mictlan more than a few times and go after every single one of those fuckers out there. But I was stuck."

"Sounds more like what Eric Carter would do than Mictlantecuhtli," she says.

"Which was part of the problem, actually. Eric Carter before coming back to L.A. was simple. He might do something like that. Eric Carter dead was a millstone around Mictlantecuhtli's neck. Eric Carter resurrected . . . I'm not even sure who the fuck I am.

"Like, just now, looking out the window. I like the new view. And I thought, hey, maybe the fires weren't so bad. Felt like Mictlantecuhtli talking."

"Is it?" she says.

"No," I say. "It's all me. Blaming everything wrong with me on the bits of leftover deity is a cop out. Still, it is a beautiful view."

"So where does this leave us?" she says. The runes on her ribbon tattoo emit a faint glow as I run my finger along them.

"Let me put it this way," I say. "Tattoos. This one suits you. The color, the design. The way it reacts when I touch it. I could do this for hours. Just watching the way the runes glow, feeling your skin under my fingers. And my eagles? They almost never do this."

"What are you talking about?" I laugh.

"That's my point. I don't think you've ever seen it. They move. All the time. When they get agitated, too pissed-off, they jump out and go on the offensive. You've never seen them do that because they don't when I'm with you."

She touches the tattoo and then pulls her finger back. "Holy shit, they moved. They . . . looked at me?"

"They must like you," I say. "They didn't try to bite your finger off. But I already knew that. I love you. I want to be with you. It took me a while to get over being pulled away from Mictlan, but you did me a favor. In more ways than one.

"We can't promise each other much of anything, that we won't die or get hurt. That's not a deal killer for me. But I understand if it is for you."

"Sometimes it feels like it might be," she says. "Not now, but sometimes."

"I can leave L.A. any time I want," I say. "You're—not stuck, rooted here. You and Amanda both. It's good that you are. You have responsibilities. You're doing good things. I could always go back to what I was doing years ago."

"Politically, it would be easier," she says. "A lot of people would like you to do that. A lot of people would also like to see you dead."

"Enh, fuck 'em."

"I have a better idea," she says. She pushes me onto my back and straddles my hips. She leans down and kisses me. "Fuck me, instead."

"This mean we're good?" I say.

"Ask me that in the morning."

Chapter 20

"**How is it out there?**" I say when I see Janna coming into the shelter's reception area. The place is a mess, but it's seen worse. The area looks kind of like a bank with only one teller. A desk at one end of the room behind bulletproof, warded glass next to a set of double doors, an armed guard off to the side.

It looks unassuming. It's just one guard, right? Yeah, not even. There are all sorts of defenses built into this room. If Gabriela doesn't want you to get through those doors there, you're not getting through those doors.

Most of the damage inflicted by Rachel's people was absorbed by the spells and wards protecting the building. It helps that it's at the end of a couple of long hallways that are filled with magical death traps. There are some scorch marks around the doors and some chips in their bulletproof glass, but that's about it. Took a while to scrape the charred bits of mercenary off the hallway walls, though.

"Not good," she says. "Tell me you people believe in coffee."

Janna looks rough. I wonder if she's slept at all. Probably not. I kind of want to drive her to a cabin for a couple of weeks and tell her to practice lifting rocks like Yoda. Maybe if we survive all this bullshit.

"Believe in Scotch more, but sure," I say. "There's a break room with an espresso machine and everything. Come on, I'll show you."

"I don't care what form it takes, I just need caffeine."

"Oh, don't say shit like that to mages. Nobody experiments with drugs more than we do. One of us might take you up on that and you won't be able to sleep for a week."

"Am I ever going to get used to this?"

"No," I say. "Especially given the people you're running with right now. Letitia deals with more weird shit as part of the Cleanup Crew than just about anybody I know. And that's saying a lot given everybody I know."

The shelter's impressive, but it's the employee break room that really hammers that home for me. It's huge. It's really more of an employee cafeteria. When the shelter's fully staffed it's never empty.

Having a building is one thing. Operating it is something completely different. That takes money, processes, people. I've never dug into how Gabriela funds this place. I know some of it, but I think that's just the tip of the iceberg. Whatever it is, she's a fucking genius at it.

"Oh my god," Janna says. "Shit. Do you guys take debit cards? I don't have any cash on me."

"The fuck are you talking about? It's free. Get coffee. Something to eat. Here, I'll get you started." I cast a small spell and a mug slides underneath one of the coffee machines. A moment later it fills up.

"I felt that," Janna says. "You used magic to make coffee?"

"If you mean, did I use magic to make coffee by moving a mug and pushing a button from over here, yes."

"Of course. God, I feel like an idiot."

"Don't. Grab your coffee. A donut, whatever." A minute later Janna joins me at a table in the back, sitting heavily in the chair opposite me.

"There aren't a lot of people here today."

"Not much reason for them to be here at the moment," I say. "Place is closed. Whoever's left is working on cleanup or helping the remaining residents find new housing, I think. It's all kind of a clusterfuck. And no, there's nobody staffing the breakroom because, ta da! Magic."

Janna looks at me, deadpan. "You need to tell me when you are and aren't joking."

"Happy to. I'm not joking. Now tell me what's going on out there."

Janna closes her eyes and sips her coffee. It's a tiny moment where she doesn't have to think about any of this bullshit and I'm not about to break that. Finally, she opens her eyes.

"It is so unbelievably fucked, you have no idea. Last I heard there's a chunk missing out of the 101, a section of Sepulveda going through the pass has turned into a dirt track. Caused a ten-car pileup. Only good thing about that is it has people staying off most of the roads, except for the 10 and the 5. They're a mess because people are trying to get the hell out of the city as fast as possible."

"As bad as it was with the fires?" I say. God, I hope not. I have enough karma to work off without this on top of it.

"Not even close. Just weirder."

"Where were you when the fires hit?" I say.

"I just got back from school. Graduated a couple months before. I was with my family at their house in Cheviot Hills. It was weird. Everybody's houses around ours went up in flames. It melted the pavement and cracked the sidewalks. But nothing so much as touched our house. Not even the yard, driveway, nothing. Not so much as a scorch mark, smoke damage, nothing."

"Impressive," I say.

"I'd call it lucky."

"It would be, if you hadn't been the one who did it."

"What?"

"I know what those flames could do," I say. "If they got that close, your place should have been ashes. You might not have known it, but you protected your house."

"That's insa—No, I guess it isn't insane, is it?" She closes her eyes, takes a deep breath. That is the look of reluctant acceptance. "So how do I control it?"

"Like getting to Carnegie Hall. Practice, practice, practice."

"I thought that was 'Always take Fountain,'" she says.

"No, that's how you get into Hollywood," I say. Points to Janna for being a Bette Davis fan.

"I don't know how Tish described any of this to you, but this is what works for me," I say. "I see magic as a negotiation with reality. You're essentially telling it to go fuck itself and do what you want it to do.

"As to how, that's up to you to figure out. Think of it like throwing a ball. You take distance, the size of your target, gravity, all that shit into account, all that math, and you don't even know it. You just need to learn to throw the ball without having to think about the math."

"How do I start?"

"You already have," I say. "You felt the spell I cast on the coffee machine, right?"

"Yeah."

"There ya go. You know that feeling. You know you can do it. You can only get better at it. Might take a while, but the more you're around it and the more you use it, the easier it gets. Provided you survive it, of course."

"You have fantastic pep talks, you know that?"

"I do what I can. Finish your donut? Good. We're going to the morgue."

"Wish you'd told me that before I ate the donut," she says, and follows me out.

We find Kyle downstairs, standing in the hallway outside the morgue with a cigarette, directly beneath a No Smoking sign. He looks exhausted.

"Oh, Christ," he says. "What now? More time-traveling corpses? Exploded mercenaries?"

"The latter. One of your new residents."

"Oh, him. You'll need to clear the drawer out first. We're triple stacked in there. Your boy's on the bottom."

"How are you holding up?" I say.

"This is the first cigarette I've had in twenty years, so you tell me." He peers at Janna. "I know you. I see you down at Mission?"

"LAPD," she says. "I was in uniform before."

"Right, right. I don't know what you're doing around this loser, but you have my sympathies. Hope I don't find you on my slab later."

"Thanks?" Janna follows me inside and when the doors close says, "What the hell was that about?"

"Kyle's a pessimist," I say.

"I heard that," Kyle yells. "And I'm a realist."

"Sounds like he has a reason for telling me that."

"Can't imagine what it is," I say. I pull open the drawer where I deposited the mercenary's corpse yesterday. There are two more on top of him. Fortunately, they're in body bags. So much shit happened yesterday nobody's had a chance to even store them properly. Not that there's room.

"Grab a gurney, would you?" I say. "My guy needs some room to breathe." I can see the gears turning, wondering if I'm joking or not as she wheels over a body carrier. I grab us a couple face shields and coveralls.

Doesn't take long before we're suited up. Normally I wouldn't bother. But the corpse was pretty juicy when I put him in there.

Janna helps me lift the two bagged corpses onto the metal tray and roll it out of the way.

"Stand to the side," I say. "This could get messy." She takes several steps back until she's at the far wall. "Not that messy."

"I'll be the judge of that," she says.

"Suit yourself." I stand to the side of the drawer and cast my spell. The corpse sits up.

"Oh, Jesus," Janna says. "Sorry, sorry. Knew that was gonna happen, just kinda didn't want it to."

"A lot of people have that reaction when I'm around," I say. Then to the corpse: "All right, Sparky, gonna play some twenty questions. First, what was your role in yesterday's little shindig?"

"Squad leader," he says. His voice is a raspy whisper. Cold vocal cords, I guess.

"Know who hired you?"

"No," he says.

"You ever communicate with them?"

"Yes."

Whether it's a ghost or a zombie, one thing is certain, the dead are as dumb as a box of hair. "How?"

"Phone."

"Awesome," I say. "Gimme the number." He recites a phone number that's almost definitely a burner phone and probably isn't even Rachel's. Any calls could have been routed through multiple numbers and locations. It's a long shot, but it's a start.

"Thanks, man. We're done here." The corpse lies back down into the drawer. I go to the bodies on the carrier and start to unzip a body bag.

"What in the fuck do you think you're doing?" Kyle says, pushing the doors open.

"Putting away your bodies," I say. "I'm not gonna leave 'em out here for you to deal with. Come on, I'm not that much of an asshole."

"And why were you opening the bag?" he says.

"Kinda hard for them to walk themselves over to the drawer if they're in a body bag," I say.

"Out."

"Look, it'll only take me a min—"

"Out. Fucking mages. Fucking *necromancers*." He pushes past me and zips up the bag.

"Oh, come on." I turn to Janna. "I'm the only necromancer he knows."

"We should probably leave," Janna says.

"Yeah, that's probably for the best."

We both begin to back out of the room. "This place was nice and orderly," Kyle says. "And then you—" The doors swing closed mid-rant and all I can hear are muffled invectives.

"So, you got a phone number," Janna says.

"I did indeed. And if I'm lucky, the phone isn't sitting at the bottom of a landfill. Ever wanted to see a two-hundred-year-old building that shouldn't exist?"

"Uh, yes?"

"Great. Let's go steal a car."

Chapter 21

"**I'm having trouble wrapping** my brain around this," Janna says. I'm driving us to the site of the adobe house in a car that I pointedly did not steal. I borrowed it from Gabriela, because apparently Janna has some problems with grand theft auto. Who knew?

"Which part?" I say. "There's a lot to wrap your brain around."

Getting Janna the hell away from Letitia for a little while was a good move for everybody. With all the shit happening, Letitia needed to focus on the Cleanup Crew, and she wasn't actually explaining anything to Janna. I could tell that Janna was reaching a point where she might just shoot her. Hell, I might've shot her.

Though I understand the urge, shooting Letitia wasn't going to help anybody. Still, I'm having some regrets. Jimmy knows Janna now. But since I can't cart her and everybody else I know off to Cabo for the next week while I figure this shit out, I might as well keep them all close.

"Okay. So we're talking about time magic," Janna says.

"Chronomancy, yeah."

"Right. And all these people and places are appearing today from sometime in the last hundred years or so."

"Except for the place we're going."

"Why haven't we heard about any of it?" she says. "Why aren't there stories of people and buildings disappearing throughout L.A. over the last hundred years? They're showing up here, they're dying. That's gonna leave a mark."

"Been wondering about that, too. I think it might not have actually happened yet," I say.

"... what?"

"When you start fucking with time magic, cause and effect go out the window," I say. "I ran into these things a little while back called reality quakes. Say you make a change in the past. The present has to change too, right? Most people aren't going to notice it. As far as they're concerned that's always been their reality. But some people, particularly if they're somehow involved in it, will see everything change around them. The past sort of catches up with the present." I can see the gears working as she processes this.

"Okay. Reality quakes," she says. "You're saying that if what's happening had happened, then this would just be the reality we've always had. But since it isn't, then it hasn't happened, yet?"

"Something like that," I say. "Did you guys check on any of the bodies you've found? Some of them had IDs on them, right? Who they are? Where they are? That kind of thing?"

"Yeah," she says. "One of them's still alive. A hundred and twenty in Boca Raton. We talked to his nurse. They hung up on me when I asked if they were sure he hadn't died in 1924."

"Same with orange groves in the Valley, the Brown Derby on Wilshire. Freeway disappearances. How many events have you heard of so far?"

"Twenty-five? Six? Probably more by now."

There's a sudden feeling like the world is being twisted around me. I slam on the brakes. Fortunately, with everything happening, there aren't a lot of people on the road right now. Janna is shoving the heels of her hands against her eyes.

"You all right?" I say.

"We need to move. Now. Back the way we came." I don't question it, I just throw the car in reverse.

"What happened?" I say.

"Look. But don't stop moving."

A twenty-story office building of glass and metal sits at the end of the block. Its base has been replaced with a much smaller building of brick and cement from the twenties. It's not just shorter, it's about half the width of the new building.

I can already see what's about to happen. I spin the wheel, throw the car into gear and stomp on the gas. It's not the best bootlegger I've done, but it does the trick.

We're a couple of blocks away when the inevitable happens. Since it no longer has a base that can support it, the new building begins to sway like a tree chopped by a drunk lumberjack who can't tell which way it's going to fall.

Finally it makes up its mind and topples down across the street, each floor like teeth on a zipper. Every impact is a new explosion of steel and glass. I don't feel any deaths, thank fuck, but I'm getting a better idea how bad it is out here.

"I think that's number twenty-seven," I say.

"You think there was anybody in there?" Janna says.

"If there were, it didn't kill them. So I'm thinking no."

"Can we get off the street?" Janna says. "I don't like the idea of dying underneath a falling skyscraper."

"But you're okay with a chunk of freeway disappearing?"

"We'll probably survive that," she says. I can't really argue with her.

The freeway is disturbingly clear. A handful of sheriff's deputies, for the most part. There's a curfew in place right now, so I've got the car covered with a don't-look-at-me spell.

The air above us, however, is filled with helicopters. Military, police, news. They're the only aircraft that haven't been grounded. A third of LAX has turned back into a wheat field, taking two terminals and a section of runway with it.

Once both our pulses return to something like normal, I ask, "Nobody remembers any of these people and places disappearing in the past."

"Not that I've heard, no. In some cases it's a full or partial replacement of the building. And when there are people in a structure—well, you know. Other times it's like at the club. The building partly changes. Old and new merging together."

"Meaning the merged buildings have been standing there the entire time. If they'd disappeared in the twenties—"

"They wouldn't exist now at all," Janna says. "Say you're right. This means we're dealing with the effect before the cause."

"Yep."

"So what's the cause?"

"Not sure. I think it's related to the spell the Blackburns cast in 1924, though. Maybe not intentionally. I think something happened that screwed things up, or they got it wrong. Having a hard time thinking a pair of grifters like them would want to bring about an actual apocalypse."

"It's something that hasn't happened yet," Janna says. "Like with the buildings and the people."

"How so?"

"If it had, then this reality quake would have happened and it would all just be our reality, right?"

"Good point," I say. I'm getting the feeling that time travel is a lot like that Abbott and Costello routine, Who's on First, only it's When's on third, in the dugout, and somewhere in the outfield picking dandelions.

"Would it, though?" she says. "Say a bunch of places start disappearing in the twenties. All of a sudden L.A. gets this reputation like the Bermuda Triangle. Why would the movie industry get a foothold? Aerospace? Finance? If this whole area turns into a sort of time pit, why would anyone ever move here? If they hadn't moved here, then we wouldn't even be here to have this conversation."

"Have I mentioned I hate chronomancy?" I say. "That's one of the reasons. What happens when I change the past so I was never born? How could I do that if I was never here in the first place?"

"What's the answer?"

"No fucking idea. Never met a chronomancer. Maybe that's the reason why. They keep writing themselves out of existence."

"I have a headache," she says.

"Don't worry," I say. "It'll get worse."

I park well outside the area that the adobe is in and get out of the car. The last thing I want is for the house to show up with the car in the middle of it. I'd hate if blowing up the house explode was the thing that made this all happen.

"This place keeps popping up," I say. "No set schedule as far as I know. At least none that Gabriela's people could figure out."

"You say 'Gabriela's people,'" Janna says. "Like she's got some huge organization. Doesn't she just run a homeless shelter?"

"Oh, wow. Letitia really has been keeping you in the dark. No, she used to run a pretty impressive criminal enterprise. Now it's more legit, but she still keeps her hand in."

"Jesus," she says. "You all really think that little of us?"

"What, the police? Yeah, pretty much."

"Normals. And yes, before you say it, I am 'normal.' At least I was. We're just a fucking joke to you people. Even the captain doesn't take us seriously."

"Keep going," I say.

"What?"

"You need to get this out of your system," I say. "You're right, we do think very little of normals. Even those of us who honestly care about them." I put my hand out, palm up, and a flame appears in the middle of it. I stretch it out, twist it into a mini fire tornado, then let it die.

"That's a nothing spell," I say. "A parlor trick. But compared to what most people can do, we might as well be fucking gods. Some of us are. There is no way any person who has even the tiniest amount of power is going to hold onto humility for very long."

"But I can't do any of that," she says.

"Yes, you can," I say. "I've seen it. You know why Tish has taken you under her wing?"

"Because she's trying to help me out," she says.

"No," I say. "Because she's fucking terrified of you. Your little invisibility trick with your car? That's really goddamn impressive. That takes a lot of power and control."

"But I don't even know how I did it."

"And that's what's scary," I say. "You might as well be a toddler with a hand grenade. If Tish were anybody else, she might have shot you just out of self-preservation. You don't understand how fucking dangerous you are."

"I know that," she says, voice rising. "I blew up a fucking building, remember? What else have I done that I don't even know about? The captain is terrified? How the fuck do you think I feel?

"I haven't talked to my parents since this all happened. They're ultra-conservative Christians. How am I supposed to explain all this to them? It was bad enough when I told them I didn't believe in god. They almost disowned me. I tell them this, or worse, I do something around them, they'll think I'm the fucking Antichrist."

"You dating anybody?" I say.

"What? I . . . what?"

"Because if you are, I'd really recommend breaking it off. Same with friends. You need to be really careful who you tell about this. Most of them, even if you show them, won't believe it. At best they'll laugh at you. At worst, they'll freak out and you'll drive them away. It's really unlikely you'll get a torches-and-pitchforks reaction, but you never know."

"What, like people will hunt me down like a Salem witch?"

"Some will, yeah," I say. "Not so much in L.A., most major cities are pretty safe, but there are some places where you really need to be careful."

She closes her eyes. Takes a deep breath. "My parents would do that," she says. "Try to save my soul by burning me at a stake. Wouldn't matter who I am. They already think I'm going to Hell. What am I going to do? I can't even talk to my fucking therapist about this."

"We'll find you one who knows about this stuff," I say.

"There are mage therapists?"

"This is L.A.," I say, stepping out of the car. "You can get a therapist for your pug. Come on, let's go do something potentially earth-shatteringly stupid."

"This doesn't look like much," she says, surveying the area. "I see tire tracks. That from the truck you found here before?"

"Yeah," I say. "You feel anything?"

"Like what?"

"Magic. Anything weird. Out of the ordinary."

"Do you?"

"No," I say. "Didn't when I was here last, either."

"I—I think?" She closes her eyes, turns a bit. She opens her eyes. "It's coming from you. I think it's your bag."

That doesn't sound good. It takes me a second, but then I feel it too and realize why I didn't notice. It's always been there, just less active.

I reach into my messenger bag and pull out my pocket watch. The hands are spinning back and forth like a top that can't figure out which way it's turning.

"What the hell is that?"

"Fucking time magic," I say. "Stand back. This could get very messy."

"What are you doing?"

"Like I said, something potentially earth-shatteringly stupid," I say. Janna takes a few steps back. I look at her until she takes a few steps further. Then a few more. I point the watch out in front of me and hit the crown.

When a spell goes off I can feel a flare of magic, like a match being lit, or a road flare. This feels like a hand grenade. A blast of displaced air hits us full-on, throwing me and sending Janna staggering against the car. My ears are ringing.

The house is back.

"Fuck me," Janna says.

"The watch stopped," I say.

"Is that bad?"

"Dunno," I say. "It's never happened before." I wind the

crown a few times until I hear it start ticking. I put it back into my bag.

"This is two hundred years old?" Janna says. "It looks almost new."

"Real adobe, too," I say.

"Now what?" she says. "We knock?"

"I think we're past that point," I say, and push the door open.

Chapter 22

I don't hear anyone yelling like last time. But I think I hear—

"Is someone crying?"

"Yeah. I think I know why. The story of this place is that a mother had a breakdown and drowned her children in the courtyard. Then her husband came home, killed her for what she'd done, and then topped himself. When my—I dunno, consciousness?—came through here, there was a fight going on outside in the courtyard about some sort of baptism."

"You think she did it?"

"Not unless she was three separate people and two of them were speaking English. Come on. Let's go see what actually happened." I push the far door open and step out into the courtyard.

This is not what I was expecting.

"There's something seriously wrong with these children," Janna says.

"Yeah, no shit."

A young woman in a blue-and-white dress, soaking wet, hair coming undone from a long braid, sits in the middle of a magic circle drawn in blood next to a fountain. Her left arm has been sliced open, from the inside of her elbow all the way down to her hand, giving her enough blood to draw the circle. She's haggard, exhausted, traumatized.

But she's not the problem. No, that would be the children. Three boys. The youngest looks about four years old, the eldest maybe seven or eight. They stand outside the circle, trying to get to their mother but unable to cross over the line.

All three of them have clearly taken a dip in the pool. Given their graying skin and the extreme cant to the toddler's head, I'd say it was a long, violent dip.

"Who are you?" the woman screams in Spanish when she sees us. "You can't hurt my children. Not anymore. No one can."

The heads of all three children turn toward us, and I can see that their eyes are glowing green.

"We're not here to hurt anyone," Janna says in Spanish. Then in English to me, "Can you back me up here?"

"We're not with the women who murdered your children," I say, playing a hunch. "We were trying to stop them. And couldn't get here in time."

"Why? Who are they? All this and they never told me who they are. They murdered my babies so that I could bring them back. They wanted to know how I did it. Wanted to learn what I know." She laughs, a harsh, unnerving sound. "So, I did. I taught them. But they didn't see everything. They didn't see this."

"Are the kids dead?" Janna says to me in English.

"Very," I say. "But that's just my take from looking at them. Magically? I honestly have no idea." They don't feel right. They're not like the corpses I animate, or what Joe is, or what any of the corpses from the twenties have been. As far as my magic is concerned, they're either not dead enough, or else so dead they might as well be a pound of ground sirloin.

"They knew I was a witch," the woman says. "They said they read stories about me. That I could bring the dead to life. But I can't. They didn't believe me."

"What did you do, exactly?" I say. The protection circle is pretty straightforward. Smart, I guess, because those kids look like they're about to go feral. But she's bleeding out. I doubt she's gonna last more than another hour with her arm like that.

"They're not real," she says. "I've stolen a piece of soul. Reached out and plucked it out of the ether. But it doesn't bring them back. It turns them into . . . these."

"And the two women want to use this spell?" Janna says.

"They want to use it to bring Willa back to life," I say. "They don't know it won't work."

"Maybe they do," Janna says. "You were saying they were trying to build up energy over time. Maybe they can do something to make it stick better if they pump more power into it?"

"Brute force a resurrection? Hope if you throw enough into it, you get something that doesn't turn into this? I've heard crazier."

"They killed my babies," the woman says. Her voice is fading. She doesn't have an hour. She may not have even a few minutes. I step up to the protection circle, pushing one of the children out of my way. He doesn't react, just shuffles backward.

"You're dying," I say. "What happens to your children when you do?"

"They'll kill you," she says. "You need to run." Her face goes slack, her eyes glaze over, and her body stills.

Well, shit.

The effect is immediate. The child I'm closest to snaps to attention, lets out a growl like a pissed-off tiger, and lunges for my face. He's not very big and goes flying with one punch.

The oldest child is a little more of a challenge. Fucker latches onto my arm with his surprisingly sharp teeth and starts gnawing at my bicep. It's not going to take him long to get through my shirt and coat.

"What do I do?" Janna yells.

"Try shooting them in the head," I say. Taking my own advice, I pull my pistol and put a round through the kid's head. It explodes like dynamite in a watermelon. The three Bs—blood, brains, bone—burst out, covering everything in gore. Okay, maybe not the best strategy.

The bullet has taken the top of the dead kid's head off, and though it's not biting anymore, its jaw has locked in place. I try shaking it off. When that doesn't work, I try beating what's left of its head with the butt of my pistol. That doesn't help much either.

I feel a pressure on my lower leg and it isn't until the little fucker starts chewing that I realize it's the toddler. Fantastic. I've got one zombie kid hanging off my arm and another wrapped around my leg, each trying to take a chunk out of their respective limbs.

"I can't shoot children," Janna says.

"Really? None of your buddies on the force seem to have that problem."

"Oh, fuck you," Janna says. "We are not all like that."

"Does that mean you're not going to shoot the dead kids?"

"No, I'm not going to fucking shoot the dead kids."

"Oh, then you're really gonna hate this next part."

"What are you—Ow! What the fuck. This little shit's trying to eat my leg."

"Ya don't say." I manage to shake the one corpse off my arm and turn to the one on my leg. It looks up at me with green glowing eyes and smiles with teeth like a shark.

I take the momentary lapse in its chewing to swing my leg around and slam it against a wooden column. A few more knocks it loose. But it's a persistent little fucker and keeps coming at me.

Let's try something different. I stop it with my hand against its forehead, my arms too long for it to get any closer. I feel around for magic, energy, anything. There's something there, faint. I've felt something like this before. A sliver of soul?

What was it she said? She plucked a piece of soul out of the ether? Okay, I can work with that. Souls are something I know how to deal with. I get a sense of its edges, grab onto it, and yank it out.

The body falls to the ground in a small heap. I turn around to check how Janna's doing, and see that the fun never stops in our wacky little adobe death house.

Daddy's home. He stands in the doorway in utter shock. A distinguished Spanish gentlemen. His brain can't process what the hell is going on. But he very quickly realizes that there are two strangers in his house, his wife and two of his sons are dead, and the third one is trying to fend off a tall, crazy woman by chewing on her leg.

He does what any man filled to the brim with grief, rage, and a little forethought would. He pulls a loaded revolver from his coat and starts shooting at us.

One bullet grazes Janna's shoulder. A second comes dangerously close to her head and blows a hole in the wall. Before he can get off a third shot I take him down with a round through his forehead.

"I don't want to hurt you," Janna is screaming at the zombie. She tries to pull it off, but it's latched on like a trap-jaw ant. "Get off me. Please get off me." She's beginning to sound desperate.

I start to head over to her and freeze when I feel it.

Janna is pumping out a metric fuck-ton of magic like a busted fire hydrant. The world around me warps in a way that makes me think of what stepping into a black hole might feel like. There's a sense of the world shifting around us and then, with a snap like breaking bones, reality becomes real again.

The zombie kid falls off her leg. One of its arms snaps off when it hits the ground, the tissue holding it together desiccated and thin. It looks like it's been mummified for the last five hundred years.

I've seen this effect before. It looks exactly as if it'd been hit with my pocket watch.

Janna is on her knees, shaking, rocking back and forth and screaming, "Why? Why?" before her voice fails her and all that comes out is a thin, whispery whine.

I run over to her, snap my fingers in front of her face to get her attention. It takes a few tries, but eventually she comes back to awareness enough to notice me.

"Can you walk?" I say. Janna nods. I help her up. She's shivering now. I walk her to the door.

"Did I kill him?" she says.

"No," I say. "He was dead long before we showed up."

Chapter 23

"She did what?" Gabriela says. I've got her on speaker. I glance over at Janna, but she's oblivious. She's leaning back as far as the car seat can go and I have her covered up with a blanket I found in the trunk. She's still shivering, though not as much as before.

I clotted the blood and got a compression bandage on her shoulder. The bullet wound's not so bad she's going to bleed out, but I'm more worried about shock. There's no way to get her on her back with her feet elevated in this car, so this is the best I can do.

I forgot to cast a don't-look-here on the car. I'm speeding down the 405 fast enough that I have three helicopters following me. Police? News? Who the hell knows?

"Basically, what my pocket watch does." I give her a rundown of the events. I wonder if we're part of the legend now. The wife died, sopping wet. The kids drowned, though it might look a little different to some. The dad took a bullet. I can see all that still fitting the narrative, more or less.

"Oh my god. Where are you now?"

"Heading down the 405. Provided there's enough of the 405 to head down. I'm probably on Channel 5. Can you have a car chase without a chase car?"

"L.A. Zen koans are a little too existential for me right now," Gabriela says. "Get her down here. I'll meet you in the parking garage. I'll get somebody over here to look at her."

"I killed him," Janna says.

"What was that?" Gabriela says.

"Janna," I say. "I assume she's talking about the kid." Janna turns to me and her eyes look like glowing lava lamps, colors shifting through them. Pretty, but goddamn that's creepy. At least mine just turn basic black.

"Huh. Her eyes are doing wacky shit."

"That is rarely a good sign."

"Hey."

"Yours aren't 'wacky,'" she says. "Just really fucking disturbing."

"Point. All right. Gotta go."

"See you in a few." The call disconnects.

Janna's still facing me, but without irises or pupils I can't tell if she's actually looking at me. Do people have the same problem when my eyes go black?

"How you doin' over there?"

"I don't know," she says. Tears slowly trickle down her face, but her affect is completely flat.

"Fair enough. Can you describe it?"

"The . . . I don't know what to call it. The zombie? It wasn't a child, was it?"

"Not at that point, no."

"Good. I'm bleeding."

"Lemme take care of that." Me and blood are on pretty good terms these days. I stop the bleeding with a small spell.

"Thank you. Was that the father you shot?" Her voice is sounding more and more distant.

"Pretty sure," I say.

"I killed a child," she says.

"I'm telling you, he just looked like a child."

She shakes her head like she's disagreeing with me and then says, "I saw him. His life. What would have happened if those two women hadn't shown up. And his father."

"Saw?"

"Saw, smelled, heard." There's a long pause then, "He left the house to haggle over the price of a couple of goats at Miguel's ranch, but they couldn't agree on the price."

Her voice picks up speed, words starting to blur together. "So, he came home, frustrated, angry. He was going to beat his wife. That's always calmed him down in the past. When he got there, he saw her, his children. His boys. His legacy. Didn't think. Shot her. And then he saw what had become of the children. Demons. He cursed them shot them, too, not to put them out of their suffering but because whatwould the otherland owners thinkandthenrealized there was no wayhecouldexplainthis away he prison familyruin name kill-onlyanswer protect the name protect the name protectthe-namenamename." Her voice suddenly stops.

She goes silent for a moment. "Then he shot himself," she says. "If we hadn't been there. I knew all that. Saw all that. And I grabbed it and twisted it. Bundled it all up like a ball and threw it at the . . . thing. I threw it. How did I throw it? I don't understand. How?"

"What exactly did you throw at him?" I say, though I already know. I'm curious if she does, though.

"Time," she says. "I threw time at him."

"For the most part, she's fine," Vivian says. Vivian and I dated in high school. She's a doctor now. We've had our ups and downs since I got back to L.A.

I got her fiancé killed. He was my best friend before I left. One of the best men I've ever known. Of all the people I can think of who shouldn't have died, he's top of the list.

So, really more downs than ups. We avoid each other these days if we can. Best for everybody.

Gabriela, Vivian, and I are in the infirmary, crowded over Janna, who's lying on a hospital bed. Vivian's given her a sedative. It seems to be helping. At least she's not shaking anymore.

"That does not look fine," I say.

"Says the man with the pitch black eyes," Vivian says. "I don't know exactly what this is, but I think it's from coming into her power. It should be temporary. I'd say let her sleep it off."

"He's not dead," Janna says, voice slow, sleepy.

"Who's not dead?" Gabriela says.

Janna looks at Vivian. "Alex," she says. We all freeze. Alex was her fiancé. The one I got killed.

"No," Vivian says, keeping her face as neutral as possible. "Alex died. He's gone."

"Here, yes," she says. "But not there." She closes her eyes and drifts off.

The three of us stand there staring at her, none of us knowing what the hell just happened.

"Let's give her some space," I say.

"Yes," Vivian says. "That would be best."

We have skipped any pretense that we're doing all right and gone straight to the tequila. We're sitting in one of the offices dotting the main hallway just past the entrance of the shelter with a bottle on the desk that's already a third gone. So far none of us have said a word about Janna.

"What the fuck was that?" Vivian says, finally.

"I'm not entirely sure," I say. "But I think she might be a chronomancer."

"That feels very convenient," Gabriela says.

"That feels very Jimmy," I say. "At this point I can't tell what's a coincidence and what's that fucking head."

"Sorry, I'm missing something," Vivian. "Who's Jimmy?"

"Guy whose head I cut off a while back in Vegas and turned into an Oracle. I don't know what the fuck its plan is, but all the changes happening right now are related to it, somehow. I'm apparently a part of its plan. Starting to think Janna is, too."

"I don't know why I ask," Vivian says. "How did she know about Alex? And what did she mean 'not here'?"

"Don't look at me," I say. "I've only known her a couple days. If anybody'll have any insight it'd be Tish. She's been working with her for over a year."

"If she's a chronomancer, she might be able to see alternate, I don't know, timelines?" Gabriela says. "Or different ways things can turn out. The way Jimmy can?"

"She's gonna love that," I say. "She's having a hard enough

time adjusting to magic as it is. Being able to see the world like Jimmy does might tip her over the edge."

Vivian's phone dings. She looks at it, stands, a little wobbly. "My Uber's here," she says. "Whatever happens, please don't make all this worse."

"Do my best," I say.

"I was afraid you were going to say that. Gabriela, let me know if anything changes with Janna. She should be out for at least four or five hours."

"I'll text," she says. "Good or bad."

"Thanks. I'll talk to you later." She leaves to go find her waiting Uber.

"She still really hates you," Gabriela says.

"She's always going to really hate me," I say. "With good reason. I was a dick when we were dating and I was a dick when I got back. Not to mention the shit with Alex."

"You can't blame yourself for everything, you know," Gabriela says.

"I don't. But I can blame myself for that. Ya know, Letitia pointed out that a lot of shit has had me as the common denominator." She waves it off.

"You don't know half what I'm responsible for," Gabriela says. "I had my own life of terrible mistakes and moral turpitude before you met me, you know."

"I'd like to hear some of the stories, sometime."

"Most of them are about as fun as yours," she says. "Though some of the shit I got up to in my sorority days was pretty wild." We sit in one of those tenuous silences where nobody wants to burst the bubble, but it has to happen, anyway.

"I have no idea what to do with Janna," I say.

"How sure are you sure her knack is chronomancy?"

"I'm not. I only saw the one event. But fuck, it was a whopper. I could be completely wrong and it was something else entirely. Whatever it was, she used a lot of power. If it had been here, today, you'd be getting phone calls from mages in Phoenix. And I didn't feel her tapping the pool. Everything she let loose, she already had in her."

"How stable do you think she is?"

"What, like mentally?" I say. "She started off pretty solid. But now? I honestly couldn't tell you."

My phone rings. A number I don't recognize. I hope it's who I think it is. "I need to take this out in the hall." I stand up and leave the room.

"Eric," says a woman. Sounds like a woman, at least.

"You *can* use a telephone."

"I figured if you can make an effort with the falcons I could stoop so low as to make a phone call."

The voice is Shait, an Egyptian god of fate. Well, a sliver of one. They came over to the U.S. with some artifacts that had been found with Tutankhamun and displayed in the Luxor, a giant, black pyramid casino on the Las Vegas Strip.

A god of fate, no matter how small, is going to thrive in a place like Las Vegas, and they did. Over the next several years they became more a Las Vegas god than an Egyptian one. Some habits are a little hard to break, though. Hence me sending them a message with the falcons.

"Jimmy," I say.

When I was in Vegas they're the one who tipped me off to the fact that Jimmy can't see me. Jimmy and Shait aren't in diametric opposition to each other, but tangentially opposed. By manipulating events, Jimmy creates certainty out of chance, and that fucks with fate. They have a vested interest in Jimmy not accomplishing whatever the fuck it is it's trying to accomplish.

"I assumed. I take it he's started enacting his plan. Why call me?"

"Is it blind to you like it is with me?" I'm playing a hunch. If I'm wrong it's back to the drawing board.

There's a pause, a resigned sigh, then, "Yes. Between you and I, for example, this phone call and immediate events stemming from it, he'll be blind to. I assume you want me to do something."

"How do you feel about kidnapping?"

"How ya feeling?" I say. I've been sitting next to Janna for the last twenty minutes or so. Her eyes just snapped open. I'm not sure what sort of answer I'm going to get. Or if Janna is even still Janna at this point.

Sometimes when someone comes into their power as an adult it can rewire their brain. Kindness becomes cruelty, murderousness becomes pacifism. I think it's largely a reflection of who they really are. A lot of new adult mages finally come out as gay or trans, for example. Magic tends to wipe away some of life's petty bullshit.

"I don't know," she says. Sounds like Janna. She sits up, swings her legs over the side of the bed.

"You might want to slow down a bit," I say. "You look a little wobbly."

She nods. "Yeah. Little nauseous, too."

"You need a bucket?"

"No, I'm good. What happened?"

"What do you remember?"

She opens her mouth to speak but nothing comes out. Finally, "Too much. But it's all a jumble. I remember the zombie. Jesus, that was fucked up. Why would someone do that?"

"Sounds like they were forcing her to show them her magic. I'm betting she was a necromancer and there were stories that said she had brought people back to life."

"Is that something you can do?"

"Not quite," I say. "Not saying it can't be done, but there are some problems with it I won't go into right now. I think they learned the spell, saw the initial results, and skedaddled. But they didn't stick around for the finale."

"The father," she says. "I saw his life. His fears. What would have happened if we hadn't shown up, if his children hadn't been killed. All these different paths his life could have taken. That wasn't all a hallucination, was it?"

"No," I say. "Sorry. Do you know what you did next?"

"I got rid of the thing hanging onto me."

"Do you remember how?"

She turns away from me, closes her eyes. "Yes. It was— Fuck."

"You said you threw time at it."

"But that's crazy," she says. "You can't throw time."

"And the dead can't talk, corpses can't be turned into feral zombies, thoughts can't stop bullets. You've seen all of these things. You've done a few of them. Hell, we were in a house that hasn't existed for a couple hundred years, dealing with people who died long before any of us were born."

"What the fuck do I do with this?" she says. "I don't know what I can and can't do. What if I screw something up and people get hurt?"

"Accept it. You will screw up, sometimes in really big ways. Tish tell you about what she and I did during the fires?"

"No. She said she'd had a hand in taking down the woman who caused the fires, though."

"The person who lit the flames is not the one who caused the fires. Her boss was pissed off at someone who didn't want to burn someplace else and as revenge sent an assassin to burn down the city. Looked at one way, and a lot of people look at it this way, the one who started the fires is the one who refused her boss."

"That was you, wasn't it?"

"Yep. The woman was a sicaria sent up to actually set everything off. Her boss was the Aztec god Quetzalcoatl. He wanted me to burn down Mictlan, the Aztec land of the dead. I refused. L.A. burned instead."

"A god," she says. "An Aztec god. I know you're not fucking with me, but I really wish you were."

"Me too. Over a hundred thousand people died that night. I felt a lot of them die."

"Felt?" she says.

"Like how you knew the father's life if we hadn't fucked it all up. I can feel when someone dies. When Vernon exploded,

I was close enough that I felt the death of everyone there, and in the surrounding areas caught in the blast."

"How did it feel?"

"Like I'd gotten smashed between two speeding trucks. Hurt like a motherfucker. Knocked me out for about six hours or so. None of that was intentional. I just made choices that came back to bite me in the ass. You're probably going to do the same thing at some point."

"Piss off gods? Burn down the city? Jesus. What I can do, that's chronomancy?"

"Sounds like. If that's your knack, you're really going to want to get a handle on it. We can help with some of it, the other sorts of magic we've all learned. A mage can learn any spell, theoretically. A knack is just something you're stupidly good at. Like you seeing possible futures."

"Or you seeing ghosts?"

"Exactly. I have a suspicion you might not be able to turn it off, or if you can, that it's going to pop up on its own anyway."

"I can't tell anyone about this," she says. "Can I even see my family anymore?"

"Sure you can," I say. "But, uh, we're going to want to handle something first." I get up, open a cabinet, find a highly polished tray, and hand it to her.

"Oh my fucking god," she says when she sees herself. "What happened to my eyes? Are they okay? I can see all right. The fuck is this?"

"Before you freak out too much, you can probably get rid of the effect. Like so." I turn my eyes black, then back again.

"That was really fucking creepy."

"I get that a lot. You try it. Just think about having them go back." She stares into her reflection and a few seconds later her eyes are normal.

"Oh, thank the Baby Jesus," she says. "I never want to have that happen again."

"I got bad news then."

"It's going to come back, isn't it?"

"With your magic, probably. Mine do, mostly when I'm pissed off, but sometimes if I do some heavy death magic. I recommend investing in a good pair of sunglasses."

"It's a lot to take in," she says.

"I know, but I have to ask you a couple other things. You said Alex was dead here, but he wasn't there. What did you mean?"

"I'm not sure. I just know he's not dead. Or he's dead but not? Or not supposed to be. It's all a jumble in my head. Sorry."

"That's fine. Last question, then I'll leave you alone. You said something about killing a kid, but it wasn't the boy in the adobe house."

Her face grows pale, eyes wide. "I said that?"

"Yeah."

"It's not what you think," she says. She's looking a little panicked.

"Whoa there. Hang on. I don't think it's anything, because I don't know what it is. Also remember that I'm responsible for over a hundred thousand dead throughout the entire county. And I have lost count of all the people and things I've killed on purpose. I am in absolutely no position to judge you."

Janna takes a deep breath, starts to slow her breathing. She'll talk when and if she's ready.

My phone buzzes. Unknown number. A text appears with a photo.

How's this?

Perfect. Appreciate it. Will be in touch.

"I'll be right back," I say and step into the hall. I copy the photo, paste it into a text for the number I got from the corpse in the morgue, and send it. Ten, nine, eight—

My phone buzzes. "Hi Rachel," I say.

"What the fuck have you done with my son?"

Chapter 24

"He's fine," I say. "Just cooling his heels. Taking really good care of him. Got his meds, keeping him fed, all that."

"If you hurt him—"

"Let's hope it doesn't come to that."

I had Shait grab Rachel's kid. He's in his twenties, but he's had a lot of bad experiences and a lot of trauma, so he doesn't interact well with the rest of the world. I told Shait to take that into account and make sure he's kept as calm and happy as possible.

He's a normal like her ex-husband, which has caused about as much strife as you can imagine.

"I'm going to find him and then I'm going to come kill you. I give a fuck what Jimmy wants."

"I think that is an excellent idea. It'll take you at least as long as I need, so knock yourself out. I wouldn't bother asking Jimmy, though. He's not going to be able to see where I've stashed him. And his powers of extrapolation might be a little strained. I'm not the one who grabbed him."

"What do you want?"

"Nothing," I say. "Save you walking away for a few days. Let's make it a week. I want to kill you, Rachel, and one of these days I will. But right now, I need you out of my hair. Jimmy's got his stone. You're dead weight at this point. Unless he needs your special skills in renting houses for him. So walk away."

"And if I don't?"

"Do I really need to answer that question?"

"You sonofabitch. That's my son."

"How many sons and daughters did you murder at Candyland? How many lives did you shatter with that stunt?"

"Oh, you're one to talk," she says. "You're a mass murderer."

"I am. But the difference between you and me is I didn't want to be. Disappear for a week. Hang onto this phone. I'd hate to have to add one more corpse to the butcher's bill."

I hang up.

"I only heard half of that conversation," Janna says coming into the hallway. "But I didn't like it."

"I'm not too crazy about it either."

"You kidnapped somebody."

"I did. Rachel's kid. He's an adult. And before you get your knickers in a twist, no, he's not going to be hurt. From what I understand he's having a great time. Don't know what he's doing. Could be Disneyland. Could be hookers and blow. No idea. I hate that I have to use him as a bargaining chip but he's the only thing I know Rachel actually cares about."

"And if she doesn't do what you want?" Janna's trying to loom over me. She's got maybe an inch or two on me, sure, but spend a few years with Santa Muerte looming over you, you acquire something of an immunity.

"Not sure. Maybe hide him in a pocket universe for a while or something."

"Why don't you think Jimmy will find him?"

"Because the . . . entity that I had grab him can't be seen by Jimmy either. They're sort of at odds with each other. How are you feeling?"

"Don't change the subject." She's crossed her arms. So I guess that means we're getting serious? I'm really not sure.

"I wasn't," I say. "I just figured the subject was over. Look, I know you don't like the idea. I don't like it either. He's going to be fine. If he's not, it's not going to be because of this. Now can we move on or are you going to let your high-handed morality keep us here for the next hour?"

"He's not a child?"

"He is not a child. He's, like, twenty-two or something. But he's had a lot of trauma, so he's being handled with kid gloves. He probably doesn't even know anything's out of sorts."

She chews her lip. I think I know what her next question is so I head it off at the pass.

"The entity I was talking about is an Egyptian god of fate," I say. "If fate can't keep him safe, I honestly don't know what can."

"A—a god?"

"Of fate, yes," I say. "Egyptian. Named Shait or Shai, depending on which gender they choose. Resides in Las Vegas."

"There's an Egyptian god of fate living in Las Vegas," she says.

"Yes. Just like an Aztec god burned down Los Angeles. He's sort of my cousin. Kind of an in-law. Can we move on now?"

"Cousin?"

"It's a long story and if you don't think it will irrevocably fuck up your worldview I'll tell you it some time."

"I—Okay." Any certainty that she had control of the conversation has evaporated.

"Good. How would you like to practice your magic?"

"Uh, sure."

"Great. Let's get some fruit."

"Janna, this is Amanda. Amanda, Janna."

"Nice to meet you," Amanda says, crossing the room to shake her hand. "I've heard a lot about you."

Amanda is almost an entire foot shorter than Janna, but it's clear which of the two of them is in charge. Amanda's a natural politician.

Gabriela, Amanda, Janna, and I are in a large office that Gabriela occasionally uses. It has a table and chairs at one end. Janna looks nervous.

"Sorry," Janna says, "Nobody mentioned you."

"Not to worry. We saw each other briefly at the club the other night when this all started. I wouldn't expect you to remember me. I understand you just discovered your magic."

"Yeah, I don't really understand it."

"Most of us don't," Amanda says. "Eric, you said you wanted to show me something."

"Janna's been practicing the last couple hours."

"I figured," Amanda says. "I could feel the spells she was casting out on the street."

"Yeah, we decided to start small."

"I'm confused," she says. "What did you want to talk about that you needed me here?"

"I'm glad you asked." I take an orange I snagged from the breakroom and put it on the table. "This is still a work in progress. Want to set expectations."

"Is my table going to explode?" Gabriela says. Janna glances at me, clearly nervous.

"Probably not."

"Is the orange going to explode?"

"Possibly not."

"I really don't think I'm comfortable with this."

"Honestly, the worst that can happen is—What's on the other side of this wall?"

"Another office. Empty."

"Worst that can happen is you get a bigger office." Gabriela gets up from her chair behind her desk and walks to the far end of the room. Amanda joins her. I can feel both of them putting up shield spells. Smart.

"Okay. Let's show them a baseline," I say.

Janna looks at the orange, I can feel magic building up. Her eyes shift to a swirl of colors. But other than that, nothing happens.

"That's just Janna on her own. But." I pull the pocket watch out of my messenger bag.

"Okay, I'm drawing the line there," Gabriela says.

"Do you trust me?" I say.

"For things like this? Absolutely not."

"Oops, my finger slipped," I say, pointing the watch at the orange and hitting the crown. A flare of magic comes from Janna, the orange shimmers, then, like a time-lapse sequence in a nature documentary, it shrinks, goes brown, splits open, goes black. "Okay, now."

There's no change I can feel in the magic Janna's pushing out, but the effect on the orange is immediate. Black goes to brown goes to orange as it plumps up and expands. It begins to shrink again and change color, but instead of the black of rot it turns green. Keeps shrinking. In a few seconds a small white orange blossom sits in its place. I stop pressing the crown on the watch.

"What the fuck was that?" Amanda says.

"An orange," I say.

"You know what I mean."

"Janna's a chronomancer. With enough training she could probably do that without the watch, but right now it acts as, I dunno, a catalyst, a power source, something."

"Okay," Amanda says. "That's impressive, but why are you showing me?"

"Because we're heading down to Union Station in 1948 and I was wondering if you'd like to join us and say hi to your dad."

Chapter 25

"**How does this work?**" Amanda says.

"He doesn't know," Gabriela says.

"Hey, I might," I say.

"Do you?"

"No. Janna?"

Janna looks nervously at the doors to Union Station. It's a sprawling Spanish Revival building meant to resemble an old California mission. Built in 1939, gorgeous interior. The old ticket counter to the left as you walk in is an Art Deco masterpiece. Pity some developers decided people didn't need to see the place. They built a bunch of commercial buildings around it. Joke's on them. They all burned down in the firestorm.

This entire area of Downtown is eerily empty, the sounds of traffic almost non-existent. Given we're right next to the freeway, it's even creepier.

The parking lot is empty and the doors to the station are locked, which isn't usual. With everything that's going on, folks have started to piece together that old L.A. is invading current L.A., so everyone is staying the fuck away from anything that smacks of old L.A. Not really how it's working, but it's making our lives easier. There's nobody here to get in our way.

"Okay, so the 1924 Harrison hotel sort of came and went, right? Instead of merging two places like with what happened at the club, it just was. Same with the adobe. After a little while it turned back."

"The leaks?" Amanda says. She had brought up this idea the other night, that whatever was bringing chunks of 1924 here was leaking into other areas and creating holes rather than just pulling things over outright.

"Yes," I say. "Good call, by the way. Holes or weak spots in time. No way to really find them, right?"

"Turns out I can see them," Janna says, sounding utterly miserable. She didn't ask for any of this. I feel for her, but she needs to learn how to control her power, which means exploring it as much as possible. Otherwise I can see her getting a lot of people killed.

Also, we need to get to 1948.

"How does that help us?" Gabriela says.

"They're fucking everywhere," Janna says. "Like Swiss cheese."

"Including here?" Gabriela says. Janna nods. "The plan is to make all of Union Station in 1948 come here?"

"Not quite," Janna says. "It's more like open a doorway, or create a bubble? I'm having a hard time putting it into words. Some of them look like they might be easier than others. Like, there's a big one right here, but it feels like it's—this is gonna sound stupid—covered in Saran Wrap. I think I can open it, but it wouldn't be easy."

"Besides, there's another one inside," I say.

"Over that way," Janna says, gesturing over to the right. "Do we really have to do this?"

"No," Gabriela says. "You're not some magic tool for us to use. We're not going to try to force you to do anything. This whole thing has been a huge ordeal for everyone, but especially you. That said, we could really use your help."

"You think this will help us?" Janna says.

"Not gonna lie," I say. "I don't know. I hope it will. Even if it doesn't work, I think it will help you learn more about your power."

Janna takes a deep breath, blows it out slowly. "Let's get this over with."

"Hang on," I say. "We've got one more we're waiting on."

A moment later a car heads into the lot and pulls up to us. Danny. He rolls down his window. Waves at Janna.

"Hola, chica," he says to her. She waves back nervously. "Y'all need backup?"

"Need somebody to watch our asses for a while. Remember the hotel?"

"Got it," he says. "You're gonna disappear in there for a few hours and you want to make sure nobody's waiting to gank you on your way out?"

"Exactly."

"Goin' on your tab," he says.

"You know I'm good for it," I say. He laughs.

"Pal, this shit's the most fun I've had since that wendigo bullshit in South Dakota. We're good. You go do your thing, I'll go do mine. If you can come out behind cover that'd be best. Text me and I'll let you know the lay of the land."

"Could be a while," I say. "Remember the Harrison."

"Figured as much," Danny says. "I spent three days in a tree in Bolivia one time waiting for a target to show. So, take your time." He drives off and around the corner.

"You think there's going to be a problem?" Gabriela says.

"At this point, yes."

I unlock the doors with a spell and we go inside. It's eerie with no one in here, lights dimmed, no footsteps, no talking, no announcements over the PA system. The terminal is a massive room with high arched ceilings and floors made of terra-cotta and beautiful Spanish tilework. The chandeliers and ceiling are gorgeous works of art. Our footsteps echo through the entire building.

"Which—" Gabriela says. Her voice bounces through the room and she drops it to a whisper. "Which way?"

"There," Janna says, and heads over to the doors of a restaurant that was opened after the station was renovated a while back. Until then the space had been closed off except for movie shoots and private parties.

They recreated the original layout. The reason I know this

is that both Amanda and I have been able to trace her father's soul after it was kicked out of his body by his brother. Spatially, it's in that room right there, in one of the booths. Temporally, it's apparently in April 18th, 1948.

"What does it look like? This hole?" Amanda says.

"A bright outline of . . . I don't know what color it is. It's really disorienting. This is going to sound crazy, but I don't think I've ever seen this color before."

"You need the watch?" I say.

"I—I don't think so," Janna says. "I don't know why, though." She steps in front of the restaurant doors. "I don't know what's going to happen. You ready?"

"Let's do it," Amanda says.

Janna closes her eyes. I can feel the magic building up. Whether she realizes it or not she's building a spell from the ground up using nothing but her own power. Going to need to show her how to tap the local pool. I get the feeling she may not need it for a while.

Sweat breaks out on her brow. She starts to shake. The build-up of energy is getting disturbingly strong. The magical equivalent of having somebody drive up to your car blasting their radio. At this point, every mage in a ten-mile radius knows something is happening.

Reality warps, twisting like a funhouse mirror, then a snap, a release.

And Union Station explodes into a burst of sound and light around us.

Voices, footsteps, announcements, music, a cacophony of activity echoing throughout the entire room. We're surrounded by at least a hundred people. Some rushing for trains, some coming in from the train tracks outside.

Men in suits and hats, women in dresses and heels, footsteps clacking on the tile floor like a dance number from 42nd Street. Everyone's smoking. Pipes, cigarettes, cigars. Nobody looks nearly as shabby as we do. We're starting to get looks. I feel a spell and the gawkers blink and move on their way.

"I put an illusion over us," Amanda says. "We won't stand out. And if my dad's here, he should recognize that spell. He taught it to me. Provided he's not, I dunno. A ghost?"

I really have no idea what state Attila will be in. I can feel something weird inside the restaurant. It's not a ghost, I know that much. It's not dead, and yet it is.

"Are we sure we're in the right time?" Gabriela says. She looks a little nervous. I walk over to a nearby newsstand and swipe a copy of the Herald Examiner, a newspaper that hasn't been around since the eighties, with a small spell to hide the theft.

I show them the paper. "Welcome to 1948," I say. "April 18th. Morning edition. You nailed it."

"I think I'm gonna be sick," Janna says. She's starting to hyperventilate.

"How about we go find somewhere to sit for a little while," Gabriela says. "Catch our breath. I don't know about the rest of you, but I'm slightly freaked out."

It takes me a second to realize why. Well, duh, we're in 1948. And why don't I have a problem with it? Because, between Mictlan and the dead side, bouncing between worlds isn't really something that bothers me much anymore. Annoys, sure. Worries? Not so much.

I feel like not worrying should worry me a little. Is this a holdover from being Mictlantecuhtli or have I just become so jaded to these weird transitions that I don't notice anymore?

"That is an excellent idea," I say, and push the restaurant doors open.

The restaurant isn't much calmer than out there in the terminal, just more controlled chaos. Every conversation collides with the others until there's nothing but an unintelligible soup of chatter and the clattering of dishes and silverware. There's an empty booth near the door. We usher Janna over to it and get her seated at the edge. She puts her head between her legs and focuses on breathing.

"I might be able to help," Amanda says. "But only if you

want me to." At this point we're all pretty clear that this is way outside Janna's comfort zone.

"Do you have Xanax?" Janna says.

"I can make you some," Amanda says. "Or I can do something else to help with your nausea and anxiety."

"Magic?" Janna says.

"Yeah."

"I'll take the Xanax, thanks." Amanda holds out her hand and lo and behold there are a couple of pills there. "You didn't pull these out of your pocket, did you?"

"I make things," Amanda says. "Change them, really. Trust me, it's real."

"Thank you." Janna takes the pills and dry swallows them.

"Everything okay, folks?" A waiter swings by the booth, a look of moderate concern on his face.

"Yeah, she's just a little dizzy," Amanda says. "Can we get some water and menus?"

"Sure thing, ma'am. Be right back."

"You want to eat?" Janna says.

"Yeah," Amanda says. "I didn't have breakfast. And when do you get a chance to dine in 1948?"

Janna stares at her, as if it's just dawned on her that she's traveled through time. Not us. Her. We just tagged along. I can see the implications starting to trickle through her head.

"Aren't you worried about . . ." Janna starts and then can't seem to think of anything to worry about.

"It's not fairy tale food," Amanda says. "Eating it isn't going to keep us stuck here."

"How do you know?"

"My dad did a lot of dimension hopping. Took me along a few times. This is kind of the same thing. Speaking of." She cranes her neck but can't see over the people. She's not very tall.

"Can you stay with Janna," I say to Gabriela, "while Amanda and I see if we can find her dad?"

"I got her covered. Go."

nd I have been to the present-day version of this
many times to make sure we can still detect her
soul that we know exactly where to go.

"Things between the two of you seem to be going better," Amanda says.

"Maybe?" I say.

"Oh, don't tell me you're doing that thing where you overthink everything and tie yourself into knots until you can't see straight."

"Do I do that?"

"Everybody does that. She looks happy, which is a rare thing, believe me. Just go with it."

"What has she told you exactly?"

She laughs. "We have better things to do than talk about you."

The booth should be over here, but for some reason there's something always blocking it from view and whenever we head in that direction, something gets in our way. A waiter, a woman with a screaming baby in a stroller. We keep getting turned around.

"This should not be this hard," Amanda says. "It's starting to piss me off."

"Somebody doesn't want us to get over there."

"Yeah, well, fuck them," she says. She lifts her leg and slams her foot hard on the floor like a toddler having a tantrum. And it's a hell of a tantrum.

A tunnel opens up in reality, the world warping around the edges. No one notices it but us. We walk through about ten feet to a booth.

"We've got the right place, all right," Amanda says, stepping out of the tunnel.

"Yeah?" I say, coming out right behind her. "Why do—Oh. Shit, I forgot about this."

Three people are seated at the booth in front of us, smoking of course. They are the epitome of 1940s fashion. Amanda's dad, Attila, is in a gray, double-breasted suit, still looking like he's in his seventies for some reason. Dude's over a hundred years old at this point and stupid powerful. He can look as old as he wants, I guess.

Then there's his sister Helga, much younger-looking than when I saw her at Amanda's estate. And holy shit. She's a knockout. A psychopath, but a knockout. I can see the resemblance between her and Amanda.

The third person is nursing a drink, whisky by the look of it. Dark gray suit, blue tie, hair slicked back and side-parted, sporting a pencil-thin mustache like an old-time movie star. He stabs his cigarette into an ashtray and throws back his drink.

He glances up and freezes. We stare at each other, neither one of us quite sure what to do. Helga glances over and sees us.

"Robert," she says. "Why does that man look exactly like you?"

Chapter 26

Attila turns, looking like he's just snapped out of a daze. "Amanda? What are you doing here? How are you here?"

Amanda runs at her dad and wraps her arms around him. "I thought I would never see you again."

"And Eric?"

"Yep. Gabriela, too."

"This is Eric?" Robert says. "I thought you said he looked like me."

"Of course you wouldn't notice the resemblance," Helga says. "You're too much of a narcissist."

"Why did I ever put up with you?" Robert says.

"Well, you won't have that problem anymore, now will you?" She looks at me. "Whoever the hell you are, you can't be a worse man than he is."

"You won't think so in about seventy years," I say. "But at least I don't have that stupid Errol Flynn mustache."

"If you're Eric," Robert Carter says, "then you're wearing my skin, so I'd be a little more grateful for it."

"I am," I say. "Means you're dead and nobody has to deal with your bullshit anymore. I got a little more than just your meat, old man. I've seen some of the shit you've pulled."

I don't know why I feel so hostile toward him. I haven't remembered everything he's done, but is the stuff I've seen really all any worse than what I've done? Robert can't keep his dick in his pants, but as far as I can tell, he's not responsible for thousands of deaths.

And then I get it. I'm this angry at him because he's this angry at himself. He knows what he's done. He knows who he's hurt. He's not all that clear why he's done it, either.

"Attila, what the hell is going on?" Helga says.

"A moment," Attila says. He presses his palm to the table, there's a flare of magic, and Helga freezes. "Much better. I've been stuck here having to listen to her yammer on and on about how unfair the world is."

"This insufferable little shit is my grandson?" Robert says.

"Yes," Attila says. "And I'm sure at some point you'll recognize the irony of that statement. How did you two get here?"

"One second," Amanda says. She opens another tunnel straight to the table we left Janna and Gabriela at and waves them through.

"Miz Cortez," Attila says. "A pleasant surprise, but still a surprise. Did you make this happen?"

"Not me," Gabriela says. "Attila, this is Janna. She's a newly minted chronomancer."

"New?" Robert says. "As in she just found out?"

"Earlier today," Janna says. "It's a little overwhelming."

"Oh, I am so sorry," Robert says, and from the tone and look on his face, I think he's being sincere. Christ, I hope he's not going to try to fuck her.

"Not helping, old man."

"In this case, he might be able to," Attila says. "You're not the only rarity in your family."

"You're kidding me. Him? He's a chronomancer?" I say. How did I not know this?

"What do you mean rarity?" Robert says. "What does he do?"

"How about we all stop for a moment," Attila says, "and take a step back. First, what are you doing here?"

"Looking for you," Amanda says. "We knew where you were, recently figured out when you were, and just now figured out how to get here."

"Your brother ganked you by taking your soul and kicking it out of your body so though your body died, your family curse didn't see it that way," I say.

"He told me he'd had you sent to this date to keep reliving

it in a loop," Amanda says. "Said it was one of the most painful days you'd had and wanted to torture you with it."

"Liam always was an idiot," Attila says. "Annoying, yes. Painful? Only insofar as Helga wouldn't shut up until we got her onto the train."

"This explains a lot," Robert says.

"I thought it might have been something like this. Robert and I both had awareness of the repeating loop, though he could step outside of it if he wanted to. I couldn't."

"If I did, it froze," Robert says. "It needed all three of us to keep going forward. I could step out but I couldn't find any way to pierce the bubble."

"And he kept having to remind me what was happening," Attila says.

"You just sat here for months?" Amanda says.

"They did," Robert says. "I was mostly outside the loop. I kept having to slide back to this date to check on them."

"It gave us a chance to catch up on a few things," Attila says. "Like letting him know about Eric."

"Though not everything," Robert says. "He kept saying 'spoiler alert.' I'm still not entirely clear what that means."

"I got it from my daughter," Attila says. "I told you that. And now you seem to have broken both the time loop and bubble. Thank you."

"We're glad it worked," Gabriela says.

"You should now be free to move about the cabin," I say.

"What?" Robert says.

"Not a thing in 1948, huh?"

"You said I was dead," Attila says, "and this is my soul deposited into my earlier self?"

"Your body's dead," I say. "It's time-locked on your estate. Your soul is here, connected to your body back there." I look, and it's faint but I can see it, a golden thread stretching out away from him and disappearing into the crowd.

"Interesting. What happened at the conclave?"

"It was about as well-managed a disaster as it could have been," Amanda says.

"You got the inheritance?"

"Yes. At the end of it the only survivors were us, Liam, and Siobhan."

"Tobias?"

"Liam pulled the same trick on him," I say. "But instead of just kicking him out of his body, Liam annihilated him, then moved his own soul in. Took us a while to figure that one out."

"That poor boy," Attila says. "I'm surprised Siobhan survived."

"It was up for debate," Amanda says. "But I decided that with everyone else gone, there was already too much instability. I've had her sitting in one of the time-frozen rooms and let her out once a week."

"Do I want to know what she did?" Attila says.

"Wanted us to kill Helga," I say. "So we did. Can she hear me?"

"No," Attila says.

"You always open your mouth before thinking?" Robert says.

"You're assuming I didn't want her to hear me."

"Both of you, please," Attila says. He holds his daughter's hand. "How are you holding up?"

"It's tough," she says. "And I miss you. And I want you to come home, but—"

"But I can't, can I?" he says. They both look at me.

"Now that I know how to get to you, I'll see what I can come up with to pull you back. But your body was dead for a couple hours before we realized what had happened," I say.

"We don't know what bringing you back to that would do," Amanda says.

"I see," Attila says. He stands up from his seat. "Let's you and I take a walk and talk about this." He turns to Robert. "I think you should take Janna here and talk to her about chronomancy. I'm sure she has questions."

"I'd appreciate that," she says.

"We also have to talk to you about some other stuff," I say.

"Trust me, you've got time," Robert says. "Miss? I promise

I don't bite." He holds his hand out to Janna and smiles at her. She looks to us and Gabriela nods.

"Thanks," she says. She takes his hand and follows him through the restaurant until they disappear into the crowd.

"What are the odds they're all planning on ditching us here in 1948?" I say.

"If they do, we take over the city," Gabriela says. "Haven't you always wanted to run a criminal empire like an old noir movie?"

"I'm not a good enough planner."

"Don't worry, I am." She slides next to me in the booth, leans her head on my shoulder. "This has got to be the weirdest day I have had in a long time."

"Right? Who knew my granddad was such a dick? I mean, besides him trying to kill me when I was a kid."

"I was talking about the time travel," she says. "And, uh, you might want to think about that statement."

"Oh, no," I say. "I know where this is going. I am not like him."

"Watching the two of you bicker like that was like watching you talk to yourself. He's more of a player, though. You see the way he looked at Janna? And did you see the way she looked back at him? Plus he's got that Errol Flynn thing going for him. He's very dapper."

"I get plenty of flashes of his memories. Guy couldn't keep his dick in his pants if he tried."

"Where's your grandmother, by the way?"

"Around now? Back east," I say. "With my dad. She kicked gramps out of the house. I don't know the whole story. My dad wasn't big on talking about him. But I suspect it had to do with the aforementioned dick-in-pants problem."

"Isn't family drama fun?" she says. "This is better than Thanksgiving dinner."

"It's not a holiday unless somebody has a tantrum and launches a flaming turkey across the kitchen," I say. "When do I get to meet your family?"

"Never, if we're lucky," she says. "I spent the earlier part of my life up here and then went down south to live with my abuela once my magic manifested. My mother and I never got along. And once that happened, she shipped my ass down there to get me out of her hair. Best thing she ever did for me."

"You ever wish things had gone differently?" I say. "Like if you could go back and change things?"

"God, yes," she says. "I can think of a couple dozen people I would have avoided meeting. Couple dozen more I'd have killed the second I met them. You?"

"Would have never made Jimmy," I say. "Kept Lucy alive. Not sure how. Probably come back to L.A. earlier. Muerte wouldn't have had a reason to kill her to get me back. Doubt it would have worked out that easily, though. Shit like that never does."

I don't think about Lucy very often and when I do it's always regret and anger. Things I should have done differently. So many things.

"You think you'd still have left?"

"Yeah," I say. "I told myself it was to protect Lucy, Vivian, and Alex. Truth is I wanted to. And even with all the shit, I think it's what I needed to do."

"How so?"

"One of my duties in Mictlan was ushering souls through their pasts. Not so much an atonement. More of a cleansing. By the time they got to Chicunamictlan they'd purified their souls.

"One thing I noticed, and this probably sounds obvious but it wasn't really to me until then—everything they did led to everything else. If they'd done one or two things differently, their lives would have been radically changed.

"I've fucked up a lot. But I have to look back at the things I've done and think if I hadn't done them where I ended up might be very different. And there are some things I don't want to be different. Like you."

"I take it back," she says. "You are totally a player. Bad at it, but still."

"Even without an Errol Flynn mustache?"

"Maybe you should try it."

"We get stuck here, I'll give it a shot," I say.

There's a commotion at the other end of the room. Raised voices, someone yelling. It takes a second to make out that it's Janna and my grandfather.

"He sounds pissed," Gabriela says.

"The fuck did I do this time?" I say.

"You don't know that it's because of you," she says, then catches my look. "Okay, yes, it's probably because of you."

"How fucking stupid could you be?" Robert says, Janna trailing behind him. She's wide-eyed and looking torn between letting him go and tackling him.

"Told ya," I say. "Hey Gramps, what's up?"

"You made a fucking Oracle?"

"People are staring," Janna says.

"Fuck 'em. Well?"

"Yes," I say. "Why the fuck do you think we're here? A family reunion? Pal, I got enough of your shit in my head already. Something happened in 1924, the effects are bleeding into our time, and Jimmy, the Oracle, is trying to do something with it. But we don't know what."

"Did you say 1924?" Attila has come back to the table with a not-very-happy-looking Amanda in tow. Gabriela slides out of the booth and goes to her.

"There was some cult—"

"The Blackburns," Attila says. "I knew that wasn't over."

"Shit," Robert says. "You stupid sonofabitch. Do you have any idea what you've—urk." Janna's LAPD training kicks in and she gets Robert into one of those chokeholds they're not supposed to do but totally do anyway.

"Before we go any further," Attila says. "I think we should take this somewhere more private."

A flare of magic, a moment of disorientation, and we're standing in the suite at the ghost Ambassador Hotel that I'd destroyed a few months ago by collapsing it on Darius. Few months. Jesus. Few decades from now.

It's a pocket universe attached to the ghost side of the Ambassador. Attila and my grandfather built it together as a trap for Darius, but never figured out how to spring it until I came along.

Speaking of, on a table near the door sits a large wooden box with latches that let the whole thing unfold. Inside there will be a bottle, Darius' bottle.

It feels weird seeing it again. Weird seeing this room again, for that matter. I was sort of in it when it collapsed, a piece of my soul embedded in a golem so I could trigger the trap.

Having an entire universe, no matter how small, fold in on you into a singularity is not an experience I can recommend.

"Oh, I missed this place," Gabriela says.

"Uh, Janna?" Amanda says. Janna is staring in shock at the sudden change in scenery.

"I think you can let him go," Attila says.

"There's no rush," I say. Robert's face has gone to a weird shade of purple and his eyes have rolled back in his head.

"Oh, god, I'm sorry," Janna says, lowering Robert to the floor. "I was a little—"

"Not to worry," Attila says. "Believe me, I've had the urge many times. Can I get anyone a drink?"

Chapter 27

"I don't normally say this," Robert says to Janna, after a few minutes of intermittent coughing and gagging, "but I'm sorry for the way I reacted back there. Thank you for stopping me."

Janna doesn't seem to know what to do with that.

"We dealt with an Oracle in France a few years ago during the war," Attila says. "A group of Nazi necromancers were experimenting trying to make one. They went through a lot of people."

I heard that Robert had a bad experience with necromancers during the war. Fucked him up enough that when I manifested my magic he freaked out and tried to kill me. Now I'm beginning to get an idea why.

"So, you really made one?" Robert says.

"I really did. And believe me, if I could change it, I would."

"Does that mean you're—" He hesitates.

"A necromancer, yes," I say. After getting that sense of self-loathing from him I feel more, maybe not sympathetic, but less hostile. "I know you had problems with them during the war, though I don't know what. I get bits of your memories here and there. Nothing from that time, though."

"Excuse me," Janna says. "But where's the blonde woman who was at the table? She didn't come with us."

"Helga," Attila says. "She's back at our estate."

Janna pinches the bridge of her nose. "Okay. Okay, sorry. I'm a little dizzy."

"It'll pass," Robert says. "You shoved your way into the past almost eighty years. You'll have the mother of all hangovers later. You might want to go lie down. And drink some water."

"No," she says. "The Xanax is helping. I want to hear this."

"The necromancers were stationed at the Keroman U-Boat

base in Lorient," Attila says. "It was too heavily fortified to bomb. So we went in with a small group of mages with commando training."

"We actually weren't there for them. Didn't even know that's what they were or what they were doing. We were looking for a relic. A timepiece that could warp time."

Janna looks at me with a question. I shake my head. I'd rather hold onto that bit of knowledge a few more minutes.

"We got there just as they were completing their ritual to create the Oracle," Attila says. "If we'd been any later, things could have gone much differently. As it is, we were able to destroy it, but we lost half of our people."

"Wait, you destroyed it?" I say. "How?"

"I rewound time long enough to prevent them from completing the ritual," Robert says. "It hadn't been aware enough at the time to do anything about it."

"That's good to know," I say. Not sure how that helps, but it's something new. "What about the Blackburns?"

"What do you know about them?" Attila says.

"May and Ruth created a crazy cult called the Divine Order of the Royal Arms of the Great Eleven," Gabriela says. "It was a grift that netted them about four or five million in today's money. Or, in our today's money."

"And they were mages," I say. "Necromancy and chronomancy. They learned a spell to raise the dead. We think to bring back a girl named Willa. But instead of just casting it, it's some kind of slow build-up across the last hundred years or so."

"That's about the size of it," Attila says. "They had this idea that if they could raise the dead, really raise the dead, they could become gods. They sold this idea of the Apocalypse in 1925. Pretty sure they actually believed it."

"I wasn't here for it," Robert says. "I heard they performed some New Year's Eve ritual in 1924."

"At the Blackburn compound in Simi Valley," Attila says. "I think they got gifted that from one of their idiot followers. Clifford something?"

"Dabney," I say. "I got questions about that."

"Willa died the next day," Gabriela says. "They must have known that was going to happen."

"Probably planned it that way. They seem the type."

"How do you know it was there?" Janna says.

"Everyone knew it was there," Attila says. "We could all feel it. They channeled a ridiculous amount of power. They'd been dropping hints of what they were trying to accomplish for weeks. Wasn't difficult to connect the dots."

"I thought it didn't work," Robert says. "Didn't they burn themselves out?"

"Yes," Attila says. "Over the next few weeks things started to fall apart for them. Some of the hold they had on their members was definitely through magic, and suddenly they didn't have any."

"Willa said that the spell was building up energy and that it was going to snap like a rubber band and change things in 1924."

"You spoke to her?"

"Her—not a ghost. I think they trapped her soul, but she didn't seem terribly concerned about it. I'm not really sure. She didn't have a lot of details. Honestly, I think her dogs knew more than she did."

"I'm going to pretend that I understood more than a third of that," Robert says. "You said 1924 is, what, bleeding into your present?"

"The spell's shedding," Janna says. "Like, it's taking the energy it's built up from 1924 and depositing what it doesn't need. How do I know that?"

"It's a really disorienting feeling," Robert says. "But you'll get used to it. Your connection to time is different now. You're going to start perceiving things differently. They won't always be in the same order everyone else sees them."

Janna says nothing for a moment, then abruptly stands up. "Excuse me. I need to—" She doesn't finish the sentence. Instead, she goes to the bathroom and closes the door.

"Should one of us go talk to her?" Amanda says.

"No," Gabriela says. "Give it a little bit. Right now, I expect she's reevaluating her life and trying to figure out how to fit it all together."

"The Blackburns have created a spell that's dumping bodies and locations from 1924 into our present," I say. "Where's all that energy going, then?"

"And what's Jimmy's connection?" Gabriela says. "Is he going to try to use that power somehow?"

"I'm still not clear on what it is," Amanda says.

"There are two things that all these events have had in common," I say.

"Death and time," Gabriela says.

"Right," I say. "I don't know what it wants with all that death energy, but time? Jimmy would absolutely want that. It's already had a device created that lets it influence a couple weeks into the past. With this—fuck, I can't even imagine what it could do."

"That explains him pulling you and Janna together," Amanda says. "Exactly how he plans on using you, I have no idea, but death and time? You're both part of this."

"Figured as much. That reminds me," I say. I pull out the pocket watch and hand it to Robert. "Is this the timepiece you were looking for? Just don't push the button."

He takes it, turns it in his hand a couple of times. "Sonofabitch. How'd you get your hands on it?"

"Miriam," I say. "Wait. I don't think you've met her yet. It was yours. Seems she snagged it from one of the vaults and a couple other items and stashed them for me to find later. She also showed me this room."

"Miriam, huh? No, I don't know anybody named Miriam yet. She say when I got hold of it?"

"No. Until today all I thought it could do was age things really quickly. But then we used this to help Janna sort of focus her magic? Thought we might need to use it to get us here, but she did fine on her own."

"Wait, did you say vault? The ones in the Valley?" Robert says.

"Yeah. I kinda inherited access to it. I think other people can get in, too, but I don't know who."

Janna comes out of the bathroom but stays away from the rest of us, as if proximity would somehow make everything worse. Can't really find a flaw with that logic.

"Oh, it does much more than that," Robert says. To Janna: "This explains how you were able to open a hole to us. You're going to find your abilities coming to you more easily. But until things stabilize, they might be a little unpredictable."

"What does that mean?" Janna says.

"It means when you used it, you got some of its power," Attila says. "I realize you didn't handle it, but you interacted with its magic."

"I've used that thing plenty of times," I say. "Nothing happened to me."

"Because you're not a chronomancer," Robert says.

"It did something to me?" Janna says.

"Nothing bad," Attila says. "Depending on your point of view, I suppose. Think of it as a supercharger. Seems to be a side effect rather than its intended use."

"It was created by a German clockmaker in the fifteenth century named Hans Düringer," Robert says. "He built an astronomical clock in Gdańsk. You can still see it. Impressive piece. It's in Saint Mary's Church. Almost fifty feet tall. But the people who'd hired him to build the clock didn't want him building anything so impressive for anyone else. They decided to blind him."

"Jesus," Janna says. "That's barbaric."

"That's the fifteenth century," Attila says.

"Fortunately, he escaped Gdańsk with his daughter before they could take his eyes and headed to Rostock," Robert says. "It gets a little blurry after that. We know he met a mage, we're assuming a chronomancer, but we're not entirely sure. Together they made this."

"They made a pocket watch in the fifteenth century?" Amanda says. "Wait. Did it used to look different? I found a reference to a timepiece that changes shape to match the times but never quite gets it right. Last I read, it looked like a Henlein watch. Sort of a copper sphere about the size of a golf ball. You flip it open and the watch face is on the inside."

"That would be it," Robert says.

"Over the years it's been a water clock, a candle clock, a sundial, various hourglasses, a few other things," Attila says. Robert hands the watch back to me.

"What exactly does it do?" I say.

"From what we know, the short of it is that it eats time," Attila says. "Stores it a little like a battery. And it can release it, too. It makes time magic easier."

"We're not sure if strengthening a mage's own abilities was what it was designed to do," Robert says. "But it does."

"I wonder if Jimmy can see it," I say. "It can't see me or the opals. I wonder if it's a problem with the amount of power something has."

"Opals? The Australian Stones?" Robert says.

"Is that what they're called?"

"I thought they were all at the bottom of the ocean."

"One of them is keeping an associate of Miz Cortez . . . stable," Attila says. "But I hadn't heard of a second in play."

"Jimmy was using it as a battery for his gizmo. I managed to snag it."

"Then Jimmy got hold of the one inside Joe," Gabriela says. "We got Jimmy's into him before things went from disastrously horrible to catastrophically horrible. Still lost a lot of people."

"According to Jimmy, it can't see the stones," I say.

"And he can't see you because you created him," Attila says. "I think it's a good bet he can't see the watch, but it's not a bet I would make unless I was absolutely sure it would tip the scales."

"How about an Egyptian god in Vegas?" I say.

"A what?" Robert says. He looks at Attila. "Is this one of your spoiler alerts?"

Attila sighs. "Yes. But there's not much point in not telling you. The short of it is that Eric was forced into becoming the

Aztec god of Death, Mictlantecuhtli, and since then he's been on a more-or-less first name basis with a number of other deities."

"Your grandson has moved up in the cosmos," Gabriela says.

I catch Janna staring at me out of the corner of my eye. That's gonna be a fun conversation to have with the conservative Christian turned atheist.

Robert looks at me like he's looking into a mirror. "Our family's really fucked up, isn't it?"

"It's been a ride, that's for sure," I say. "The god in question is Shait. They're a sliver of the god from Egypt who came over in an exhibit of Tutankhamun's and made a home for themselves in Las Vegas. They're in opposition to each other, more or less. Jimmy can't see them either."

"Is that because of their nature or because they're too powerful?" Gabriela says.

"Or because they're a god?" Amanda says.

"Possibly all three," Attila says. "Robert?"

"Power, definitely," he says. "I did a lot of research on Oracles in the early days of the war. The Army wanted anything that could turn the tide. I dissuaded them. With other very powerful items or people, it's like staring into the sun. It's not so much that the Oracle can't see as they can't look."

"Interesting," I say.

"You're thinking again," Gabriela says. "Should I be afraid?"

"I promise it's not about raising the dead. Or me dying again. Well, not exactly. I gotta look into a couple things first." The conversation about death energy with the spell has given me an idea. If it's the way I think it is, I might be able to solve two problems at the same time.

"So, what do we do about it?" Janna says.

"I think we can't do much until Jimmy makes his move," Amanda says, "whatever that happens to be."

"Sounds like it's going to be in one of two places," I say.

"The house in Venice where Willa's stashed or near the adobe in Simi."

"Simi," Gabriela says. "Willa doesn't get moved to Venice until after the first of the year."

"We have a where and a when," I say. "What day is it now? In 1924, I mean. If that has any meaning whatsoever anymore."

"Should be the day after Christmas," Janna says. "The dates were syncing up from that first night. Don't know if that's still the case."

Something about dates syncing up. Then I have it. Shit. "How long have we been here? In this year?"

"One hour, forty-eight minutes, thirteen seconds," Janna and Robert say simultaneously.

"That wasn't disturbing at all," Amanda says. "Is there a problem?"

"When I went into the Harrison I was there for a few minutes. When I came out, hours had passed. If the same is here, it could be a lot later than we think it is out there."

"Could we have missed our window?" Gabriela says.

"No," I say. "Jimmy won't let that happen. It'll find some way to twist things around. That said, we should probably be going. There is one thing we need to figure out, though."

I've been dreading this part of the conversation. It's going to suck no matter what anybody wants.

"Me," Attila says. "Amanda and I talked about it. I can't stay here. This version of me, at least. It could cause too many changes down the line and I don't know what that would do."

"I might not exist," Amanda says.

"You basically have two souls sitting in one body right now," I say. "That's not going to be sustainable. I can separate them easily enough, and I'm pretty sure I could pull you back. But I don't know what that would do."

"I've lived a long time," Attila says. "I think I'm ready to move on. What happens to the me from 1948?"

"You from 1948 is still in there. If I pull your soul out,

you'll probably still remember bits, but I don't know how much. I mean, I'm still getting memories from Mictlantecuhtli and this asshole."

"I think we can work with the memories," Robert says, ignoring me. "Suppress them a little. Minimize the possible changes down the line."

"You realize that you'll die, right? The you that I'm talking to right now. I don't know how it all works with the two of you but I think at some point the different pieces will merge. It's still the same soul."

"I don't understand," Janna says. "Where will it go?"

"No idea," I say. "Where it's supposed to. Some people it's Valhalla, some people it's Heaven. I know of five or six different places that could be considered Hell. I don't know what determines it."

"God doesn't exist?" Magic, time travel, and now questions of faith. Janna's hit the Existential Jackpot.

"He does. Look, it's complicated. And I think we should have this conversation later. With alcohol." I turn to Amanda. "Are you okay with this?"

Amanda looks at me, surprised. "No," she says. "But it's not my call."

"All due respect to your dad, here, yes, it is," I say. "I'm not doing this if you say no. You're the one left behind. You're the one who's got to grieve.

"I do this, you very well might hate me. It's happened before. Which is fine. I'll take that hit if it helps you deal. But I need to know you're okay with this enough for me to do it."

"What happens if I say no?"

"He'll stay like this and, I don't really know. Two souls that are essentially the same sitting in one body? I don't think it can last. It'll probably kill him. Today, tomorrow, seventy years from now, I don't know."

Gabriela touches Amanda's shoulder and Amanda grabs her hand tight. "Yes," she says, tears forming around her eyes. "Let's do it."

Chapter 28

It doesn't take long. Amanda, Attila, and I go into the bedroom and Attila lies down. I don't know if it will hurt, so Amanda puts a sleep spell on him after telling him she loves him.

She sits by his side holding his hand, and I slowly, as gently as I can, pry apart the two souls inside his body. I did something like this to a friend who was dying slow and hard. His granddaughter asked me to. I'm glad I did it, but it was tough.

"Hey," I say. "Gimme your hand." I can show people the ghost side from here if I want to. This doesn't seem like it would be any different.

"Is that him?" she says.

"Yeah," I say.

I lift his soul out of his body. Souls always look so fragile. I've destroyed a few of them. They all look like nets of gold filigree. Some more complex than others. Attila's has patterns in it that would give Escher a headache.

"It's beautiful," Amanda says.

"All the ones I've seen are," I say. "Even from the worst people. But this is the most complex one I've ever seen."

"That's good," she says. "Souls should be beautiful. Even from the ugliest of us."

"You ready?"

"As ready as I think I can ever be." She reaches out to touch it but stops short. Instead, she leans down and kisses Attila's forehead. "Goodbye, Daddy. I love you."

I let go. It floats over my hand like it's caught in a gentle current, then dissolves into motes of light and disappears.

I almost say, "Hope I got the right one," but she wouldn't appreciate the joke. Hey, I can grow.

I go to the door and open it a crack. Gabriela is right outside, waiting. I open it to let her in and step out after her. This isn't a place for me. My part's over. Now the hard bit begins.

"She okay?" Janna says.

I shrug. "As okay as she can be, I guess. How about you? How you holding up?"

Janna looks at Robert and I in turn. "Honestly, seeing two of you is freaking me out more than anything else at this point."

"If it helps, it's freaking me out a little, too," I say.

The bedroom door opens and Gabriela and Amanda step out. Amanda is dry-eyed with a warrior's gaze. I've seen it before. I have a feeling that when we get back her uncle is in for a world of hurt.

"Let's get out of here," she says. "I'd like to leave before he wakes up."

Robert gets us back to Union Station the same way we arrived, through a portal that was apparently built into the room. Wish I'd known about that. Would have made getting in and out of that little bolthole a lot easier.

Union Station is just as busy as before. It was the most important transportation hub Los Angeles had. LAX would only have started commercial flights a few years ago, and flying was a luxury.

"Do you think you'll need the watch?" I say. Janna shakes her head.

"Kinda wish I did, but no, I'm good." She turns to Robert and unexpectedly hugs him. "Thank you. The talk helped. And, uh, sorry about the chokehold."

"Believe me, I've had less beautiful women do far worse." Janna blushes a little. "If you need to or just want to, you know where you can find me. Or when, rather."

Oh, for fuck sake. "We good to go?" I say.

"Not yet," Robert says. "I know you think you know me. And to an extent you do. And from what I understand from Attila, you and I are not that different. I know I was, will be, not a great parent. I hope that whatever damage I'll do won't stain you too much."

"No worse than simply being me," I say. "I don't even remember you snapping when I resurrected a dead frog. I think it was a frog. Maybe a duck? I don't remember. Miriam told me about it, who by the way is a fucking treasure and you better remember that. Anyway, point is you can't fuck me up anymore than I fucked myself up."

"Does your dad hate me?"

"I think hate's a strong word," I say. "He never talked about you much."

"Talked. Past tense."

"Yeah. He and our mom both. I hunted down the guy who killed them. There were repercussions. I left L.A. for a long time. My sister died a few years ago because of me. There's been a lot of violence."

"I'm sorry to hear that," he says. "From what Attila's told me and what I've learned tonight, I know that you've been at the center of a lot of momentous, sometimes terrible things. For what it's worth, I'm glad I met you. And I'm very proud of you. Go fix things." He nods toward Gabriela. "And don't let that one go. Trust me on this."

I was not expecting that. "I'm not going to hug any man with a mustache like that," I say. "General rule. Sorry. Oh."

I pull a sharpie and a sticker from my messenger bag, and root around until I find a folded-up napkin with a phone number. I copy it to the sticker.

"Hang onto that," I say. "You're going to set up a phone line in a few years for Miriam with that number and leave a cocktail napkin from Kelbo's for me to find."

"Kelbo's? Tiki Bar on Pico?"

"That or the one on Fairfax." He pockets the sticker.

"I'll make certain of it. And I won't ask what 'Hello, My Name Is' is supposed to mean." He puts out his hand and after a beat of uncertainty I shake it. "Goodbye and good luck."

I feel Janna build her spell. It seems to be taking less time and less strain on her. A flare of magic and that feeling of a soap bubble bursting around us and we're back. Union Station, empty, in the dark, the sounds of conversation and the echoing clatter of footsteps still ringing in my ears.

My phone buzzes. Danny. The phone hasn't caught up with the local time yet, so I don't know how long ago he texted.

"How long have we been gone?"

"Four hours, thirteen minutes, twelve seconds," Janna says. She frowns. "Shouldn't it be longer?"

"I would think so, yeah. I was in the Harrison only a few minutes and it was something like four or five hours later when came back out. I would have expected most of a day had gone by, at least."

"What's Danny got to say?" Gabriela says.

"Seems Rachel is outside with a couple squads of pissed-off mercenaries. Twenty people, maybe?"

"What do we do?" Janna says.

"I'll go out and talk to her," I say. "I'm the only one we're sure Jimmy absolutely needs." Not entirely true. I could be here in order to make something else happen before whatever the main event turns out to be.

"How did she know where we were?" Janna says.

"Jimmy, undoubtedly. Just because it can't see me doesn't mean it can't figure out where I am. It might not know what we were doing, though."

"I'm less worried about how and more about why," Gabriela says. "They already have the stone."

I'm about to say something but it all flies out of my head as everything distorts around me like a wave passing through the world. Amanda and Gabriela don't seem to notice, but it takes Janna and I to our knees.

"What the fuck was that?" Janna says.

"What was what?" Gabriela says. "Are you okay?"

"Reality quake," I say.

"Fuck," Amanda says. "It's what happens when changes are made in the past and they catch up to the present. Eric felt it because of his connection to Jimmy and presumably you did because of your connection to time."

"What changed?"

"Don't know," I say, "but I got a couple ideas. I had some leverage on Rachel to get her out of our hair. I think I've been outplayed. I think Jimmy made a change two weeks ago that basically kept what I had going from even happening."

"Do I want to know what it is?" Gabriela says.

"You might not like it."

I text Danny.

> Coming out. When I scratch my head you start dropping her support team.

I get a thumbs up emoji in response.

"I'm going to go out there, Danny's going to start evening the odds. Once the gunfire starts, come out swinging."

"Do we care about keeping her alive?" Gabriela says.

"I can't think of a reason to. But let's make sure she's dead. Last time didn't stick."

"Remember," Gabriela says.

"Don't die. I got it."

I pull one of the doors open and step outside. Rachel's leaning against the hood of a Jeep Wrangler, an M-4 carbine slung across her chest with her finger resting just above the trigger. She's in all-black BDUs with a black Kevlar vest.

The parking lot lights hide most of her face in shadow, but I can still see the half-sneer her mouth has burned into it and her once-thick red hair is shot through with streaks of white and patches where I can see her scarred scalp.

"The lighting here suits you," I say. "Still really fuckin' ugly, though."

"Yeah, well, I got you to thank for that, don't I?" She has a couple dozen people with her scattered around the lot. Mean-looking motherfuckers.

"Happy to oblige. Jimmy do his hop-to-the-past trick and get your boy outta Dodge before I could grab him?"

"That's what he tells me. I don't remember it. But then, I wouldn't. You really did that?"

"I really did. Or I guess I didn't. Since he's been gone for, what, a couple weeks now?"

"Just about."

"Did Jimmy promise to keep your boy safe if you came to work for it?"

"Only thing I've ever cared about, Eric. I'll do anything for him."

"Yeah, I guess you will. So, what are you doing here? Jimmy's got an opal, your kid's safe and sound, I'm drawing a blank."

"I've come to collect you. You and the cop."

"Might have to narrow that down a little. Lotta cops in L.A."

"Your cop friend. Does that help?"

"Weirdly, no. Who'da thunk a guy like me could be friends with police officers. Hell, I've got a bigger kill count than all the LAPD combined for, Christ, I don't even know how many years. Not for their lack of trying, of course."

"The one that's with you."

"What's their name?"

"Didn't get a name," Rachel says.

"That doesn't sound like you. You like having as much information as possible. You didn't get a name? Or did Jimmy not know the name?"

"Jimmy knows everything," she says.

"Yeah, it likes people to believe that. I think that what happened was Jimmy did know the name but then something happened. And now it doesn't."

"I don't know what you're talking about."

"Yeah, you really don't, do you?" I say, and scratch just above my ear. "Might as well get this over with."

Gunfire from the roof. It's suppressed but still loud as fuck. Four of her people drop in the first half-second. Three more go down before they realize what's happening and return fire.

By that time Gabriela and Amanda have come out, shields raised. Amanda turns one of the mercenaries to glass, and Gabriela makes snakes burst out of another one's stomach.

Rachel and I don't move. Chaos all around us, but we're

locked in, each waiting for the other to make a move. I don't get a chance to.

Janna comes out of the building, her eyes swirling with that lava-lamp glow. She starts walking toward us.

"I think you mean this cop," I say.

"Shit," Rachel says. "I was hoping you'd just get in the van, but you have to make everything difficult, don't you?" She raises her gun and fires a single round at Janna. Low enough to wound, but not kill. Only Janna's not there.

Rachel blinks. This is not something that happens to her. Like Danny, she's a combat mage. She hits what she wants to hit, whether she was aiming at it or not.

Janna keeps walking toward us. Rachel fires. Janna isn't there. It's like she's moved at just the right time and in the right way for the bullet to miss.

And then I get it. That's exactly what she's doing. She can see the shot before it happens and not be where she shouldn't be when it does.

That doesn't seem very sporting. But that's okay, this isn't, either. I draw my gun and shoot Rachel. Two rounds hit her in the chest, knocking her back across the Jeep's hood. The look of shock on her face is priceless.

She recovers fast, though, and unloads a burst of fire right at me. My shield catches most of the bullets, but it's Rachel we're talking about here. There's at least half a dozen ensorcelled rounds in her magazine. A bullet tears a furrow through my left side along the ribcage, my tats doing their job and deflecting it as best they can, but goddamn that's gonna leave a mark.

But then Janna's on her. She grabs the gun with one hand, undoes the buckle attaching it to the sling with the other, and throws the gun away. Rachel goes in for a palm strike, but finds only empty air. Janna has sidestepped and delivers a vicious kick to the side of Rachel's knee that drops her to the pavement.

Down, not out. Rachel's had to deal with worse, I'm sure. She rolls, comes up onto her good leg right inside Janna's guard, and slashes out with a serrated blade you could probably saw through bones with.

Janna's learning fast, but she's still learning. She doesn't get away in time and takes a slash across her belly. Fortunately, it doesn't look too bad. She was already moving when she got hit.

I've already sealed the wound in my side as I run up, manifesting the straight razor in my hand. Rachel's focused on Janna. She doesn't notice me until I've taken her arm off above the elbow.

Rachel screams, blood spurting out of the stump of her arm. She turns enough to see it, then falls against the Jeep's hood.

"That was for Lucas," I say. Janna has stepped away from us, shocked out of whatever temporal fugue she was in. Good. This is going to get messy.

"Dammit, Eric," she says, gritting her teeth through the pain. "I had to. It was the only way."

"The only way to what? Tie you to Jimmy for the rest of your life? Because you know that's where this was going, right? You step out of line, displease your master, and your son has an 'accident.'"

"What was I supposed to do? You think he could live this life? You saw him. You know what he went through."

"You know what else I saw?" I say. "I saw photos of Lucas's kid and how fucking proud he was to be a father. I saw dozens of dead men and women shot in the back, taken by surprise because Rachel's part of the family. She couldn't do anything bad. Hell, they tried to protect you because they thought you were a target, not the killer. This is for them."

She raises her remaining arm to ward off the razor, but that just makes it easier because I wanted that arm anyway. This time I slice through just behind the wrist. She grits her teeth to hold in the scream.

"I want to know something," I say, "before you bleed out on the pavement here and I piss on your corpse. Why the Twins? You tortured them. Why?"

"You want to know the reason? I wasn't their friend." She's gritting her teeth, sweating from the pain. "They were fucking freaks. Everybody in that place was. I hated them. Every single, fucking, sick one of them. When we were doing jobs for the Twins I liked their money, but I fucking hated them."

"Do you have any idea what you put them through?"

She laughs. "Of course I do. Why the fuck do you think I did it? I hated them. What the hell even were they? Men, women? Human? I don't fucking know. You tell me. What the hell were they?"

I want to make sure I'm the last thing she sees. I take the top of her head off just above the eyes, the look of surprise frozen on her face. Her body tilts and falls to the ground.

"Something more beautiful than you could possibly understand."

Chapter 29

"Are you okay?" I say to Janna. The front of her shirt is completely soaked with blood.

"It doesn't seem too bad," she says, "but I'm feeling a little woozy."

"We'll get you stitched up. In the meantime, this should hold you." I clot the blood in the wound. She gasps as it seals up. Should have warned her it might hurt.

Gabriela and Amanda come over, both of them looking a little disheveled. Gabriela in particular is spattered with blood and carrying a glowing blue machete.

"You two all right?"

"There were a couple mages," Amanda says. She looks absolutely exhausted. "Stronger than I was prepared for."

"Best fight I've had in a long time," Gabriela says. She's beaming, energized. Her machete evaporates.

God, that's hot.

"Holy shit, chica," Danny says, hopping down from the roof of the building. "That was some damn fine footwork."

"I didn't see," Gabriela says.

"I could see where she was going to strike and I made sure I wasn't there," Janna says. She looks down at her bloody shirt. "Mostly."

"What did Rachel want?" Danny says.

"She was here to collect me and 'the cop,'" I say. "Seems Jimmy didn't give her your name."

"But he knows my name," Janna says.

"I think it *knew* your name," I say. "And when you started throwing around time magic, in its mind you stopped being you."

"He forgot who she was?" Danny says.

"He can't see her," Gabriela says.

"Don't know for sure, but I think so," I say.

"Did she say where she was supposed to take you?" Amanda says.

"No," I say. "I figure it's somewhere she could do whatever it is Jimmy wants us for. Or Rachel was becoming more troublesome than she was worth. I'm thinking the latter."

"Let's take this somewhere else," Amanda says. "I'm about to pass out and I need—I just need to go home. Everyone's welcome to stay. God knows I have plenty of room."

"Thanks, but I'll pass," Danny says. "I gotta get my gear cleaned. Never know when I'll get a chance to shoot more motherfuckers in the face. Goddamn that was fun."

"Right?" Gabriela says. They high five each other.

"What about the bodies?" Janna says.

"We can let Tish know about them," I say. "Not much point, though. I guarantee they're dealing with bigger shit."

"I suppose you're right. I should get home. I—Shit, my car's back at the shelter."

Amanda opens a portal to her estate in its own pocket universe. Through the portal I can see the view looking out from one of the balconies of her Neuschwanstein fairytale castle.

"You live there?" Janna says.

"I do. Coming?"

"Fuck yes." She winces. "But I think I need to go get stitches first."

"We'll get you taken care of," Amanda says.

"You have a doctor?"

"Sort of," I say. "When it's not trying to murder you."

"Ignore him," Amanda says. "I do."

A knock on the door. It's an impressive door. Thick oak, tall, with a decorative jamb that curves up into an arch.

The rest of the room is just as grandiose. Four-poster,

curtained bed, a vanity you'd need a crane to move. Everything out of a fairy tale. I half expect to see talking mice.

"It's open," I say. I'm sitting on the bed putting a salve on the bullet wound. It was too wide and shallow to bother with stitches. A graze sucks less than having a bullet in me, but it's still not fun.

Gabriela pokes her head in. "You decent?"

"I'm not even respectable. Come on in." She steps inside, leans against the door jamb. She sighs and closes her eyes.

"Amanda?"

"She's finally asleep," she says. "Before, she could sort of pretend he wasn't gone. Now she knows for sure and, fuck, she feels so alone. I don't know what to do for her."

"Listen," I say. "Be there. Make sure she knows it. Above all, be patient. Believe me, you hang around enough dead people, you see a lot of people grieving. She might go a little crazy."

I try to get a bandage over the wound but it keeps flopping over. Gabriela sits next to me on the bed and takes the bandage from me. She gets it set right, smooths out the tape.

"Crazy?" she says.

"Lashing out, being impulsive. Letting her anger and grief make her decisions for her. She has a pretty good lock on things, though."

"Crazy," she says. "Like trying to bring back a dead necromancer who's turned into a god?"

"Definite possibility. That's her, how about you?"

"I've never been on this side of things," she says. "I want to help. I also want her to get over it. I know she can't and I know it's a dick thing to think, but I do."

"Bringing some shit up for you, is it?" I say.

She doesn't say anything for a long moment. "At what point did you lose count of the people you'd killed?"

I haven't thought about this in years, but the memory comes through like it happened yesterday.

"I forget the date, but it was winter. South Dakota.

Snowing and fucking cold. I was with Danny. We were hunting a wendigo. It'd been tearing through one of those pop-up oil towns that house workers and their families on the rigs and pipelines.

"Every few nights it would take one of them. When it snagged somebody's kid they called in a bunch of hunters. Most of them never made it back out. Danny got called and I went with him."

"Don't wendigos hunt with some kind of mind control?" Gabriela says.

"Yeah, crude. It's like really loud suggestion. Easy to ignore if you know what it feels like. Otherwise it can make people do impulsive shit they wouldn't otherwise. Makes its prey come to it. Turns out it can also convince an entire town that you're the monster they need to kill."

"Oh, no."

"Yeah. They followed Danny and I out to one of the oil rigs. There were a few hundred of them, I think. Danny set explosives on the rig and I lured them over. Got close enough, I hit the detonator and slid over to the other side. Even over there I felt their deaths.

"Almost knocked me out. If it had I would have been fucked because I'd just created a whole buttload of new ghosts and they were already looking hungry. I have no idea how many I killed. A lot. You?"

"Not quite like that," she says. "A town in Mexico. Cartel run. Filled with toxic masculinity and testosterone poisoning. You know the type. I was seventeen and passing through. A couple guys decided they wanted a 'date' when I was trying to get some lunch."

"They must have been surprised when you turned them down," I say.

"They were. I melted the skin off their bones in front of about twenty people. All of a sudden they're screaming 'Bruja' and running for the doors."

"Torches and pitchforks?"

"AKs and hand grenades, actually. They were between me and the road out of town. I don't know who was left once I got out of there."

"How'd you feel about it?"

"Angry. Angry that they made me do that. They just wouldn't stop. Wouldn't listen to me. It's never gotten easier."

"No, it hasn't," I say. "Even after I spent time in Mictlan and have a better idea of what death can mean, it's still tough. I figure when I need to, the best I can do is make it quick."

"That fucking head," Gabriela says. "That thing has caused nothing but misery, hasn't it?"

"Guy I know called it what happens when a monkey's paw fucks a hand grenade. I think that's about right."

"How do we kill him?"

"I honestly don't know. I've been going through the spellbook and the best I can think of is to never have made it in the first place."

"You think he actually sent Rachel to bring you and Janna in?"

"No," I say. "I think it sent her so we'd kill her for it. I'm not sure why it's doing it, though."

"Cleaning house?" she says.

"Now that's an interesting thought. But why is it cleaning house? Jimmy's not going to do it just to do it."

"He's removing potential obstacles," Amanda says. She stands in the doorway, wearing what I've thought of as her Xena Warrior Princess look: steely gaze, don't-fuck-with-me posture. But she's also in a thick robe with bags under her eyes. "Right now, you're a wild card. You and Janna both. Wild cards are only as good as the other cards in play make them."

"You are supposed to be asleep," Gabriela says.

"It didn't last," Amanda says. "Obviously."

"It's trying to get rid of anyone we could have as allies?" I say. "I'm not sure Rachel qualifies."

"He probably saw some scenario where she might be," Amanda says.

Is that why so many people have died? They knew about Jimmy and might have been people we could use to influence things? That makes sense. It made changes that affected the avatars of Las Vegas. They shift around so often it didn't take much. But it couldn't do anything to Shait. Probably somewhere between it not able to see them and not being able to reach back far enough to have an impact.

"Why hasn't it made a move on the two of us?" Gabriela says.

"We were useful," Amanda says. "We helped get rid of Rachel. We still are. What happens if either one of us goes down?"

"I'll go to the ends of the Earth to find a way to rip Jimmy apart piece by piece," I say. "It wants to piss me off, but not so much that I'll really fly into a rage."

"I think it's more that you'd fuck everything up for him just out of spite," Amanda says. "You almost let Darius loose from his bottle simply to prove a point because a bunch of assholes were insisting you sacrifice yourself. I think Jimmy's treading carefully here."

"You think his plan's that fragile?" Gabriela says.

"Yes," Amanda says. "Everything we know points to a plan someone else set in motion that has who-knows-how-many moving parts to it. He can plan all he wants, but the more complex a system, the easier it is to break. And when the people he needs are ones he can't even see, he's got to be really careful to keep control."

"Easy to break, but I can't go in there swinging a sledgehammer," I say. "That's something I might normally do. It would have adjusted for that, have some way to counter it."

"There's going to be a lot of improvisation," Amanda says. "Now, who wants coffee?"

"Hang on," I say. "I want to get this out here before we don't have a chance. Whatever you're dealing with, however you are with it, know we've got your back."

She gives us a smile that looks genuinely happy. "I know. Thank you. Now let's go get some caffeine and figure out a way to kill this thing."

We find Janna sipping coffee in a kitchen that looks out onto snowcapped mountains. "Sorry," she says. "There was coffee already made and cups so—"

"You are welcome to it," Amanda says. "Really, don't worry about it. You're a guest. If you need anything, ask Bigsby, the butler who helped you last night, and he'll get it for you."

"Thanks. Are those real?" she says, nodding toward the mountains.

"Partly," Amanda says. "The property doesn't go as far out as you can see, but where it does, they're there. Same with the height. We're high up, but we're not Bavarian Alps high."

"I'm sorry about your dad," she says.

"Thanks," she says. "But deep down I already knew he was gone. How's your stomach?"

"That butler of yours is really good with a needle and thread. It looks like it's almost healed, actually."

"It should be," Amanda says. "Bigsby's able to speed up the healing process."

"He also gave me a room and said it wouldn't be a problem if I destroyed it practicing magic, in case I screwed it up."

"Did you?" I say. "Screw it up, I mean."

"Couple times. Accidentally turned the bed into a really shitty antique. And there's a hand mirror, but I can't tell if I aged it so much it disintegrated or if it went backward so far it turned back into sand."

"Try anything with the watch?"

"That thing scares me."

"It should," I say. "But if anybody can get a handle on how it works, I'm betting on you. Use it in good health."

"You're not giving it to me, are you?"

"Sure," I say. "The fuck am I gonna do with it?"

"Thanks," she says. "I think. I know we need to figure out this whole mess but when it's over, can I—Shit, I dunno, pick your brains on this?"

"Gabriela's probably your best bet on that," I say.

"Nuh uh," Gabriela says. "She's your apprentice."

"The fuck she is. If anything she's Tish's."

"How much has Letitia taught you?" Amanda says.

"Fuck all," Janna says.

"And Eric?"

"Almost everything I know."

"It's settled," Amanda says. "She's your apprentice."

"This is going to end badly, you realize," I say.

"Absolutely," Amanda says. "And yet you're still the best candidate for the job."

"Jesus. That's scary. Fine. But later. Right now we need to figure out what to do about Jimmy."

"What's the best guess on what he's trying to do?" Amanda says.

"It has something to do with time magic," I say. "I'm thinking to get rid of any constraints on his abilities to go into the past. And there's something with necromancy. Best I can figure, the spell is designed to bring Willa back to life. But fuck if I know what Jimmy could use it for."

Janna's face goes a little slack and her eyes turn into multi-colored lava lamps. "It's tainted," she says.

"She do this often?" Amanda says.

"Don't know. I don't think 'often' is something that applies to her yet."

"The time is tainted with death," she says. "It's useless if it's not separated." Of course. That's why he needs both of us. Pieces start to fall into place.

"Oh, shit. I think I know what Jimmy's trying to do," I say. "And how it's going to do it."

Chapter 30

"You think Jimmy could get in here?" Janna says, looking nervously at the sky. We're surrounded by high peaks, walking along the shore of a clear mountain lake.

"Oh yeah," I say. "I mean, it wouldn't be here on its own or maybe even be here at all, it'd send a proxy like Rachel, or cause some kind of accident."

"But he won't because . . ."

"No point. Jimmy doesn't need to come to us, we're going to Jimmy."

"But we know he's doing something," she says.

"Yeah, which I think is part of the plan. Okay, the book on the Blackburn Cult that Danny and I found? I thought Nicole put it there for us to find. But now I think Rachel put it there on Jimmy's orders."

She thinks about it. Picks up a stone from the shore, throws it sidearm into the lake, where it skips a few times before sinking.

"It was a breadcrumb," she says. "If you hadn't found it, we wouldn't know about the spell and who was behind it."

I pick up my own stone, a thin, flat rock that looks perfect. I throw it out. Eight skips. Might be a record for me.

"Right," I say. "We might have figured it out eventually, but Jimmy deals in certainties. It doesn't gamble if it can help it. It sets up a path of events that inevitably leads where it wants to go. Getting Gabriela's soul trapped so I had to go find it and get it out of a vault in Vegas, for example."

I've been wondering about the book for a while now. Conceivably, Nicole could have left it for me to find, but Jimmy couldn't control her actions. It could influence events that would force a particular action, but that's not the same thing.

It's felt awfully convenient. And convenient feels awfully Jimmy.

"Why do you keep calling Jimmy 'it'?" she says. "I thought he was a person. Everybody else is calling him, well, him."

"I used to," I say. "When everybody around me saw the Oracle as a thing, imagining it was like some sort of Magic 8-Ball. But it started off as a person, so that's what I thought of it as. Now everybody else seems to think of it as a person and I'm the one who thinks it's a thing.

"Its old handler, Nicole, who created it with me, summed it up really well, and I didn't see it for what it was for a while after. She was telling me about how there are side effects to the things Jimmy makes happen. One time, to win a bet for someone, the side effect was crashing a jumbo jet and killing everybody on board."

"Jesus. What the hell was the bet?"

"I don't remember. Something like making sure a football team won a tournament. Something stupid like that. I asked Nicole if Jimmy felt any remorse about what it had done, and she said, 'Jimmy doesn't feel.' And that's the thing. Jimmy doesn't feel. It's an object. An artifact. I couldn't even tell you what it wants. Does it want like a person? With goals and hopes? Or does it want like a shark? Nothing but unending hunger? Hell, does it want in a way you and I could even understand? I don't know."

"Was it something that needed to happen?"

"Needed? I don't know," I say. "It just did. Like, maybe the most convenient future that had all the things Jimmy wanted happened to be one where an airplane crashed."

"It killed someone for my dad," she says. "To get him that liver. Didn't it?"

"Yeah. Probably did something like having somebody's car keys moved a little to the left so they fall behind a desk. Makes them a couple minutes later going through an intersection than they would have been. Plows into a motorcycle ridden by a guy who just happens to be a match for your dad."

"It killed a man with just a twitch."

"Twitch is all you need most times. Pulling a trigger's just a twitch, too."

"We're not just out here taking in the fake, bracing mountain air, are we?" Janna says.

"No. Wanted to talk to you alone. Or as alone as we can be with the estate watching, but probably safer than anywhere else. Amanda's dad. Do you understand what happened to him?"

"Better than I want to," she says. "You could have pulled his soul back. I could have, which blows my mind. I mean, I know we would do it differently, but the fact is that I could see how. I still don't understand why we didn't."

"You'll have to talk to Amanda about that. But the spell that put him there, think you could recreate it? Do the same thing with a soul and pull it back?"

"Like I said, I understand it better than I want to. It's funny. You call it a spell and to me it doesn't feel any more complicated than tying my shoes or throwing a ball. Do you get that?"

"Yeah. It's like that for a lot of people's knacks. I don't try to see ghosts. I just do."

"I understand why you don't want to say it out loud, but I think I know what you're planning. I can . . . see it? I don't know that it will work. There will be consequences."

"Good or bad?"

Janna shrugs. "Both. Neither. I can't tell."

"Willa said the same thing. What was it? Something like if you mend a cracked cup the crack is still there."

"Yeah," Janna says. "That sounds about right. We're going to need to stop the spell before we can stop Jimmy."

"I kinda figured," I say. "Can you see why?"

"It's fuzzy. But he needs time. The death will make it useless for him."

"I'm honestly more concerned about keeping Gabriela and Amanda safe."

"They will be," Janna says. "I've got that covered. I think."

There's a pop of displaced air and Bigsby, Amanda's pseudo-butler, appears in front of us. He's the epitome of old English gentility. Only he's part of the house, servant, security system, occasional homicidal maniac.

"Excuse me, ma'am, sir. But Miss Amanda requests your presence in the drawing room. Shall I bring you there?"

"I'll walk, thanks," Janna says. She looks up at the castle high above us. "Part of the way, at least."

"Of course, ma'am," Bigsby says. "Sir?"

"You want company?" I say.

"No, I need to think some things through," Janna says.

"Then I'll see you in the drawing room," I say. "Bigsby, let's go."

"Of course, sir." And we're gone.

Janna joins us about ten minutes later in a room that probably didn't exist before a few minutes ago, porting in with Bigsby at her side.

"That's a really steep hill," she says.

"Could have gotten you a carriage," Amanda says.

"Is it shaped like a pumpkin?" Janna says.

"No, but it is drawn by sparkly crystal unicorns that put a Lisa Frank notebook to shame."

"Oh, hell yes," Janna says. "I'll remember that. This is a drawing room?"

It doesn't really look like one. You expect a Victorian salon with chairs, teas, maybe a fainting couch. This is more of a conference room with a long table in the middle, chairs pushed to the side.

"Pretty much any room that doesn't have a specific purpose gets called a drawing room," Amanda says. She unrolls a large map onto the table showing a group of buildings, a chapel, dorms, stables.

"This is an architectural drawing of the Blackburn compound," Amanda says.

"It looks rough," Janna says. "Where did you get it?"

"Friend of mine does automatic drawing," Amanda says. "She goes into a trance and pulls images out of the past."

"It's accurate?"

"She's got about a ninety-five percent hit rate," Amanda says. "Anyway, this is the spot I wanted to point out." She taps a circle behind the main house.

"Firepit?" Janna says.

"Ritual circle," I say. "That's where they'll . . . that's where they did the ritual that got all this started."

"Okay," Gabriela says. "Why are we looking at this?"

"We're gonna party like it's 1924."

"You have a plan," Gabriela says.

"I do."

"And you're not going to tell us what it is."

"I am not. I made a mistake telling Rachel about her kid and she went to Jimmy and basically had it erased."

"What did you do to her kid?" Amanda says.

"Had somebody I know Jimmy can't see pick him up. Idea was to sit on him a few days and force Rachel to back the hell off."

"And instead, she talked to Jimmy, who went into the past and stopped you?" Gabriela says.

"Sort of," I say. "Hid him before I could get to him, effectively erasing what I'd done because he wasn't where he would be for me to grab him."

"That was the reality quake last night," Janna says.

"I can't even feel those things and I hate them," Amanda says. "Okay, what can you tell us?"

"I need to get us to 1924 in Simi," Janna says. "Why did they do this in Simi? Isn't that girl buried under a house in Venice?"

"Not for a few weeks after she died," Gabriela says. "I don't know if there's a particular significance to it being Simi beyond proximity to the adobe. Might just be because that's where they had the space."

"How many people are we looking at?"

"At least May and Ruth. Not sure how many others, though. At the time they had not quite thirty members that I could find," Gabriela says. "At least two of them, May and Ruth, are mages."

"Probably more," Amanda says. "My dad told me L.A. was crawling with them in the twenties and thirties."

"We're supposed to go in blind," Gabriela says. "Get into a fight with a few dozen people, two or more mages, so you and Janna can go do whatever it is you need to do? And you're not going to tell us what it is."

"No, we're going in blind," I say. " This is going to be me and Janna. You and Amanda are hanging out here. We're the ones Jimmy needs."

"The fuck we are," Gabriela says.

"You need to," I say. "I need you to. This won't work otherwise."

"Why?"

"If I don't think the two of you are safe I'm not going to be able to do what I have to do."

"Goddammit, Eric, I'm not some damsel you have to protect."

"I know that," I say.

"If this doesn't work," Janna says, "the results could be catastrophic."

"Catastrophic how?" Gabriela says.

"Us never having existed catastrophic," she says. "What Eric should have opened with is that we need an anchor to now. It will keep all of us safe. Safer, at least."

Gabriela clenches her hands, working to keep her anger under control. "I suppose if it works, you'll tell us later," she says.

"While we get very, very drunk," I say.

"I still don't like this."

"Nobody likes this," Amanda says. "But Janna seems to have a good idea of what's going on."

"Or she's lying through her teeth."

"Why would I do that?" Janna says.

"You wouldn't," Gabriela says. "I just don't like being sidelined."

"You're not being sidelined," I say.

"Then what am I?"

"Load bearing support," Amanda says.

"What?"

"Not every role is running up to slay the dragon," Amanda says. To Janna: "I take it this isn't just hopes and prayers on our part?"

"No," Janna says. "I—I don't know how to explain it. Give me your hands." Amanda does immediately. Gabriela takes a few seconds, glaring at me the entire time.

Janna's eyes go all glowy lava-lamp. There's a pulse of magic, but not strong as far as I can tell.

"Is that it?" Amanda says. "I don't feel anything."

"I think," Janna says. She turns to me. "Is there anything we need?"

"Need to make one stop," I say.

"Where am I sending you?" Amanda says.

"Strip mall on Normandie near Eighth. Need to talk to the ex-wife."

"Somebody actually married you?" Janna says.

"Oh, I like you," Gabriela says, laughing.

"Fuck both of ya. It's complicated," I say.

We're standing outside a strip mall on Normandie Avenue in front of a botanica with a sign above the doors that reads *Santuario De La Santa Muerte*. To one side is a coin-op laundry. On the other, a Chinese fast-food place. They do a pretty decent orange chicken.

"Your ex-wife is a priestess for Santa Muerte?" Janna says.

"No," I say. "Come on. Let's see if we can get an audience."

"Audience?"

I push my way through the doors. There are a few people inside looking at prayer candles, statuettes of Santa Muerte anywhere from five inches to five feet tall. A man at the counter notices us and straightens, eyes snapping wide. He bows his head as I walk up to him.

"My Lord," he says.

"Don't do that," I say. "You know I'm not."

"You may believe that," he says. "No one else does."

"Not even your Lady?" I say.

"I would not know Her thoughts."

"Yeah, well, she's pissed off at me and I need to talk to her. Anybody inside?"

"The temple's empty. Go ahead."

"Much obliged."

Janna and I head over to a door in the back of the shop. "What language were you speaking?" she says.

"Nahuatl. I forget I'm doing it sometimes."

The door opens onto a temple space with pews, a podium, white Christmas lights and sheets of black tulle hung from the walls. At the head of the room stands a seven-foot-tall statue of Santa Muerte with a dented brass plate at her feet holding half-smoked cigars, rum, bullets, and a nickel-plated .38.

"Are we meeting her here?" Janna says looking around. "Where is she?"

I'm sure Janna's LAPD training is kicking into gear with the Satanic Panic level of paranoia regarding Santa Muerte. It's amazing the disinformation being spread about her. Not that she isn't worshipped by a lot of cartel folks, and how they see her influences who she is, but that's just one small part of her.

"She's right there," I say. Janna stares at me, then at the statue.

"Is this a joke?"

"No, Detective Benson, it is not a joke." Janna whips around to see a petite Korean-American woman sitting in the front pew.

"You're Asian."

"Part of me was," Muerte says. "I'm an amalgam of several

things. Santa Muerte, the Aztec goddess Mictecacihuatl, and this woman, Tabitha Cheung. How all that happened is a pretty involved story."

"This is your wife?"

"Ex-wife," I say.

"I'm having trouble with this," Janna says. "You're telling me a short Asian woman in her, what, twenties, is the Grim Reaper?"

"Oh, no," Muerte says, laughing. "My form as Santa Muerte owes a lot to the Grim Reaper, yes. The Spanish brought him over here. But he and I are very different things. I thought seeing me like this at first might make things a little easier for you. Perhaps I should have shown up like this instead."

Muerte's body stretches as flesh melts away from her bones and a white wedding dress and veil flow out from nowhere to drape over her skeletal frame. In a few seconds she's an eight-foot-tall skeleton bride carrying a sickle in one hand and a globe of the world in another.

"Is this better?" Muerte says, her voice deeper with more reverb than usual.

"Cut that the fuck out," I say. "One, you're not scaring her. Two, you're wasting all our time. And three, you're being an asshole."

In a blink, Tabitha is back. She and Janna are staring at each other. I don't know which one's going to blink first and I don't really care.

"We're here for a reason," I say. "How's my better half doing?"

"Still Asleep," Muerte says. "More so, in fact. Mictlan wants you back. It's getting harder to maintain. Any progress?"

"Possibly," I say. "I won't know for a little while. I just need you to stick him in his tomb and be ready."

"For what?"

"I can't say, but you'll know it when you see it."

"You two are going to do something monumentally stupid, aren't you?"

"Would you expect any less of me?"

"You, no. But her? You realize there's a very good chance you won't walk away from what's about to happen."

"Yes," Janna says. "I'm doing it anyway."

"Good," Muerte says. "Don't fuck it up. Anything else?"

"As a matter of fact, yes," I say. I hand her a small book bound in human skin. "I need you to do something to this."

Chapter 31

I text Amanda and she opens a portal back to the estate and then another onto a dirt road with old, charred oak trees on either side showing season after season of wildfires. A low metal gate for keeping out vehicles blocks the road.

"This is it, huh?" I say.

"This is it," Amanda says. "Near enough, at least. There's something blocking the portal from going any further in."

"Imagine that. We'll let you know how this all shakes out."

"Good luck," Amanda says.

"Be careful," Gabriela says. "Both of you." We step through and the portal closes behind us.

The Simi Hills are technically mountains. They're part of a low, rocky range northwest of Los Angeles. A lot of open, undeveloped land, perfect for shooting Westerns. A few sets from old television shows are still up there, preserved as tourist attractions.

What used to be the old Blackburn compound is a now shuttered Boy Scout camp sold off to pay for the lawsuits against all those pedophile scout masters they insisted didn't exist.

"Am I supposed to get nauseous stepping through these?" Janna says.

"If you're not used to them," I say.

"Do you feel that?" Janna says.

"I don't feel anything," I say. Nothing seems out of place. I don't sense any ghosts. We're far enough from just about everything that it's a little odd but not too concerning.

"It's like at the train station," Janna says. "There was a hole that felt like it was covered over. Only it's everywhere. Like a bubble."

"Can you get us through to 1924?" I say.

"Yeah, but not out here." She steps over the gate, takes two steps, and stops. "I'm through." She sounds surprised, as if she didn't expect it to be that easy.

"What exactly is it?" I say.

"It's like if you made a snow globe out of time," Janna says. "We shouldn't travel from here, though. There are . . . things. We need to get further inside."

"Things?"

"They look like gargoyles," she says. "I don't know what they'll do if I try to move us over near them, but I think it'll be bad. Maybe they're just an alarm system. They look pretty nasty for an alarm system, though."

This must be what it's like talking to me. I'm used to being the one who can see what nobody else can. Being on this side of it's a little disconcerting.

"This way," Janna says. Instead of going down the road, she winds her way between trees off to the side. "Otherwise, they'll see us. Or maybe they'll just see me."

"At this point I figure it's pretty much the same thing," I say.

The air gets thicker and quieter the further in we go. Birdsong disappears, the air goes still, even our feet crunching through dried leaves and twigs is muffled. I catch movement out of the corner of my eyes.

"I thought I saw someone chopping at a tree with an axe for just a flash and then it was gone."

"You did," Janna says, her voice sounding distant and disconnected. "There will be more the closer we get. Ignore them. They're safe."

"You okay there?" I say.

"Yes," she says. "There's just a lot to pay attention to. Come on. We're almost there."

I follow Janna deeper into the trees, my paranoia screaming that we're walking into a trap. And maybe we are, but I don't think it's Janna's.

I start to hear people. Chanting, hymns. Fleeting images

there and gone too quickly to follow. The trees open up onto a dirt clearing with half a dozen clapboard buildings arranged around a circle of large white stones, filled with a covering of smaller rocks, a flagpole in the middle.

A large wooden sign declares that this is CAMP BLACKBURN.

"That the ritual circle?" I say.

"It's the same here as it is there," Janna says. "We're in sync now. A minute here and a minute there are the same. They're almost done." She walks to the circle and stands next to the flagpole. I follow her inside.

"What are we doing exactly?" she asks.

"I thought you could see it."

"I can, but there are a few things I don't know."

"For starters, we need to stop them from finishing the spell," I say. "After that we need to do whatever it is with the spell's leftover energy to, fuck, I don't really know. But after that happens, I need you to do that thing we talked about by the lake."

"Okay. I'll need to use as much power as I can get from the spell for my part," Janna says. "We can't stop it too soon."

We've circled around my plan without saying much out loud. Does she get what I'm thinking? Only one way to find out, I guess.

"I'm going to be busy," she says. "Do you think you can interrupt the spell on your own?"

"If it's one thing I'm good at, it's fucking up other people's plans." I draw my gun, check to make sure there's a round in the chamber.

"Okay, I've—S-shit."

I hadn't noticed it before, but now it's too much to ignore. Janna's beginning to shake. "You okay there?"

"I'm getting pulled in. I can't—I can't control it," Janna says. She grabs my hand with a grip like a vise. She convulses and her body jerks up a foot off the ground—then hangs there. The world closes in on itself, the buildings warping together. A bright spring day twists into a cold, dark night. Torches and candles light the grounds, revealing two dozen people in hooded black-and-red robes surrounding us. The flagpole is gone and in its place is a pulsing blue light the size of a basketball. The chanting stops.

Janna falls to the ground, barely keeping her balance, her hand still locked on mine. I help her stand straight. Her eyes are glowing like thousand-watt lava lamps.

"You good?"

"Yeah," she says. "Just feel a little sick."

"What happened?"

"I was trying to find something of the spell to grab hold of."

"And it grabbed you instead?" I say. She nods. "Okay. I got this part."

I look around, turning to take in the crowd surrounding the circle. "Sorry for the intrusion, everyone," I say. "You don't know me and I realize that you're probably expecting a different result. But not to worry. We've got it handled.

"Couple things. First, what is it with cultists and robes? Is it tradition? Air of gravitas? Because y'all just look kind of stupid. No? None of you?"

Muttering, confusion. The amount of magic they've channeled is almost blinding. My head is starting to hurt.

"Okay, moving on. Second thing, which of you are the Two Witnesses? This is all about you, after all."

Two women lower their hoods and step forward. A sour looking woman with white hair hanging down to her shoulders and a much younger woman with black hair pulled back in a bun. Definitely May and Ruth.

"Excellent! So very glad to meet you," I say, stepping to the edge of the circle, taking care not to step over. Would it do anything? I don't know, but I don't really want to find out.

"Who the fuck are you?" Ruth says.

"Interested third party," I say, and shoot them.

May drops with a round through her head. Ruth takes one in the chest, but there's a flare of magic. Reality freezes and begins to reverse.

"No, I don't think so," Janna says. A stronger spell pushes

time forward again. Ruth is fighting it. Back and forth, the bullet reversing and then continuing its trajectory. I can see waves rippling from the bullet as it displaces the air. Janna is using more power, but from the backward movement of the bullet Ruth is clearly more experienced.

I wonder how far that time reversal goes. I fire three more rounds. Ruth catches one of them in her net, but the other two she takes in the chest and head. There's a loud snap as frozen time catches up with the present and the first two bullets join the rest. Ruth hits the ground next to her mother.

"That was easier than I expected," I say, and because the universe is a dick, it immediately proves me wrong.

May raises up, levitating quickly like Dracula coming out of his coffin to hover a few inches above the ground. The hole in her head closes.

She's put up a shield, but she's spent a lot of power. Even the local pool of magic is bordering on empty. Takes a few rounds to break through, but this time when she goes down she stays down.

All of the Blackburn cultists are screaming, running for the road, the buildings. I see somebody with a shotgun. By the time he fires I already have a shield up.

I can feel the power concentrated here, but at the same time it isn't. I can see two shifting shapes on the edges. They have the feel of Wanderers, but not quite. They feel too far away, but far more cohesive than any Wanderers I've met. Actual souls? Or something weirder?

A wind picks up, blowing leaves off trees, like a Santa Ana wind and a tornado combined. The man with the shotgun has had enough, turns tail and runs.

"That's part one," I yell to Janna, trying to be heard over the rushing wind. "I'm seeing something near us. How about you?"

"Yes. I think it's the same thing, but I doubt we're seeing it the same way."

"Care to do the honors?"

She grabs my hand. "Let's go finish this."

Pain rips through me like at the club and the car crash but a thousand times worse. Everything disappears around me.

"Hello, Eric," Willa says. The compound with the ritual space and its torches has been replaced by a candle-lit church. She sits cross-legged on the altar, underneath a large cross, holding one of her dogs. I'm sitting in the front pew.

"Where's Janna?"

"I'm having a conversation with her somewhere else," Willa says. "We're between ticks of the clock, so to speak. Do you understand what's happening?" Her puppy squirms in her arms, whimpering. "Hush, Re."

"The spell started in 1924," I say. "But it's supposed to be finishing up a hundred years later. Then the power will snap back on itself and bring you back from the dead. But May and Ruth fucked it up. It won't work. It was never going to work."

"No, it won't work," she says. "But it's not over. What happens depends on what you do here. I can't tell you what to do, and I don't know exactly what will happen, but I do know that if you're not careful, a lot of people will die."

"What about the intrusions from your past to my present?"

"That depends on what you do here, too. Work things correctly and they'll be gone when—if—you get back. If you hadn't killed May and Ruth, the changes would have kept coming until your past was completely overwritten. If you do nothing else, it won't get worse. But it won't get better, either."

"You sound different," I say. "A lot more knowledgeable about all this than I would have expected."

"Because I am. You met me a long time ago, by my clock. Though it's only been a few days for you, it's been almost a hundred years for me. At least looked at one way. Looked at another, it's been thousands."

"How many times have we had this conversation?"

She smiles like a teacher who's just watched a struggling first-grader grasp addition. "This is the first time. But you're close. I told you that the spell is like a rubber-band. I've managed to keep it from snapping by turning it into more of a yo-yo.

"I'm still alive. In 1924. They have me in the chapel right now."

"Is that why this is a chapel?"

"Yes. It's easier for me since I'm in multiple places. I'm not in the void yet. That will be tomorrow morning, when I die. It happens every time. I die, I wait, I reverse the years, I die again. I can't break the cycle."

"So, these incursions have happened before, but you've been turning back the clock each time."

"Yes. I don't remember the first time, exactly. They tried to bring me back and couldn't do it. They hunted for another way until they eventually found the stories of Juanita Hernandez, where she lived. They were able to go back to learn her secrets. The effort almost killed them. It left them too weak to work the spell here even with the energy of everyone around the circle. If you hadn't killed them just now, they would have used up all their power in the attempt."

Which is how they originally burnt themselves out. They must have made the trip back to the adobe and then turned around and tried the resurrection spell right away. Too much magic too quickly.

"Is that why there were the incursions from the past?" I say.

"Yes," she says. "It started the cycle. The next part of the spell that they would have to cast later, would have focused the energy. Kept it from leaking out."

"They kicked everything off, but they weren't able to control it."

"That's right. This cycle's been going on and on for a very long time. But now you have the potential to break it," she says. "This time is different. I always knew it was going to happen, though when, I wasn't sure. Time is a hard thing to track in this state."

"Different because Jimmy's here?" I say.

"Different because you, Jimmy, and Janna are here," she

says. "Every time is a little bit different. Jimmy's been here before. Fleetingly, though I'd never met him. He wasn't able to make the changes he wanted to make. But this time you and Janna are here. I think some of that's luck and some of it's Jimmy's doing. You need to go now. I'll see you in a moment but might not remember that we had this conversation. I'll try. Jimmy's pulling hard to bring all of us together."

"I get why me and Janna, but why you?"

"I'm tied to the spell," she says. "At this point we might as well be the same thing."

"But, what if—"

Reality warps and when it rights itself I'm standing inside the ritual circle again with Janna. Two bodies lie on the ground just outside it. The rest of the Blackburn cult has already scattered. The wind has died down. At least around us. The sky looks like the eye of a hurricane. I can see trees on the edge of the compound bending in the gale, their branches completely stripped.

There are two new figures standing at the edges of the circle, just on the other side. Willa in her white nightgown and flower wreath, puppy in her hands. And Jimmy, looking like Jimmy did thirty years ago, head firmly attached to its neck, stupid Billy Holly glasses perched on its nose. Neither of them is moving, frozen.

A ball of energy sits at the center of the circle, glowing. Janna has her hands around it, moving like a sculptor shaping clay, but not touching it. At least not in any way I can see.

"Good conversation?" Janna says.

"Yeah," I say. "You?"

"She told me we're fucked if we make the wrong choice," Janna says.

"Same. Seems this particular bit of time fuckery has been going on for a really long time."

"I can feel it," Janna says. "Did she . . . try to pull it back and then let it go forward again? I was going to ask but I didn't get the chance."

"Yeah," I say. "She said it's like a yo-yo."

"That makes sense. Good intentions," Janna says. "But instead of one loop it's gone back and forth so many times I don't know that anyone can control it now. You still want to do this?"

"Do we have a choice?"

"Not really," Janna says. She's straining with effort, doing some magic I can feel but can't see. "You ready to try this thing?"

"Let's see if we can get any insights before we pull the trigger."

Janna nods. There's a sound that isn't a sound and for a moment it feels like I'm going to be torn apart again, but then the pain is gone just as quickly as it came.

"Eric," Jimmy says. It doesn't seem to notice or maybe care that it was frozen in time for a bit there. "Officer Benson. I'm sorry, it's Detective now, isn't it? Congratulations on your battlefield promotion. How's your father feeling?" Janna says nothing.

"How are you walking around?" she says.

"I'm not," it says. "I just look like it for the sake of this conversation. Willa and I, we're not actually here. Projections, echoes of time."

"Well, we're here," I say. "What now?" Willa is looking confused, holding Re up to her ear, listening intently.

Jimmy shrugs its shoulders. It's weird to think of Jimmy with shoulders. "You have choices to make," it says. "If you do nothing the spell will grow in power until it can't be contained any longer. In fact, it's getting to that point very quickly."

"And it'll kill a lot of people," I say. "The spell's been picking up bits and pieces of people's deaths over the last hundred years. Those bits of soul Juanita told us about, that she animated her children with. Only it's not just the last hundred years. It's that multiplied by however many times it's looped around." A hundred years of death accumulated by this spell, Tens of thousands of dead every year from everything from old age to gunshot wounds for a hundred years, over and over again.

"Those deaths, those bits of soul as you say, they're just potential right now," Jimmy says. "If the spell finishes, it will finally pull all of them together. And not just in L.A. All through Southern California. Some in Arizona, Nevada, Mexico. Can you imagine how many people that is?"

It hasn't been pulling in tens of thousands a year, but hundreds of thousands. "We're talking millions dead in a split second. Like a bomb going off."

"That's right," Jimmy says. "One that will tear time apart. But you have another option."

"We give all that energy to you," Janna says.

"Yes," it says. "After a bit of cleaning, of course. All that death wrapped up in it makes the energy I need useless."

"Cleaning," I say. "By pulling the death energy out of it. I see a flaw in this plan."

"There will be a hell of a lot more energy than at the club," Janna says. "You'll die."

"You probably will, too," I say.

"If you don't, millions die," Jimmy says. "Now, I would expect Eric to let them, he's certainly cold and vindictive enough. But you, detective? You still care about people. And even if you didn't, there's your father to consider. It'd be a shame to waste the opportunity he was given for more life, don't you think?"

"You're an asshole," Janna says.

"Why are you doing this?" I say.

"I'd think if anyone would understand it would be you, Eric," Jimmy says. "I'm going to become a god. I'll control the entirety of fate. It's what May and Ruth wanted, after all. If it's good enough for them, I think it's good enough for me."

"Eric?" Janna says.

"Yeah," I say. "I don't see we have a lot of choice. Let's do this. How do we handle it?"

"Just grab it and pull it apart," Jimmy says.

"If I survive this, I'm going to fuck you up," I say.

"Then it's a good thing for me that you probably won't."

I really hope Janna understands what the plan is. Not being able to tell her without possibly tipping off Jimmy is risky. And even if she does get it and does what we need, there's no guarantee that it will work.

"Okay," I say. I reach out just as Janna does. I find the edges of that same energy I pulled from the corpses in the past. There's just a lot more of it. I start to reel it in as Janna does the same with the other half.

"You know, Jimmy," I say, straining as I pull in more and more of the energy. "You only showed us doors number one and two."

"There aren't any other doors, Eric."

Jimmy's right about one thing. All this energy won't just kill me, it'll incinerate my soul. There's only way I can think of to survive it: treat it like a river. It just needs to be diverted.

"Now that's where you're wrong," I say, drawing on the first trick I ever learned as Mictlantecuhtli. "There are lots of other doors. Like this one."

I open a hole into Mictlan and send the energy I've pulled through the opening, letting my grip on it go. It continues to flow like a high-pressure stream forced through a cracked dam. The energy isn't death so much as the potential for it. Those earmarked bits of soul don't exist, yet. But even that potential should be enough to wake Mictlantecuhtli. If nothing else goes right here, at least I'll have done that.

"What are you doing?" Jimmy steps closer but pulls up short when it hits the circle.

"Not playing your game," Janna says.

"I have been looking for a way to destroy you for a while now and you know what? I haven't found one. But then my grandfather said something about how he had to deal with an Oracle that stuck with me."

Janna's been pulling in more and more energy from the

glowing sphere. It dims occasionally, but there's an incredible amount there. She's sweating.

"We can't destroy you," I say.

"But we can make sure you were never made in the first place," Janna says. She releases all that energy in a blinding blast of time.

Chapter 32

I feel a wrenching in my gut, a sense of falling, then a hard snap as I land in a way that I know isn't anything like falling or landing, but that's the only sensation my brain can translate it into. I stagger and grab the nearest solid thing to keep myself upright, a stack of drywall on a pallet.

I smell sawdust, fresh cement, off-gassing plastic. It takes me a second to orient myself. Dry, hot air. A house still under construction. What should be the living room covered in clear plastic tarps.

I'm in Las Vegas. Thirty years ago.

I check my messenger bag. It's not the same one I had with me in Simi Valley. I lost this one in Connecticut a few years after this happened. I have a gun in there, a semi-sentient Nazi pistol. A Browning Hi-Power that's about as evil an artifact as you'll ever see.

There's also my straight razor. This one's normal, not like the one I could manifest when I need it. I push my way through the tarps, knowing I'll find something that will figure in some of my more prominent nightmares for the next few years, an autopsy table covered in leather straps with grooves leading down to a fluid drain at the bottom.

Jesus. I actually did this? I strapped a man down and cut off his head because he asked me to?

Jimmy was the second man I'd ever killed. The first, Jean Boudreau, who killed my parents and left my sister Lucy and me as orphans, I murdered for vengeance. Jimmy I killed for expediency. I had screwed up a dry run of the spell and accidentally summoned the demon that I was going to use. I had no sacrifice and only avoided getting eaten through sheer luck and some quick thinking.

I got a short reprieve. I hadn't planned on going through with it. But now I had to or I was going to be the demon's next meal.

"Do you think this will actually work?" I look up from the table to see Sebastian McCord, a thick slab of a man, muscles slowly going to fat, hair graying. He's in his fifties. Owns the Gold Rush Casino. He's the one who pulled me into this whole mess after he caught Jimmy cheating at his casino. He and his girlfriend, Nicole, had the spellbook I used to make Jimmy.

By this time I'd already discovered that neither of them could be trusted. They both had come to me with a proposition that I use the other to make the Oracle.

I could see where that was going a mile off. If I'd actually gone with either of them I'd have had a knife in my back soon enough.

"Yeah," I say. "Pretty simple once things get moving. Where's Nicole?"

"She's grabbing a couple things from the car," he says. "Is everything ready?" I can tell from the way he says it that he's not talking about the ritual. I told both him and Nicole that during a toast to this bold undertaking I will have spiked the other's drink with a paralytic, then haul them onto the table and take their head.

What really happened is that I spiked the entire bottle of champagne and depended on the protective charms in my tattoos to protect me. The two of them went down, I propped them up in a corner so they could watch the proceedings.

Then I taped guns to their hands with fingers on the triggers. Whichever one woke up first had the option of killing the other and taking the Oracle for themselves.

Sebastian lost that particular battle, but Nicole lost the war. She thought she was getting something to make her rich and powerful, but instead she got a controlling monster that made her life a living hell.

"This looks so medieval," Sebastian says.

"It is," I say. "I'm cutting a guy's head off. With a saw. While he's awake. There's no way to not see this as fucked up."

I remember this conversation going slightly differently, which makes sense, I suppose. I'm a different person than I was last time.

"Sorry I'm late," Nicole says, stepping through the break in the plastic behind me. "Funny thing just happened." I turn to her and freeze.

"Nicole, why do you have a gun?" Sebastian says.

"Because she just met Jimmy," I say.

"Who?"

"A friend of Eric's," Nicole says. "He was waiting for me as I came in. Had a really interesting story to tell me about how you two were going to drug me, then put me on that table."

"Let me guess," I say. "He offered to go on the table himself because he's sick and dying. If we're being all truthful here, Nicole, maybe tell Sebastian what you and I discussed for him."

"I don't know what the hell you're talking about," Nicole says.

"Christ, you know, you aren't any better a liar thirty years from now. See, Nicole and I talked about doing the same thing to you, Sebastian. In fact, I think she came to me first."

"Nicole, what the fuck?"

"Me?" Nicole says. "What about you? You were gonna cut off my fucking head."

"You talked to him about it first," Sebastian says.

"If it helps any, I wasn't planning on cutting either of your heads off. In fact, I wasn't planning on cutting anybody's head off. Though you both do really bring out the urge."

"Then what the fuck were you going to do?" Nicole says.

"Initially, I was going to skip town, but some things didn't go as planned. So I was going to have to use one of your heads. Until Jimmy showed up. You see, he's dying. Thought this was his shot at immortality."

"That's an overly simplistic way of looking at it," Jimmy says, stepping into the room behind Nicole. He looks the way

I remember him, just the way he looked when I left him at the Blackburn compound. He sounds smarter than when I was here last. No doubt he is.

"I'm talking about the you now," I say. "Not the you in thirty years," I say.

"What the hell is going on here?" Sebastian says.

"Nicole, you should just shoot Sebastian now," Jimmy says. "You're going to anyway and there's really no reason you should have to wait."

"Think you're being a little premature there, Jimmy," I say. "I don't have to do anything to you. Literally. I can sit here doing nothing and it'll solve the entire problem."

"What the hell are you talking about?" Sebastian says.

"You already did it," Nicole says. "You already created the Oracle and now you're back? From thirty years in the future?"

"Via a detour about fifty, sixty years in the past?" I say. "I'm really bad at math. See, Sebastian? You never stood a chance. Nicole was the smart one in your relationship."

"Which is why I chose her," Jimmy says.

"You're here to stop the creation of the Oracle," Nicole says to me.

"What? Why?" Sebastian says. "Hell, how?"

"Jimmy and I are from the future," I say. "If I don't create the Oracle, then Jimmy dies. Jimmy has created nothing but misery over the last thirty years. I'm here to end it."

"This is insane," Sebastian says.

"Give it a rest, Sebastian," Nicole says. "Thirty years? What happens to me?"

"You have unimaginable power," Jimmy says.

"Actually, you're dead. It has you killed for figuring out what I just figured out. And up to that point you were basically its prisoner."

"You can't believe him," Jimmy says.

"I don't even know who the fuck you are," Nicole says. "I don't trust him, but I trust him a hell of a lot more than I trust you."

"Eric, you can't do this," Jimmy says. "If you destroy me, everything changes. The world you knew will be gone. You have no idea all I've done, how many lives I've made better."

"Or how many lives were cut short to fix a football game, but I don't really need to. One's more than enough."

I'm looking at Jimmy, but I have both Nicole and Sebastian in my peripheral vision. I don't know what would happen if I died here, but I suspect it would mean dying permanently. And seeing as I'm not likely to go to Mictlan, that's something I'd like to avoid.

"You know, the question you should be asking," I say, "is why is Jimmy here hoping to stop me? Doesn't seem to get that I have all the power in this situation. I don't have to kill you, Jimmy. I just have to do nothing."

"No," Sebastian says. He's pulled a pistol from the small of his back. "You're going to make the Oracle and then the Oracle and I are going to leave."

"I like that plan," Jimmy says.

"Shut up," Sebastian says. "You're just here to make a fucking tool."

"You kill me," Nicole says. She's peering at Jimmy, trying to make sense of it. "You really kill me."

"Of course not," Jimmy says. "Eric wants all the power for himself."

"That's what I thought," Sebastian says.

"God, you are dumb as a box of hair," Nicole says. "If he wanted all the power, why bring this guy here? Why not take him to the middle of nowhere? Why be around us at all?"

"Shut up, Nicole. You think I don't know what you're doing? The sort of person you are?"

"Baby, I—"

"Don't you fucking say that to me," he says. "You're just using me. Well, that's not gonna happen again, you bitch."

"I'm telling you, Nicole, you should shoot him. He's only going to be trouble."

"And you shut the fuck up," she says to Jimmy.

"Are you going to do it?" Sebastian says. "Or do I have to find another fucking necromancer?"

"No," Jimmy says. "He has to do it now. You can't wait."

"Because if he waits he might not end up with you being the Oracle," Nicole says.

"Of course not. It's just that the magic is more stable tonight."

"Are you going to do it?" Sebastian says to me.

"No," I say. I dive for cover behind the autopsy table. Sebastian fires, a bullet ricochets off the stand. Two more gunshots. I draw the Browning out of my messenger bag. I'd forgotten how nasty it feels to hold. There's so much misery and hatred infused into its frame.

I roll to the side, coming up with my gun pointed at Nicole's face, her gun at mine. I wasn't sure who fired after the first shot, but seeing Sebastian on the floor between us with a bullet through his eye tells me it wasn't him.

"Put your gun down," Nicole says. "And I'll put mine down. Sound good?"

I spy a limp hand poking out from behind a pile of lumber in the corner.

"Sounds good," I say. We both slowly lower our weapons.

"He was really gonna kill me?" she says. I walk over to the lumber and look down at Jimmy's corpse. The back of his skull is missing.

"Oh yeah. It was trying to become a god or some shit. It fucked up a lot of lives on its way."

"So what now?" she says. I pull the spell book for creating an Oracle out from my messenger bag. It's a small book, bound in human skin.

"Here," I say, and hold it out to her. "I don't want this."

"This some kind of trap?" she says.

"Just take the book," I say. She does. Opens it slightly with her thumb to confirm that it's the right one.

"Thanks," she says.

"Sorry," I say.

"Why?"

"Because you were right. It's a trap." The book bursts into green flames that run up her arm, covering her completely in less than a second. I throw up a shield to ward off the exploding bullets as her ammunition cooks off. She doesn't even get a chance to scream. She's nothing but ash in less than a minute.

I wasn't entirely sure what was going to happen. I asked Santa Muerte to do something to the book so it could take down Nicole or Sebastian, whichever one of them was left. I honestly didn't expect green flames.

In the present, Nicole told me she had cancer. Had it when Jimmy had been created and that only Jimmy's power kept it at bay. Without it, her cancer was going to eat her alive. I tell myself that I did her a favor. But I really have to wonder if that's true. Because it feels a whole hell of a lot like vengeance.

Very satisfying.

I'm staring at a blue sky on a cool spring day. I can smell wildflowers, manzanita, oak. I sit up. I'm at the camp about a hundred feet from the ritual circle.

"You're awake," Janna says. "I figured it was time to pull you back when I felt the reality quake. Hell of a big one, too. For a second I thought it was a real earthquake."

"It worked?"

"I think so. What happened exactly?"

"Jimmy was able to follow me. Tried to convince the two people who'd helped me create it that I needed to go through with it."

"You shoot him?"

"No, one of them did. She realized that it was blowing smoke up her ass. So she shot the sonofabitch. Also shot her boyfriend."

"Hell of a way to break up. How about her?"

"I lit her on fire."

"I take it you weren't close."

"No, but I did her a favor. She was gonna be dead in a few weeks anyway. How are things here?"

"Don't know yet," Janna says. "I wanted to have you wake up before trying to get hold of Amanda or Gabriela."

"Think they remember?"

"They should. Though they might have a few doubled memories. I'm feeling a few myself."

"Yeah? Like what."

"Lot of buildings that burned down in the fires didn't burn down. Death toll was still pretty bad, but not as bad as I remember."

No shit? Jimmy actually made all that worse. If that's the case, then what else has changed? And does the good outweigh the bad?

My phone rings. I pull it out of my pocket. Gabriela.

"Hey," I say. "How are you doing?"

"You got him?"

"Yeah."

"Okay, good."

"You all right?" I say.

"Yeah. Amanda and I are checking on some stuff. Seems the fires weren't quite so bad. I still have the shelter, her dad's still gone. Died at their family conclave instead of before. This time around Liam's dead, too. Without Jimmy to give him the spell to shove the soul out, he tried something that didn't work as well.

"He tried killing Attila and transferring his consciousness to Tobias at the same time. We're not sure if the spell went south or if he ended up triggering the family curse anyway."

"That's good news."

"Yeah," she says.

"Okay, you're sounding weird," I say. "What the hell's going on?"

"There's somebody here you need to talk to," she says. She's rarely at a loss for words, but she really does sound tongue-tied. "I've explained what I knew to her as best I could but—Here, just talk to her."

"Her who?"

"I can't explain it," she says, "so, here." She hands the phone off to someone else. What the fuck is going on? What changed because I didn't create Jimmy?

"Eric?" A woman's voice I don't recognize. "Hi. Uh, Gabriela told me what happened. Mostly. Are you okay? Please tell me you're okay." Who the fuck is this person?

"Sorry, do I know you?"

"Oh," she says. "She said you might not remember because—Shit. You really don't know me?"

I wrack my brains trying to figure out who she should be. She sounds important. She sounds like someone I'm supposed to know, but for the life of me I can't place why.

"No," I say. "I think I should, though."

"It's Lucy," the woman says. "Your sister."

If she says anything after that I don't hear it. My mind is filled with a grinding buzz.

Lucy. My sister.

My *dead* sister.